Years ago she'd settled down to single motherhood, sure she'd never be attracted to another man.

Until now.

For the first time Kate admitted to herself that she *could* love again. And—*oh, dear God, help me*—this was the man. She wanted to touch Ian, heal all his hurts.

He looked up at her, his beautiful hazel eyes troubled. "You're a good friend, Kate."

A good friend. She made herself say it. "Well, friends help friends, Ian. And you know how fond I am of young Raymond."

"You've been a godsend to my boy. I could never repay you for what you do for him."

"I understand," Kate said gravely. But, her heart whispered, I don't want you to pay me. I want you to love me. Love me to distraction. The way I love you....

Books by Virginia Myers

Love Inspired

Helpmate #36
The Dad Next Door #71

VIRGINIA MYERS

Virginia Myers has been writing since childhood. As an adult she has published ten novels, contemporary and historical, for the general market. She has now written three novels for the inspirational market.

Active in the writing community, Virginia developed a course in popular novel writing, which she has taught in several Washington colleges. She has lectured, taught writing workshops and served for two years on the board of trustees of the Pacific Northwest Writers Conference.

She lives in Longview, Washington, where she is active in her community and a faithful worker in her church.

The Dad Next Door
Virginia Myers

Love Inspired®

Published by Steeple Hill Books™

STEEPLE HILL BOOKS

Steeple
Hill™

ISBN 0-373-87071-X

THE DAD NEXT DOOR

Copyright © 1999 by Virginia Myers

Printed in U.S.A.

Blessed are the peacemakers: for they shall be called the children of God.

—*Matthew* 5:9

In memory of my aunt, Lillian Harrison Hardesty,
a woman of peace

Chapter One

Kate Graham glanced out the window at the weather. Seattle was having a fierce February for the second year in a row. She draped a scarf over her light brown hair, which was pulled back in a ponytail secured by a rubber band. As she tied the scarf beneath her chin, she wished—again—that she was pretty. She could be a lot better looking if she worked at it, the way she had when Claude was alive. But now...

Half a dozen of her sister Jill's well-meant comments on the subject flew through her mind. Of course, Jill was beautiful. She snatched up her umbrella, picked up the windbreaker jacket she had found in Raymond's closet and rushed out the door to meet the middle-school bus. She had wasted too much time looking out the window at Ian's house next door, and planning what she would have for dinner. Ian always came over for dinner when he got home from a business trip.

It was ridiculous. Her daydreaming about Ian McAllister. She was a respectable widow with two children of her own. Maybe she should talk about it to Pastor Ledbetter. He had so much good sense and was always so willing to help. He had been a tower of strength for her when Claude had died. She had needed all the help she could get then. Dad, Mom and her younger sister, Jill. Then Jill's husband, Greg Rhys, a CPA, had sorted out all the insurance so that she had the steady small income that paid her little family's bills, if she was very careful.

She wondered again if she had taken on Ian McAllister's son, Raymond, to bolster the family budget or because she was sorry for the lonely child of a broken marriage. Or was part of the reason that it kept her in regular contact with Ian? She had certainly never regretted the arrangement. Raymond was such a changeling of a child, bright, sensitive, responsive, with Ian's blond good looks and hazel eyes, and so in need of love. He was twelve, but a very young twelve. She had always felt a wave of protectiveness toward him, from the first time he'd appeared in her kitchen.

She stopped halfway up the block, in front of the second-from-the-end brick house, as Raymond had instructed. He was afraid of some of the bigger boys at school, who often harassed him when they got off the bus at their corner, but he was, after all, twelve and it was unthinkable that he should be met at the bus.

"I'm in middle school!" he had said, his voice rising in panic. "Nobody's mom meets the middle-school bus!" Her heart had ached. He had started calling her Mom the way her own children did. He was such a waif, with no real mother and his father away on business half the time. He was trying so hard to grow up and also trying to hold on to the childhood he had never really had during his parents' turbulent marriage.

They had settled on her standing half a block down, so if the bigger boys started hassling him, she could start walking toward the corner. At the sight of an adult, even a short one, approaching, the tough kids would skulk off and leave him alone.

She stopped at the designated place. The bus was late today. She needn't have hurried. The rain was light and intermittent, but the wind swept it this way and that up under the umbrella. Kate shivered. Raymond had worn only a sweater this morning, so he would probably be cold.

The great yellow lumbering vehicle appeared down at the far end of the street. *Hurry.* This was a hot-chocolate day for sure. Her own two children, Tommy, eight, and Joy, six, were already home and were alone in the house. She had left firm instructions *not* to turn on the burner under the pan of milk until she and Raymond got there. They were pretty good kids, and she was reasonably sure they would wait.

The bus stopped at the corner, its air brakes letting out a whooshing sound. The kids, in their hideous collections of many-layered clothing, began to get off the bus. Something was different today—they didn't loiter at the stop. Some of the bigger boys got off and fairly ran from the area. She waited for Raymond to get off, straining to see. The driver was an older woman who took a real interest in her charges. Kate watched now as the driver got out of her seat and went toward the back of the bus. The bus was still about half-full of kids, who seemed unusually subdued.

Something was wrong.

Kate took a chance of embarrassing Raymond and hurried the half block to the bus. Surely Raymond hadn't missed it. No. As she came up to the open bus door, she saw the driver coming back up the aisle, her arm around Raymond's shoulders.

"See. They all went. And here's your mom. It's okay," the driver was saying.

Kate's heart was suddenly pounding. "Raymond! What happened!" She could hardly recognize him. His face was swollen and bruised, badly scraped on one side. Blood was smeared over his sweater and T-shirt. He was limping.

"Oh...Raymond." She held out suddenly shaking hands as he got off the bus. He shrugged away from the driver's protecting arm, looking sick and miserable.

"I'm so sorry, ma'am," the driver said. "I told him he should see the school nurse, but he said he didn't know where she was, and he couldn't miss the bus. I wanted to go find her myself, but I'm not allowed to leave the bus when there are kids on it."

"But what happened?" Kate gasped.

"Nuthin'. It's okay. I wanna go home," Raymond said.

"It's those tough kids, ma'am," the driver said. "They can be so mean. It's because he's skinny and he won't fight back. If he'd just fight back a little, I tell him. It awful to tell peaceable kids to fight back, but how else can they cope?" Her kindly eyes filmed over with tear

"I wanna go home," Raymond muttered, twisting the strap of his backpack with a thin hand.

"Thank you," Kate managed to say to the bus driver. "Come on," she added to Raymond. "We'll go and see to that swelling." Both his eyes were almost shut.

"Here," Kate said. "Put this on." She draped the windbreaker around his shoulders. *What will Ian say?* A wave of belated fury rushed through her. "Who did this to you?" The bus roared away and a shudder went through the boy. He looked after the bus with sheer hatred showing through his slitted eyes.

"I'm not going back!" he said through his teeth.

"Who did this to you? Tell me what happened!"

"Okay, but at home. Let's go home." He was watching the bus disappear out of sight around the corner.

"All right." She put her arm around him, trying to shelter him with the umbrella from the dashing rain, but he pulled away and started a half run back toward the house. He *was* limping. She hurried to follow him and they reached the door together, which Tommy held open. The wind and rain blew Tommy's light brown hair. He was her own small image, whereas Joy had inherited Claude's dark hair and bright blue eyes.

"What took you so long?" Tommy demanded. "We waited and waited..." He fell silent when he saw Raymond's face.

"Keep quiet!" Raymond commanded. "Do you want the whole neighborhood to hear?" He darted into the house and Kate followed, pausing only to partly close her umbrella and shake out excess water onto the porch. Inside, she dropped it into the umbrella stand.

"Settle down, you two. Raymond will tell us about it when he's ready to. Go in the kitchen and wait. We'll make the cocoa after I see to Raymond. Raymond, you come with me into the bathroom. I've got to look at that scrape."

"I'm okay," Raymond muttered, but followed her into the bathroom, as did the other two children, ignoring her command to wait in the kitchen.

"No, you're not okay. Now, I've got to get you fixed up. I mean it." The "I mean it" was the no-nonsense code phrase that usually got results.

Raymond submitted, somewhat sullenly, while the other children watched. The bathroom was crowded, but Kate managed to wash the caked blood from Raymond's face and observe the extent of the damage. She did the best she could with water and disinfectant. In a few hours, when the bruising surfaced, he was going to be a sight. She wished that Ian wasn't coming back to Seattle tonight. When she had done the best she could, they went into the kitchen.

"Raymond, I need to know what happened. Your dad is coming in tonight. What am I going to tell him?" She kept her voice steady with an effort because she wanted very badly to cry. He looked so pathetic, trying to pretend it didn't matter. Since before Claude's death, when her life had collapsed, and through her long journey with her grief to this present point of acceptance, if not content, she had become very good at not crying in front of the children.

Tommy and Joy were unusually silent as they stared at Raymond's battered face. Raymond, *twelve,* and in *middle school,* was their hero. They were both deeply shocked.

"Okay," Raymond said through swollen lips. "So I got beat up. It's no big deal."

Kate turned from the stove. "It *is* a big deal, Raymond. It should never have happened. Tell me how it did."

"Well," he said reluctantly, "there's this bunch of big kids, see. They're really big guys." He paused, seeming tired, and pushed one grubby hand through his fair hair. "Well, what happened is they want to get in this gang. In that school, if you're a guy and you're not in a gang, you're nobody. So there's this test, this initiation."

"Initiation? What kind of initiation?" Kate felt a sudden chill. These were children they were talking about. Kids, just about to enter their teens, like Raymond.

The boy sighed. "Is the milk hot yet? I'll never get warm again."

"Raymond, what initiation?"

"Well, it was three guys." It seemed the boy was pushing the words out, one at a time. "These three guys can get in this gang if they can prove they're tough. Really tough. If they can deliver. If they can follow orders. So they had to beat up somebody. Really bad. To prove it, you know."

"*Three* of them had to beat you up to prove *they* were tough!" Kate sat down suddenly in a chair. She was physically sick. They could have killed him.

"Now, what's going to happen is this," Raymond added. "I'm not—repeat *not*—goin' back to that school! Ever!"

Tommy broke the silence that followed. "Ray, when I get to middle school I'll help you."

"But Tommy, I'm not going back. Ever."

Joy spoke softly. "Mommy, the milk is moving." And Kate returned her gaze to the milk pan, watching the surface of the milk in its preboiling state. Raymond cannot go back to that school, she thought. Nor did she want Tommy and Joy continuing in public school after the primary grades. Something was very wrong. She'd have to face it. This was not the way her children were going to grow up. They must not be cheated out of their childhood.

Kate lunged forward to pull the pan of suddenly-boiling milk from the burner, and poured the hot milk into the big metal pitcher over the sweetened chocolate.

"Well, you certainly don't need to go back to school tomorrow anyway," she said to Raymond. "We'll talk to your dad about it tonight." Kate poured chocolate into a mug and handed it to him. "Don't drink that yet. It's too hot." She poured two more mugfuls for her children.

"I wish he wasn't coming back tonight. I'd like to heal up a little first," Raymond muttered.

"Oh, Raymond, I'm so sorry." She poured another mug for herself. She shouldn't have. She was getting too rounded again and she had made a resolve not to eat between meals anymore. But she needed this.

"Your father's going to be upset. He'll think I'm not taking care of you."

"Not your fault," Raymond said quickly. "You can't help what those goons at school do. Dad will just have to understand it. See, Dad's always been first string. In *everything*. All his life he's total success. So he freaks out when I can't cope, which mostly I can't. But he's gotta face it. I'm an inferior kid. He can take it or leave it."

"You're *not* an inferior kid. You're a great kid. I wouldn't want you to be any different than you are. Your father wouldn't, either!"

"Don't sweat it, Mom. It'll be okay."

Kate wondered again how Ian's former wife, Marsha, could have simply walked out on this boy. He was struggling so hard for some sort of family. Thank heavens Ian was paying Marsha so much alimony that he couldn't afford to send Raymond to boarding school. That would have stifled the boy completely.

"Help yourself to seconds," she told the children, getting up. "I have to make a phone call. But let Raymond pour. It's hot."

She sent up a silent prayer that Pastor Ledbetter would be in and available, not counseling parishioners or doing any of the thousand and one things that filled his days. Recollecting his kindly face, his graying hair and nice blue-gray eyes, Kate felt her tension easing.

"Congregational Church. How can I help you?" She

silently thanked God that the pastor had answered the phone himself. The church secretary must have stepped out for a minute. Words tumbled from Kate as she poured out her story and resumed the talk that had started when Raymond had first realized he was being targeted.

Kate heard Ian's car come into the driveway next door just minutes before the dinner hour, and she forced herself not to look out the window.

"He's coming!" Tommy shouted. "Finally! I'm starving!"

"All right, Tommy. He's a little late," Kate admonished. "Don't make a big thing of it. Where are you going, Raymond?" But Raymond had retreated down the hall toward the bedroom the two boys shared. Kate went after him and Raymond turned.

"You talk to him first, okay? Kind of break it to him that I'm not exactly Mike Tyson in a fight. Then I'll come in later. When he's ready to take it."

"That's not a bad idea," Kate agreed. The moment she did, Raymond ducked into the bedroom and shut the door. "Call me when it's time," he said through the crack.

Joy had opened the front door at Ian's ring. Both of her children adored Ian, and Kate felt a little breathless herself every time she saw him—tall, a bit over six feet, well-built, with the unusual combination of blond hair and hazel eyes. Kate had met his former wife, who was jaw-droppingly gorgeous. What a stunning couple they must have been.

"Hi, kids. Boy, am I glad to be back." He glanced around. "Where's Ray?"

Before Kate could answer, Joy said, "He's hiding, because he—"

Tommy clasped his hand over her mouth just in time and pulled her over to the big chair by the fireplace and pushed her into it.

Ian glanced a question at Kate.

"Actually, I guess he is, in a way," Kate said. "I need to speak to you about something, Ian. Raymond had some trouble at school."

"What kind of trouble?" Ian's voice was guarded.

"There was a fight at school," she admitted weakly, feeling guilty.

"Three bigger boys jumped him," Tommy interjected, unable to resist.

"He'll be all right," Kate said quickly. "He's—"

But Ian was heading for the boy's room, and she followed helplessly, with the children close behind her. Ian opened the door and went in. When he saw Raymond lying on the bed he froze. Raymond cast Kate a look of dismay.

"It's okay, Dad. It's no big deal."

Kate went sick at the shock on Ian's face as he sank to his knees beside the bed and reached out to his son.

"Oh …*no*," he whispered, his hands hovering over the boy, as if he were afraid to touch him.

"Look, it's okay, Dad." Raymond struggled to a sitting position. "I'll heal up…." But as he said it, his voice broke and tears started from his swollen eyes. He went into his father's arms, muttering, "I'm sorry. I'm sorry."

Kate pushed her kids out the door. "Come on, kids," she said softly, shutting the door behind them.

"What about dinner?" Tommy wailed. "I'm starving."

"We'll wait a while," Kate said firmly.

But they didn't need to wait long. It was only a matter

of minutes before Ian and Raymond came into the living room. Raymond threw himself into his favorite chair.

"What happened, Kate? All he'll say is that he got into a fight." Ian's voice betrayed a forced calmness. He wanted to explode at what had been done to his son. His eyes showed it.

Kate glanced at Raymond. "You should have told him," she said. "Well, Ian, I may as well give it to you straight."

"I'd like that," Ian said with faint sarcasm, going over to the fireplace.

"There seems to be some gang activity over at the middle school."

"You must be kidding." He turned to look at her.

"I only wish I were. As I get the story, three of the boys—bullies, really—were in some form of initiation. They had to 'beat up' someone to prove themselves. They chose Raymond. There were three of them, all bigger boys than he is." In spite of her effort at control, her voice rose in anger.

"That's sick," Ian said shortly. He was filled with seething rage. Kate could feel it.

"I know how you feel," she said.

Tommy interrupted. "He didn't have a chance, Ian. He was outnumbered. He was ambushed."

"I'll go over to that school tomorrow," Ian began grimly. "I'll—"

"No!" Raymond sprang out of his chair, wincing as he did so.

Kate despaired. She was handling this badly. Later she would think of dozens of things she should have said. She often had long imaginary conversations in her head with Ian, in which she was clever, witty, intelligent and very composed. And he was always so appreciative and admiring. Now she moved forward and caught Raymond by the arm.

"Listen to your father," she said, pushing back his fair hair. Raymond calmed down and looked sullenly at Ian.

Ian retreated. "Okay," he said gently. "What do you want me to do?"

"Well, first, just let it alone," Raymond muttered.

Joy piped up, climbing back into the big chair by the fireplace and smoothing her skirt down primly. "Raymond is never going to school again. He's through."

"Through with school?" Ian asked.

"That's what he said," Joy answered.

Kate interposed. "He doesn't really have to, you know." She swallowed hard and braced herself.

"Okay, I'm listening. Why doesn't my twelve-year-old son need to go to school anymore?" Ian asked quietly.

Her mouth was suddenly dry. "I was talking with Pastor Ledbetter earlier. This has been coming on for a while. We were talking about homeschooling and—"

Ian didn't let her finish. "Maybe we'd better have dinner first. It might calm us down. This looks like a long discussion coming up. And I think I heard Tommy say he was starving."

"I am," Tommy said promptly, and both boys headed for the dining room, followed by Joy.

Kate gave up and followed the children, with Ian beside her. He was anything but calm; she could sense it.

Dinner was a disaster. Only the children could eat, and watching Raymond struggle to eat through his swollen lips made her sick with anger. She noted that Ian couldn't do anything either but push the food around on his plate. Well, her precious roast of beef wouldn't be wasted. She would use the leftovers for baked hash. The children loved it. When the endless meal was finally over Kate stopped herself from mentioning homework—after all, Raymond wasn't going back to school anyhow.

"I brought back a couple of videos. If you kids want to go watch them, they're on the hall table," Ian said. The children rushed out. And he added to Kate, "Want some help with this? You don't have a dishwasher."

"I'm the dishwasher," Kate murmured. Ian was being kind; he had never offered to help before. It probably meant he was going to reject the homeschooling idea and wanted to let her down easily. But Raymond couldn't go back to that school. She had seen this coming. She should have acted sooner.

In the kitchen, Ian waited until he was drying the last glass. Then he hung up the dish towel on the rack and turned to her. The sounds of cartoon voices and singing came to them from the boys' bedroom.

"Let's stay in here, Kate. They'll be busy for another hour at least." He pulled out a kitchen chair for her and she sat down. He took the opposite chair. He was waiting politely for her to begin.

She cleared her throat, trying to remember some of the things she had learned from Pastor Ledbetter. She wished Ian knew him better, but Ian was seldom in Seattle weekends and, although he had attended church with them a few times, it was not a priority with him.

"You were talking with your pastor," Ian prompted.

"Earlier, about a month ago, this trouble started and I—Raymond and I—worked it out that I'd meet the bus, but this apparently happened at school. I'm worried about Tommy and Joy, too. They're just in primary grades and, so far, things are going well, but I'm trying to prepare for their future, too. Pastor Ledbetter is a former teacher and he's been advising me."

Ian was at least listening, she hoped with an open mind.

"We can't—just can't—make Raymond go back there. Once those toughs have targeted him, they'll show him no mercy. They're bullies. And I don't think it will do much good for you to go down. Schools don't seem to pay much attention to parents anymore."

"So, tell me about this homeschooling."

"Pastor Ledbetter said that in a few years' time over a million families will be homeschooling their children. There is a wealth of material available, for all grade levels, with loads of teaching aids. It started with Americans in Europe homeschooling their children. It's a growing trend now, especially among Christians, very widespread." She went on, remembering more and more of what Pastor Ledbetter had told her.

"You've thought about this for quite a while, haven't you?"

"Ever since this trouble started. Today, with Raymond coming home like he did, that was the last straw. I realized that I'd have to do something."

"Would you do the teaching yourself?" Ian asked, and Kate could hear the doubt in his voice.

"Oh, yes," she said firmly.

"I didn't know you had a teaching credential."

"I haven't. I don't need one. The homeschooling materials are so well prepared—I mean, they are designed for use by nonteachers."

A silence lengthened between them. Finally Ian broke it.

"That's a wonderful offer, Kate. And you are a very kind and generous person to make it but, I have to ask it, how far did you go in school?"

Kate felt her face getting hot. She knew that Ian had

an M.B.A., as well as having had specialized training for his work.

"I…had two years at community college, but Claude and I wanted to get married and…I needed to get a job. I mean, he didn't have his degree yet and…one of us had to go to work…." Her voice trailed off. Memories surfaced of herself and Claude and all their great plans, the too-early marriage, the unexpected pregnancy with Tommy. Then, later, the planned pregnancy with Joy, after Claude was established in his job. Then—oh, why do these things happen to people—Claude getting sick. Everything had been going so well. It was unbelievable that it should collapse around them. If it hadn't been for the strong support of her close family she didn't think she could have made it through.

Kate suddenly got up from the table, trying to shut out the flood of memories of Claude's long illness, his bravery. Her caring for Claude as his life slipped away into merciful death. Caring for the rowdy little Tommy and the infant, Joy. Pinching pennies, trying to get by on Claude's disability payments. The nights she had fallen into bed too exhausted to sleep.

"Would you like a cappuccino?" she heard herself asking.

"Yes, thank you, I would. Do you think of Claude often?"

"Sometimes. Not as much as I used to." She set about making the coffee.

"How long has it been since—"

"Over six years now. Joy doesn't even remember him at all, of course. She was too little." *Do you think of Marsha?* The question remained unasked in her mind. There was no way he could forget Marsha, because Marsha came back into his life now and then on her occasional visits to see Raymond and toy with motherhood.

A silence grew between them as she finished making the cappuccino, and when she had put the pot and small cups onto the table, he said, "That smells good."

She poured the steaming coffee into the little cups.

"I guess I agree that Raymond can't go back to that school," Ian said, his voice sounding tired. "But to be honest, I can't see this homeschooling idea for him. For one thing, his grandparents would raise the roof."

"Why? What have they got to do with it?"

"Well, when Marsha wanted out of our marriage, they gave me a lot of advice about Raymond. Justin, Colonel Justin Greer, my ex-father-in-law, who is a nice guy, really, is retired army. And they always—this is my reading of it—they feel embarrassed about Marsha not staying with the marriage." He was choosing his words carefully, and Kate respected him for it. He was trying not to say anything disparaging about Marsha. He never had, but Raymond wasn't so careful, so Kate knew a great deal about the rocky marriage.

"You see," Ian continued, "they feel apologetic about Marsha. They needn't. It takes two to make a bad bargain, and I've tried to take my share of blame with them. You see, Marsha didn't really have a very good life. She was an army brat, shuffled around abroad when they were stationed abroad, or warehoused in some boarding school when they were stationed some place where they couldn't take her. But they really are concerned about me, a single parent, raising Raymond. With the travel and all. They wanted—still want—him placed in a good military school. And they do care. They do keep in touch…have input into his life."

Kate was well aware of that. Raymond got at least a

couple of letters a month from his grandmother Greer, and the VCR in the boys' bedroom was one of his grandparents' gifts.

"Don't drink that yet. It's too hot," Kate said almost mechanically, and saw Ian trying not to smile. He probably thought she was just everybody's mommy, and it wasn't how she wanted him to think of her.

"Will you do me a favor?" she asked with a sigh.

"Sure. If I can. What is it?"

"Can I set up an appointment for us both to visit with Pastor Ledbetter? I've already decided it's something I want to do for my kids a little later, in the upper grades, and I may as well start with Raymond. I'd just like you to hear what he has to say. Just consider it."

"Okay, if you want me to, Kate, but…" His hazel eyes fell to look at the cup before him with its still-steaming coffee. "But I really don't like the idea of homeschooling him and…" He paused and she saw color rise into his face. "My disposable income will shortly increase considerably." His tone was carefully neutral, but there was a grimness about it.

"You got a raise? You got a promotion?" She couldn't keep the eagerness out of her voice, and was about to congratulate him.

"No," he said flatly. "Marsha is getting married again. She's found…Mr. Right."

"I don't understand," Kate said faintly, afraid that she did understand.

"It means I'm off the hook for alimony, Kate. I don't have to pay it after June. I'll have enough to send Raymond to a good private school. I guess I'll have to give in on that point. It'll please his grandparents, anyhow…. Kate? Are you okay?"

"Yes. Yes, I'm okay," *Over my dead body. That boy*

needs family. "Is that absolutely carved in stone? Can't we just go and see Pastor Ledbetter?"

"If you want me to go, Kate, I'll go. But let's be honest. I've pretty much made up my mind. I had to, as soon as I saw Raymond's face tonight. He'll be much better off in a good boarding school."

Chapter Two

After Ian had gone and the children were in bed, Kate started her evening routine of living-room tidy-up. She was tired but not sleepy, having just successfully completed one of her mental conversations with Ian, during which she said all the things she should have said. Halfway through her task she noticed the time. Eleven o'clock. She might as well get tomorrow's weather report. She flipped on the TV and sat down, straightening the newspapers she held for the recycle bin, only half listening.

There was another freeway drive-by shooting. A serial arsonist was taken into custody. The city council was deadlocked about something. A Siberian cold front was moving down from Alaska. Kate's hands became still and she watched the screen. Snow! A real blizzard! Oh, wonderful news. None of the kids would go to school tomorrow. In a heavy snow Seattle came to a dead stop until it was over. The news media would give constant updates twenty-four hours a day, and at some point some news anchor would interview somebody from Minnesota who was having a good laugh at Seattle's snow hysteria. Seattle was a city of many hills and had never come to terms with the occasional heavy snowfall. Yes, the anchor was now listing the school closings for tomorrow. Kate listened for and heard what she wanted to hear. Raymond would be elated. So would the other two.

But this left uncertain their appointment with Pastor Ledbetter for early tomorrow. Before Ian had left, she had called the pastor at home. He, hearing the concern in Kate's voice, had agreed to meet them for an early-morning appointment. Now if the streets were impassable maybe they couldn't go. But even as she thought it the phone rang. She flipped off the TV. It was Ian.

"I knew you were still up. I saw your lights on," he began. "Were you looking at the news?"

"Yes. Snow. The kids will be over the moon. I'll have to dig out the snowsuits and extra sweaters. I thought winter was winding down."

"Does this do anything to our early appointment with your pastor about the homeschooling thing? Will he be in the church office?"

"Yes. The parsonage is right next door. He'll just shovel a path through. He did last year."

"Well, we can keep the appointment, then. I'll use my sports van. It'll get us anywhere. Haven't used it in a while." There was a hint of wistfulness in his tone. The sports van, purchased just after Marsha had left and he had received the promotion that required traveling, had been another good idea gone wrong. He had bought the sports vehicle planning good-father fishing trips with Raymond to some of the many rivers nearby, but it hadn't worked out.

Kate knew Ian was on the fast track at his company, being groomed for bigger things. He was employed by a manufacturer of security and surveillance devices, and the latest in laser and other equipment. His travel was usually as a consultant to rural police forces needing to upgrade their equipment for new procedures.

It wouldn't have worked anyhow, since Raymond was a child who disliked fishing intensely. He had sat politely in the boat—another wasted effort—because he didn't want to disappoint his father. But he had managed to cut several fingers on fishhooks, become nauseated at the motion of the boat, gagged when he watched Ian remove the fishhook from the fish's mouth, and had spent the rest of the day under a tree on the riverbank reading a book he had brought along. Kate thought again that Ian should have taken Tommy, who was the nature boy, with his rock collection, his leaf collection and his dead-fly collection.

"Fine," she said. "We'll go as scheduled, then."

In the morning they awoke to a world of white. The children were elated, and by the time Kate and Ian had left for their seven-thirty appointment, all three of them were out in front, building a snowman. Ian had contributed a rakish, broad-brimmed safari-type hat she had never seen him wear and a red muffler. Kate got the feeling that he would rather stay with the snowman and the kids, but he dutifully drove her to Pastor Ledbetter's office.

"It'll be warm in a few minutes," Pastor Ledbetter said as they settled themselves in the chairs around his small conference table. "I just turned on the heat."

Everything in the pastor's office had the look of leftover rummage sale, from his battered, paper-strewn desk to the refinished kitchen table and odd repainted chairs he used for conferences.

"I've laid all this stuff out for you," he said. "There

are many curricula and plans to choose from. If you want my recommendations, I'll give them to you. But I need to start with a few cautions."

Ian was leafing thoughtfully through some lesson plan material. "This does look very thorough," he commented.

"It's prepared for nonteachers," Kate said hopefully.

"What cautions did you have in mind, sir?" Ian asked.

Cyrus sat down. Kate wondered again how old he was. He certainly never seemed to run out of energy. She knew this was the beginning of another long day for him.

"First and foremost, school authorities oppose homeschooling on principle. They are convinced that only credentialed teachers should teach, which has been proved to be invalid. With all the built-in wasted time in some of the large structured school districts, plus busing of students, often from a long distance, surveys have found that some students are spending less and less actual time in the classrooms. But they routinely object to homeschooling."

"That seems a bit much," Ian said. "Do you think this school district would actively object if Kate homeschooled Raymond?"

"Maybe. Maybe not. But remember that homeschooling is perfectly legal in this state. Sometimes a district can put up roadblocks, but usually they can't stop you. You can take precautions."

"What precautions?" Kate asked, feeling a distinct qualm.

"I would suggest the first thing you do is join the Home School Legal Defense Association. It only costs a hundred dollars, and they are your counsel, your protection, just in case. If necessary they'll go to court for you, but it doesn't usually come to that. It sure beats hiring your own lawyer if push does come to shove. You need to first bone up on your rights, so you can't be bluffed.''

"My rights?'' Kate asked faintly. Suddenly the idea of homeschooling Raymond seemed very intimidating.

The pastor leaned over and patted her hand. "Don't give in to faint heart yet, Kate,'' he said, smiling. "Homeschooling is a grand solution in some cases and I think, in the case of your Raymond, it should work. Some public schools are very good. Some aren't.

"Everything—remember this—everything depends on your child passing the exams. If he or she can pass the exams at the proficiency level for his or her grade, then the goal of teaching has been achieved, regardless of how, or where or from whom.''

Kate felt a bit overwhelmed. She'd be taking on a huge responsibility here. She wasn't sure she was up to it.

"Do you know anything about actual results?'' Ian asked. "How do homeschooled students compare with children from public and private schools?''

"Well, you can't compare public and private schools— that's apples and oranges. But statistically, homeschooled children can always outperform public school children.''

"Always?''

"According to everything I've seen so far.''

"That's certainly food for thought,'' Ian said. "Raymond is, I regret to say, just a so-so student—''

"Raymond's been under a lot of stress,'' Kate interposed quickly. "He wouldn't be if…'' She faltered. Was she *really* capable of taking on the teaching? Again, she wondered about it. She felt color rise into her face.

"Look at this new series,'' the pastor was saying with enthusiasm, pulling out a brochure and unfolding it.

"This looks like an awfully good approach to the teaching of chemistry."

"Chemistry?" Kate asked faintly.

"Kate, don't worry about it," the pastor said. "Your home is full of chemistry experiments. This looks very practical. And remember, it's designed for home teaching."

"Let's have a look," Ian said, reaching for the brochure. "You know, Kate," he added, "I could help out when I'm home. I remember I was fascinated by chemistry, got pretty good at it, and I didn't blow up anything. And they offer this whole kit of stuff. See?" He handed the brochure to her.

Kate looked at it without really seeing it. Was he coming round? Was he accepting this? And could she do it if he agreed?

"And look at this," the pastor said. "This comes with a complete set of videos. It would be like having your own private lecturer come into your home. All interactive with the students. And do you have a computer? They have a lot of things geared to the home computer."

"I don't—I don't have a computer," Kate said.

"I could get you a computer," Ian said. "That's no problem."

"Me learning to use it might be a problem," Kate responded without thinking, and Ian laughed.

"I'll bet the kids could pick it up quickly," he said.

The pastor plunged ahead, explaining, illustrating, advising.

"I think I'm sort of convinced," Ian said after a while. "At least as a stopgap, for the time being. My boy's grandparents want me to place him in a good military school, but my gut feeling is that my kid is not a military type. He'd hate it, but I do think just a good boarding school might be the solution for him.''

Kate's heart, which had lifted, sank.

"Why don't you give it a try?" the pastor asked kindly. "Be guided by his test scores at the end of the school year."

"That would be the acid test," Ian agreed.

"That and the fact that Raymond might thrive on it," Kate heard herself saying somewhat testily. Boarding school, indeed. He had mentioned last night that Marsha had been "warehoused" in boarding schools, yet somehow he saw it as a good solution for Raymond.

The church secretary popped her head in the door.

"Mr. Barnes is here about the room dividers."

"Oh, dear," the pastor said. "Well, think about it. Take all these things with you and go over them. Take your time. Here, I think I have some sort of case." He got up and rummaged in a closet, bringing out a battered old leather briefcase. "Put them in this."

Kate and Ian helped arrange all the items in the case.

"Call me if you have any questions," the pastor said optimistically as they left.

Going home, Ian didn't say much. Driving was difficult. Snow had started coming down heavily again, and the windshield wipers couldn't handle it. Kate hoped the children had gone inside. Twice they had to detour because the street was barricaded due to an accident, although traffic was very sparse. They encountered three city buses, stalled because they couldn't make it up the hills. And once Ian had to slam on his brakes because two children on a sled careened down a hill into the middle of the street. They both breathed a sigh of relief when they drove into Ian's driveway.

"I may not go in to work today," Ian said as they

were making their way through the snow to Kate's porch. "I can dictate my reports from home. You didn't have time to get Raymond to the doctor yesterday, did you?"

"No. He seemed all right. Not all right, really, but you know what I mean." Ian had taken her arm to help her. It was a warm, comforting feeling. She had been so alone, so long. The snow was swirling around them.

"Yes, but I saw him undressed," Ian said. "I'm glad you asked me to look at his body. He's one big bruise." Ian's voice was briefly unsteady.

"He was still limping this morning," Kate said as they got near her front porch. "Come in and we can call the pediatrician. See if they can fit Raymond in. Did you have breakfast?"

"No, and I'm starved."

"The kids probably are, too. They couldn't wait to get outside this morning. Look at that!" They both stopped to look at the snowman. He was about four feet tall, a series of large snowballs. His round face was topped with Ian's now somewhat damp and limp felt hat. Kate saw that he also wore her fancy sunglasses that she had bought at a sale and had never yet used.

"Dad, don't you have an old pipe?" Raymond shouted. "Don't snowmen always have a pipe?"

"Maybe this guy's a nonsmoker," Ian said, smiling at his son's enthusiasm. "We can get him a pipe later, if you want to." Raymond's face looked terrible today. "Kate said something about food. Is anybody besides me hungry?"

This brought on an interval of happy holiday-type confusion, which included Kate coping with wet snowsuits and sweaters, Ian calling the pediatrician and everybody ending up in the kitchen, either helping or getting in the way. With a lot of laughter and noise their new master plan was decided. They would have a large brunch now, a later skimpy snack and a regular dinner with the two mandated veggies.

This is what the good life is like, Kate thought, piling the just-right scrambled eggs onto the platter beside the bacon strips. Ian had washed the large bunch of grapes she had bought for school lunches, breaking them into small individual bunches and piling them onto another plate. Raymond was pouring orange juice into glasses, and Tommy and Joy were working on buttered toast, and a crooked pile of it was now ready.

If only…if only… Kate thought as they all sat down around the table to devour the spread. When the fun-filled meal was finished and the children were on the service porch struggling into their still-damp snowsuits, Kate and Ian lingered at the table. Ian picked up a leftover curl of bacon and put it down again.

"I can't eat that. I'm stuffed," he said, smiling a bit wistfully. "Kids… Raymond's having a ball, isn't he? He…seems to have forgotten yesterday."

"Children are so resilient," Kate said. Ian really had beautiful eyes, especially when he was looking thoughtful.

"You're sure doing a great job as surrogate mother, Kate. Raymond's lucky to be with you when I'm away."

"Did…the pediatrician have any time for him today?"

"Yes, she did. I didn't want to mention it in front of the kids. Raymond won't want to go. The nurse said they have nothing but time today. Several people have canceled because of the snow."

"When is your appointment?"

"Three o'clock." He glanced at his watch. "Let me help you clear up this mess."

"No. I can do it," Kate said. "I suggest you go out

and help with what's-his-name, the snowperson. It might be a good idea to kind of prepare Raymond for the idea of going to the doctor.''

Ian laughed. ''I expect a battle. But okay. Thanks for the reprieve.''

As Kate cleaned up the kitchen she could hear shouts and laughter from the front yard. As three o'clock approached there was, as Ian had predicted, a brief battle, which Ian won. He took her children with them, as they had never ridden in the sport van and wanted to. The company also provided a much-needed distraction for Raymond.

''Drive carefully,'' she said, waving them off.

A peaceful silence settled over the little house. She used the time to call her sister, Jill, for a good gossip. Jill, the bright, bold, beautiful sister, had been the one who had got her and Ian together for the care of Raymond. And before Jill had given up her restaurant to become a stay-at-home mom, she had helped out financially from time to time after Claude had died. They covered all the family news, her plans to plunge into home teaching and were winding down when the doorbell rang.

''Is that your doorbell?'' Jill asked. It had been a loud and prolonged ringing.

''Yes. I'd better run. It can't be Ian and the kids back so soon. Probably someone selling something or offering to shovel snow.'' They rang off.

The doorbell rang again insistently as she was opening the door. For a moment Kate didn't recognize who it was. She had met Marsha only a few times, very briefly.

''Thank heavens you're home. Ian isn't. I rang over there a dozen times. And like an idiot I let my cab go.''

''Marsha!'' Kate gasped.

''Yes, the infamous Marsha. Please invite me in. I'm

freezing.'' She was the same lovely, charming, impeccably groomed woman Kate had last glimpsed. Her exquisite cameo face, framed with near-black hair, her startling violet-blue eyes, her flawless skin. Today she looked like Little Red Riding Hood, enveloped in a capelike coat in vivid scarlet, with a hood trimmed in white fur. Her knee-high black boots were also trimmed in white fur.

"Yes, of course.'' Kate stood back to let her in.

"Better get that, too,'' Marsha said, coming in. "It has my jewel case in it. I dragged it clear over from next door.'' It was then that Kate saw the large suitcase on the bottom step. Kate sighed, then darted out into the icy air to get it.

"Where's my son? Is he home from school yet?''

"School is closed today,'' Kate said, shivering as she shut the door, "because of the snow, but Raymond isn't here. Ian took him—Ian has all the kids out. I expect them back any time.''

"That's quite a snowman out there,'' Marsha said, shaking out her dark mane of hair as she took off the hooded coat.

"Oh, the kids love it when it snows.''

"Yes, I saw some sliding on the hills when I was coming in from the airport. You did say Ian would be back. He's not off on some business jaunt. I was rather hoping he would be. Sometimes he can be...a little hard to persuade.''

"No. He just came back from a business trip. Would you like some coffee or something? Have you had lunch?''

"Nothing, thanks. I'm okay. I had something or other on the plane. In one of those little plastic dishes. It wasn't too bad, and I have to watch my weight.'' She glanced over Kate, assuring herself, Kate felt sure, that she was the thinner of the two. "I suppose you're wondering why I popped in like this." Marsha sat down in the big chair by the fireplace.

"It did cross my mind," Kate said, sitting down opposite. Marsha was really so lovely and so poised and confident. No wonder Ian had fallen in love with her. Was he still?

"I...don't know if Ian has mentioned it or not, but I..." Marsha began.

"Ian mentioned that you planned to marry again," Kate said. "Congratulations. I hope you will be very happy."

"I will be. I am." Marsha smiled her beautiful smile. She held out her elegant left hand. Marsha's slim hands, always beautifully manicured, made Kate want to put hers in her pockets. "You see," Marsha continued. "We didn't wait until June, which was the original plan."

"Oh? You've moved it up?"

"Very much so. We've already done it." And Kate really looked at the hand, with its sparkling diamond solitaire and slender circlet of diamonds that was the wedding ring. "Chet, my husband, is down in Virginia now, explaining things to his family."

"Wonderful," Kate said, since that was obviously what Marsha expected her to say. At the same time her heart plummeted. Ian was now no longer liable for alimony payments. He could put Raymond in a boarding school immediately if he wanted to.

"What, er, made you speed it up?"

"Several things. It seemed foolish to wait for a June wedding when it's a second time around for both of us. Did Ian tell you who I was going to marry?"

"No, he didn't." Kate thought it best not to mention that Ian had referred to him as Mr. Right.

"Chet Burgess. Chester Burgess." Marsha paused, and Kate realized she was supposed to recognize the name.

"I'm afraid that doesn't ring a bell," she said apologetically.

"Well, perhaps it wouldn't," Marsha conceded. "Chet is with State. The State Department. You've probably seen him on TV. He sometimes makes statements, you know, about the nation's position on this or that or the other thing. He's an undersecretary. Not that he needs to work. The Burgess family is old money. But all the Burgess men serve the nation in some way—army, navy, government, whatever. I'll love living in Washington. I mean D.C., of course. Chet and I have bought this perfect little gem of a house in Georgetown. It cost the earth. It's going to be a wonderful life. I've finally got things right." Her lovely face was glowing.

"Good," Kate said woodenly. "I'm happy for you, Marsha. I think I should mention that Ian took Raymond to see the pediatrician. I'd better prepare you. He looks pretty awful. He got in a fight at school yesterday. He's all bruised."

"A fight. Good heavens. Well, I guess boys will be boys. Ian has him in a public school, hasn't he?"

"He has been, yes," Kate said, deciding not to mention the homeschooling plan.

"Well, I can take him off Ian's hands now that I'm married again. Chet..." She paused, as if deciding how to phrase her next sentence. "Chet is very *family*. I mean he—he *wants* a family." Her tone implied that she didn't quite understand this but was willing to accept it.

"What do you mean, 'take him off Ian's hands'?" Kate asked, knowing the answer before it came.

"Why, I can take him back to D.C. with me, of course. Chet's prepared to adopt him. Legally. He'll inherit from

Chet. When I explained to Chet how difficult it had been for me to be without my son, he understood immediately.''

Kate felt her mouth go dry. "I thought," she said carefully, "that Raymond was placed in Ian's custody at the divorce. Because you…didn't want his care."

"Yes, he was. But that's all changed now. I want him back. He's my child. I…have to get him back." Suddenly she sat up very straight and looked squarely at Kate.

"Woman to woman, Kate. Wasn't your time being pregnant the awfulest, most dreary time in your whole life?''

"No," Kate gasped. "I loved being pregnant. It was…wonderful." She just managed to keep from saying, "I wish I were pregnant now. I want Joy to have a sister, as I have."

Marsha stared at her, confusion in her lovely eyes. "I…don't understand that," she murmured at last. "Well," she added briskly, "it's academic now. My parents are elated, of course, at my marriage. My father— he's a retired army colonel, you know—wants Raymond in a good military school. Chet agrees. Chet is so hipped on family." A shadow of worry came and went in her violet eyes.

"Of course, I promised Chet we would have our own children—child, but later. Not now. We deserve a bit of time together…without…" Her voice dwindled off.

Kate held her peace with an effort. She wanted to scream at the other woman, reprimanding her for her selfishness. Chet wanted a family and Marsha was willing to provide him with a ready-made son—Raymond, who would be warehoused in some cold, austere military school, to be brought out on occasion for display. No longer able to stay seated, Kate got up.

"Marsha, please excuse me. I have a million things to do. Ian will be back soon. There are—there are magazines here on the coffee table." She indicated the littered table and fled to the kitchen. She stood by the kitchen sink, her hands gripping the edge of it.

Oh, Ian, don't let this happen.

Chapter Three

When Ian returned with the children they came in the back door, Ian having parked his van in his own driveway and cut across the backyards. Kate was surprised that they came in so quietly to the service porch, then she saw Raymond's scowl. She quickly shut the door between the service porch and kitchen.

"What's the matter?" she asked, starting to help Joy take off her wet snowsuit.

"You'd never guess," Raymond hissed angrily. "She made me take off all my clothes! *And she took a picture!*" He flung his damp watch cap into the corner.

"Cool it, Ray," Ian pleaded, picking up the watch cap and draping it over the edge of the washer. "The 'she' my son so disrespectfully refers to is Dr. Madison. And Dr. Madison explained about the picture. It's a child-abuse precaution. Raymond is one big bruise. Doctors have a certain responsibility."

"It was gross! I'm twelve years old! And there's no point. I'm not going back to that dumb school."

"You are also covered with bruises and abrasions and

the doctor was only doing what she's required to do, and—''

"And Dad *has to* go over to the school, but *I'm not going back!*"

"All right, Ray, I've agreed to that, but as the doctor pointed out, I have an obligation here. The school authorities should be told. It might save some other boy from getting the same treatment you got. You certainly understand that, don't you?"

"Oh, I guess so," Raymond admitted reluctantly.

Kate stroked his tousled head. "Look, Raymond, you don't have to go back, so what do you care? You'll never see those kids again." His bruises looked far worse today.

"Yeah, okay," he said in a small voice.

Kate wondered nervously how she was going to break the news to both of them that Marsha was waiting in the living room. She knew that Raymond regarded his mother, whom he always referred to as "Marsha," with an odd mixture of natural love and cautious distrust. And Ian? What did Ian really feel about Marsha? He had always been so careful not to betray his feelings.

Tommy said, "Mommy, we don't need a snack. Ian got us some big pretzels from this vendor guy—"

"And apple juice," Joy interrupted. "The thick kind, you know."

"Just a minute, kids. Ian, I want to tell you—"

"I didn't eat the pretzels," Raymond said. "I got those soft little cupcake things—"

"Okay, wait a minute," Kate said desperately. "Ian, you and Raymond have company. Marsha is—"

Ian's face, half-smiling at the children's chatter, seemed to close. "What about Marsha?"

"She's here," Kate said helplessly. "Ah...she came a while after you had gone. I...she's in the living room."

"Marsha's *here?*" Raymond asked, suddenly seeming oddly more composed. The complaining child of a moment ago seemed to have changed. Instead there was a cautiousness, a tentativeness about him. He was standing quite still, not leaning against the washer anymore. "She's not gonna like the way I look," he added. "Dad?" He looked up at Ian. "Maybe you'd better kinda break it to her..."

Kate, too, glanced up at Ian's face. He was slightly flushed and—oh, no—just for an instant had she seen a glint of eagerness? Happiness? Hope?

"Okay," Ian said. "You're right. Stay out of sight until I talk to her." He put his hand on Raymond's shoulder and gave it a little squeeze. He was looking at Kate intently.

"Kate? Is there anything else you want to tell me? Before I go in there?"

Kate swallowed. What could she say in front of the kids?

"I...you mentioned that she had found, uh, Mr. Right. Chester Burgess, she said his name is."

Raymond muttered contemptuously, "Chester Burgess. I met that Chester Burgess. He's a stick."

"Well, she told me that, uh, they had been going to marry in June, but they, well, they decided to go ahead with it, and they're already married."

Ian started to say something, but Raymond interrupted. "You gotta be kidding! She married that stick? When she coulda had Dad?"

Could she have, Kate thought with a qualm. Would Ian have taken her back?

"Cool it, Ray," Ian said quietly. "Kate? What else?

There's only one reason for her to come back here after she remarried.''

Kate nodded. He was too perceptive. Her gaze flicked over to Raymond for an instant. She couldn't help it.

Ian looked grim. "Well, she can forget that."

"Dad?" Raymond knew immediately what had been left unsaid. "Don't let them mess with our custody deal, okay...? Okay?"

Kate's heart went out to him. Children were so at the mercy of adults.

"Don't worry. I'll handle it." Ian opened the door to the kitchen and strode through.

"Shut the kitchen door," Kate said to his retreating back, not sure he had heard her, and making a grab for Joy, who had started to follow him. "Stay here," she commanded. "We're going to stay in the kitchen."

"What's up?" Tommy asked, frowning. "Why are you so antsy?"

"But what'll we *do* in the kitchen? We're not going to eat yet. There's nothing to *do* in the kitchen."

But there was. Before Ian had taken two steps he met Marsha coming into the room.

"Ian?" she said pleasantly. "I thought I heard voices back—" She stopped, because she had seen Raymond, who had also followed Ian. She gave a cry of horror and covered her face with her hands.

"It's all right," Ian said, taking her into his arms. "It's all right. He's okay. I know he looks—"

Kate was startled at the wave of pure jealousy that swept through her as Marsha broke away.

"Don't!" Marsha cried. "What have you done to him! What have you done to my son!"

Raymond groaned. "Marsha, it's no big deal. Don't make a big deal of it, okay?"

Kate came forward and took Marsha's arm. Seeing your child in Raymond's condition would be a shock—to any mother, even a part-time one. "Sit down here, Marsha. Remember I did tell you that Raymond had been in this school fight. Raymond will be fine. Ian's just taken him to the pediatrician."

Marsha sat down at the kitchen table, her head in her hands. "I can't look," she moaned. "I can't look."

"Well, don't look," Ian said coldly. "Just listen. Ray got beaten up by some tough kids at school, and—I've taken him out of that school. He won't be going back. Everything is under control."

Marsha peeked through her fingers at Raymond and slowly took her hands away from her face. She was trembling. "How could such a thing happen? What kind of school was he in? You should have listened to Daddy. Daddy always said—"

"I know what Daddy always said," Ian answered. "But let's forget that. Ray doesn't want to go to a military school and I agree. But I, we've, made other arrangements." He turned to Kate. "Do you mind if we use your living room? It's such a mess outside. By the time we get over to my place we'll be frozen."

"Please do," Kate said. She turned to her children. "Go watch a video in your rooms or something. Go on, now. Go." And with obvious reluctance Joy and Tommy left the kitchen.

"I wanna stay here," Raymond said tentatively, looking at Ian.

"Sure. Your mother and I need to talk things over. Come on, Marsha. Stop dramatizing. We can talk about this sensibly." He waited with obvious impatience while she got up and, still casting horrified glances at Raymond, preceded him back toward the living room.

Kate went to look out the window over the sink. It was coming down more heavily now, almost a curtain of white with little chips of ice in it. Her heart was pounding. *Dear God, please forgive me. I have no right to be jealous of Marsha.* But Ian had reached out to her, taken her into his arms when she had been upset about Raymond. Kate picked up a glass and ran some water into it, took a sip and put it down. She heard Raymond behind her, flinging himself into a kitchen chair.

"They're gonna have a fight," he muttered. "I always *know* when they're gonna fight. I get the vibes." He was clicking something. Kate could hear the rhythmic little clicks.

"I don't care, you know?" Raymond was saying. "They can fight all they want. I don't care." His voice sounded oddly thick, and she turned around.

"I don't care," Raymond was repeating, and Kate saw tears rolling down his battered face. His thin hand was grasping the saltcellar, which he was hitting the table with again and again. "I don't care."

Kate rushed to him and took his bony, shaking body into her arms to hold him close, while angry words came to them from the living room despite the closed door. She wondered frantically if Tommy and Joy had really gone to their rooms.

Marsha was fairly screaming. "He could have been killed! My only child! How could you..."

Then Ian's voice, lower, controlled. "Keep your voice down!"

"Daddy told you and told you..."

Ian's voice was saying something they couldn't hear.

"...Chet said...Chet will adopt him. Chet cares about my son. Chet..."

Kate felt Raymond stiffen against her. "Over my dead body," he muttered. "That stick."

"Shush," Kate said into his hair. "Your father will handle it. Don't worry."

Marsha was crying now, great rasping sobs. "My child," she moaned. "You can't be trusted to take care…"

Again they couldn't hear Ian's response.

"…he'll put a stop to this…" Marsha's wail came through.

Then Ian's voice, angry. "Stop it! Stop this! Hysterics don't work with me anymore. You're talking nonsense!"

Kate was holding her breath, waiting, but no further sound came, and she heard Ian's firm footsteps coming toward the kitchen. Raymond straightened and grabbed a paper napkin to blot his face, but not soon enough.

Ian came over to the table. His face was flushed with anger, his eyes glinting. His hands rubbed over Raymond's thin shoulders. "Forget whatever you heard, buddy," he said. "We're a team. Nothing's going to change that. Okay?" He turned to Kate. "I'm sorry. This is embarrassing."

"It's all right," Kate said quickly. "Can I help? Can I do anything?"

"No. I mean yes. Maybe you can. She'll have a splitting headache. She always does when she has one of these screaming fits. I'm sorry. I'm really sorry about this."

"No problem," Kate said, taking a clean glass down from the cupboard. She was aware that her hands were slightly shaking.

Somehow she got the aspirin bottle and a glass of water into the living room without mishap, feeling a surge of mixed emotions. Marsha was sitting on the couch, leaning forward, her hands braced on the coffee table.

"Here, Marsha. Take a couple of aspirin. You'll feel better," Kate said. She couldn't help feeling sorry for her.

"I need some tissues," Marsha said piteously. "Have you got some tissues? Ian is such a beast. He never understands." She started to cry again.

"I'll get some," Kate said, putting down the water and aspirin. When she came back with the box Marsha was putting the glass back down on the table.

"I took two. You said a couple," she said, like a little girl who had done as she had been told and wanted praise for it.

"Good. Now here are the tissues," Kate said. "Would you like to freshen up a bit?" She didn't want to tell Marsha that her eye makeup was smudged below her lovely eyes.

"I'm...probably a mess," Marsha said tiredly. "Yes, I should...freshen up," she added without moving. "I'm just so beat. I've been on the go for twenty-four hours. If I weren't so tired I...wouldn't have lost control like that. But seeing Raymond..." Her voice dwindled away.

"Would you like to lie down a while?" Kate asked.

"I'd like to...go to bed," Marsha said. "Would that be asking too much?" She started to say something else, but Ian came into the room.

"Don't be ridiculous," he said. "We've imposed on Kate enough. She doesn't have any spare rooms. Come on. I'll take you next door."

"Don't *you* be ridiculous," she said, anger underlying her tone. "*I'm Chet's wife*. I don't think he'd take kindly to that." There was just a hint of smugness as she watched Ian's face flame.

"You can have my room," Kate said quickly. "It would be better than trying to get a cab in this weather to find some hotel. It's all right, Ian. This couch is a makedown and very comfortable. Don't worry. Come along, Marsha. You'll feel better after you've had some rest. I'll bring you something to eat later."

Ian still loves her. Kate forced herself to be calm and composed. She showed Marsha the bathroom, got her clean towels and washcloth. She made up her own bed with fresh sheets.

Keep busy. Don't think. Why do I feel this way because Ian loves Marsha? She wondered. He's only my neighbor. I don't care. I mean, I shouldn't care. But I do. I do. I care. She was vaguely aware that Tommy and Joy had gone back to the kitchen to be with Raymond and that the children were talking, but she couldn't hear what they were saying. Where is Ian? What is Ian doing? she thought. Was he still in the living room? What was he thinking? Was he racked with jealousy because of this Chet person? *Chet's a stick, Ian.*

Marsha was showered and sweetly fragrant when she came into Kate's bedroom and saw the turned-down bed.

"Oh, Kate, thank you. A bed never looked so good. It just came over me all of a sudden. I just hit the wall. I've never felt so exhausted. I used your hair dryer, I hope that was okay. I thought I'd brought mine, but I couldn't find it in the bag."

"Of course, that's okay. Just get into bed. I'll bring you something to eat later."

"No, please don't. All I want is sleep. You're an angel to do this." Marsha slipped out of her elegant peach-colored robe, revealing an elegant peach-colored nightgown, and got into Kate's bed with a sigh. "I'll have to call your hairdresser tomorrow," she said tiredly. "Turn off all the lights, will you? I don't sleep well with any light on.''

I don't have a hairdresser, Kate thought. Can't you tell by my awful hair? She hurriedly got her own nightclothes and took them into Joy's room until she needed them. Somewhere in the back of her mind she was hearing her sister Jill's voice, and Jill was saying something about *highlights* and *glints*. She was saying, *No, I don't mean dyeing. I mean just adding a touch of light here and there. I see you with short hair, a layered, smart-looking style.* And at some time or other Jill had offered to do what she called a ''makeover.'' Bracing herself, Kate went back into the living room. Forget makeover, Jill. I can never compete with Marsha. Not in a million years.

Ian was slumped on the couch. He was putting the glass down on the table. ''I took some of your aspirin,'' he said bleakly. ''I'm really embarrassed about this. I can usually manage to keep my troubles to myself.''

Kate sat down opposite him. ''Don't worry. These things happen. I'm sorry I couldn't warn you in front of Raymond, but Marsha mentioned that adoption idea to me, so I knew it was coming.'' She glanced at her watch. It was only four forty-five. Not time to start dinner yet.

''I shouldn't be surprised,'' Ian muttered. ''Marsha's always got an angle. My guess is that Burgess wants a family—he's a bit older than she is.'' He looked at her questioningly.

''I...I think that's what she said. She plans to have their own baby,'' Kate said, to be fair. ''But not immediately.''

''Don't take any bets on it,'' Ian said. ''Raymond was what they call an 'unplanned pregnancy.' I'm sorry. I shouldn't be dumping on you like this.''

''It's all right. This is stressful for all of you,'' Kate

said. She knew all about Raymond's beginnings. They had been too careless, not realizing how quickly he understood the nuances. *I heard 'em fighting, see. I almost got aborted. Marsha's always bringing it up to him. How he told Granddad and Granddad put a stop to it. There's lots of money on the Greer side and Marsha's an only child.* Raymond hadn't missed much.

"How's Marsha doing?" Ian asked.

"She took a shower and went to bed. She *did* seem exhausted."

"I'm sure she is. That's vintage Marsha. She's probably bushed. She does that, goes and goes and goes and then crashes. This is an old rerun. Burgess didn't come with her? Did she say where he is?"

"I think she said he had gone to break the news to his family about the marriage, about not waiting for the June wedding."

He was quiet for a time, slowly twisting the water glass on the coffee table, around and around. He looked desolate, and it tore her heart. She was accustomed to seeing him as Raymond saw him—confident, successful, always in control. *Dad's always been first string. In everything. All his life he's total success.* She wanted desperately to comfort him in some way. Almost six years ago when Claude had died she had settled down to a life of widowhood and motherhood, sure she could never be attracted to another man.

Until now.

For the first time she admitted to herself honestly that she could love again and, *Oh, dear God, help me,* this was the man. She wanted to touch him, push back his hair from falling over his forehead, reassure him, heal his hurt.

He looked up at her, his beautiful hazel eyes troubled.

"You're a good friend, Kate."

A good friend. She made herself say it. "Well, neighbors help neighbors, Ian. And you know how fond I am of Raymond."

"You've been a godsend to my boy. I could never repay you for what you do for him."

I don't want you to pay me. I want you to love me. She wasn't looking at him anymore, for fear of what he might see in her eyes. Sounding practical and neighborly, she said, "What will you do now? Don't you think you'd better try to nip this adoption idea in the bud? Can you do that?"

"Yes. Absolutely. I mean, I'm pretty sure I can. I know I'm just a working stiff and I'm up against people who can usually get their way, but I don't think Justin—Marsha's dad—will go for that. He's a pretty fair-minded guy. Things like old-fashioned honor count with him."

"Where is he? Can you reach him?"

"What time is it?"

"Almost five."

"They're over in Scottsdale for the winter. They like the sun. He'd just about be coming in from the golf course, I think. May I use your phone? Now, where's my phone card?" He had taken out his billfold and was shuffling through credit cards. Kate got up to leave and he glanced up. "Would you mind sticking around? I...kinda need some moral support."

"Of course." Kate sat back down, feeling a warm glow in spite of herself. It was nice to be needed. She watched him covertly, seeing the hard clear line of his jaw, the breadth of his shoulders, the way he moved to the little phone table near the door, the way he picked up the phone and punched in the numbers. Apparently someone answered almost immediately.

"Lydia? Ian here. How are you? Getting enough sun over there?" Then a pause. "Yeah, we're snowed in." Then a longer pause. "Actually, I'd like to speak to Justin if he's available. Oh, fine. Yes. Marsha's here. She's told me about the marriage." Longer pause. "Of course I'm glad she's found someone. I wish them every happiness. I... Oh, okay. Hello, Justin. Yes, I was just telling Lydia that Marsha came here to Seattle."

There was a much longer pause as he listened intently to his former father-in-law. "Yes, she told me that, too. It's out of the question, of course. I would never agree to give up my son. Never." Then he listened quietly for a long time. Finally, his tone sounding relieved, he said, "Thank you, sir. I appreciate your support on this, and I will think about some sort of boarding school, but for now I have another arrangement I want to try. Why don't I call you again when I've got it firmed up? Raymond's pretty upset. There was some trouble at school and he got the short end of it."

They talked a while longer and Kate felt a growing sense of relief. Apparently Marsha's father was in agreement with Ian. When Ian rang off he came back to the couch.

"Well, that's that for now," he said with a sigh. "I wish the weather would break so I could get Marsha to some hotel. I know she can't get out of Seattle yet. We had the news on the radio coming back from the doctor's and Sea-Tac is snowed in. Nothing's coming in or going out. Which reminds me. I didn't finish telling you about what Dr. Madison said. I really have to go down to Raymond's school. They don't want the gangs to get down into the middle schools, or next it's the elementary schools. The world's gone nuts. I understand that the Seattle police have a special gang unit that needs to know these things.''

''That's encouraging, at least,'' Kate said. ''When you told Colonel Greer you had another arrangement you wanted to try, was that...?''

He grinned. ''Yeah. Raymond's so stressed-out I guess I'd better go along with the homeschooling. At least for a while. When he's with you... Kate, you have no idea how much you mean to that boy. And since you offered, I...''

''Oh, yes, I'm eager to try it, Ian,'' Kate said, feeling a rush of excitement. ''School is closed for students now, but I'll bet the administrative offices aren't. I'll talk to someone tomorrow. I'll check with Pastor Ledbetter for some coaching first,'' she added. Somehow she had to make this work, for everybody's sake.

''Justin means well, but he's one of those people who thrive on stress and pressure. He doesn't really understand that some people can't. He made it through seven years as a POW in Viet Nam. You've never met him, have you?''

''No. Mrs. Greer was here once, to see Raymond, and I met her, but not the colonel.''

''He's one of those thin wiry guys, quiet, soft spoken, never hurried, never rattled, a real old-line gentleman, but hard as nails underneath. His idea, and he honestly believes it, is that a good military school would 'toughen Ray up'—his phrase, not mine. I think I know my boy, and that toughening-up process kids in a military academy go through would scatter what reserves Ray has left. If I have to settle for a boarding school it's going to be one more laid-back than that.''

''You won't have to settle for any boarding school,''

Kate said firmly. *Oh, God, please help me. I'm not sure I know what I'm doing.*

"I'll help you all I can between trips. I wish…"

"You wish what?"

He sighed. "I wish I hadn't pushed so hard for this promotion that keeps me on the road so much. But it's part of the game. And it'll be a while before I move past it. Thank heaven you stepped in to take over Raymond's care. You just looked at your watch. Am I keeping you from something?"

"I was just checking to see how much time I have until I start dinner. And I've got almost an hour yet."

"Time to look over that homeschooling stuff again?" he asked hopefully.

"Yes. I was just thinking that." And a few minutes later they were seated at the dining-room table with the contents of Pastor Ledbetter's battered briefcase spread before them.

"I talked a bit with Dr. Madison about this," Ian said, "and she thought anything that takes the pressure off Ray would be good. You and he get along so well. He does things for you that he'd dig his heels in about with anyone else. This may be the answer, at least for the time being."

They studied the material together, finding little nuggets of agreement and encouragement.

"Your pastor is right about the less rigid system. You and the kids don't want to burn out trying to imitate a school," Ian said.

"And look," Kate said. "Look at the educational stuff available at Seattle Center and the Pacific Science Center. I'll call tomorrow and get on their mailing lists."

They were interrupted by the phone ringing. It was

Kate's mother, Beth, who ran a successful bed-and-breakfast about ten blocks away.

"Kate, dear," she said, "can't you get through with the muffins?"

"Oh, good grief, Mom. I got involved with... something here and clean forgot. Don't tell me you actually have more guests. How did they get through from Sea-Tac or wherever?"

Beth laughed. "They didn't. These are the ones who can't get out. So they are staying on until meltdown. I'm temporarily a boardinghouse, serving three meals a day. It's only humane, since they're stuck here playing Scrabble and doing your dad's old jigsaw puzzles."

At the mention of her late father Kate felt again the sense of loss. How she would have loved to talk things over with Dad. She could certainly use his gentle common-sense wisdom now.

"Just a minute, Mom," she said, turning to Ian. "Ian, I make those miniature muffins twice a week for Mom's guest house. You know the ones I mean. I was supposed to be making them today. I can whip up a few batches now. When they're done could you take me over in your van? It got through fine this morning."

"Sure. No problem."

"Mom, do you need anything else besides muffins? You know I have a lot of canned summer fruit and frozen vegetables from my garden. Maybe you'd better give me a list."

"I was going to ask you. Yes, I'm short a lot of things, since I only usually do breakfasts." She gave Kate a list of things to bring.

The children were elated at the late muffin-baking time and pitched in to help. One of the specialities of Beth's bed-and-breakfast was the wide variety of the two-bite-size muffins. Kate had been supplying them and other baked goods since the business had opened. She was the best cook in the family and it added to her small income.

Now Tommy and Joy set the table and Raymond prepared the dinner vegetables and, between muffin batches, Kate made hash from leftover roast beef. Ian watched them.

"I didn't know you were so good in the kitchen, Ray," he said, and Raymond laughed.

"I help a lot. I know how to do a lot of things, Dad. I'm not a washout in everything."

"Oh, I believe it, buddy. You've got success genes you haven't even used yet."

The dinner was rather fun, with a lot of joking and laughing because the timer kept ringing and Kate would have to jump up and take a batch out of the oven or put one in.

It was almost nine o'clock before the muffins were all baked and the children put to bed. Raymond usually slept at home when Ian wasn't away. But tonight, because of the snow, he stayed. Raymond often found excuses not to stay in the big house next door. Ian helped with bedtime, and Kate was filled with a warm glow. It's almost like family, she reflected. This crisis, unpleasant as it had been, had been a kind of breakthrough. I know now, she thought. I know. And she hugged the knowledge secretly to her heart.

Her private joy lasted until Marsha came softly into the kitchen in her lovely peach-colored robe, her dark hair tousled from sleep. "What in the world are you doing?"

"Oh, dear, did our noise wake you?" Kate asked.

"It didn't matter," Marsha said, sitting down at the

kitchen table. "I think I got hungry after all. What is that heavenly smell?"

"Muffins. I make them for my mother's bed-and-breakfast. They are so small her guests get a kick out of having several different kinds. Would you like some? I've got banana, orange and nut, cinnamon and blueberry tonight."

"Yes, could I have some? I think the blueberry. No, maybe the cinnamon." Marsha settled back in the kitchen chair, looking around Kate's old-fashioned kitchen. "Where's Ian?"

"He's probably in the boys' room with Raymond. They don't get enough time together, with Ian traveling so much." As soon as she said it she was sorry. *Bite your tongue, Kate.* "Here you are," she added brightly, handing Marsha a small plate of four tiny buttered muffins. "Would you like some tea?"

"That would be lovely, thank you."

At that moment Ian came back into the kitchen. "Oh, hi, Marsha. Couldn't you sleep through our racket?"

"I did sleep a while, and I'm going back to bed as soon as I finish these. They're delicious. Did you have some?"

"Yes. I've had them before. Kate's a generous cook."

Marsha said she would stay up until they came back from delivering the muffins.

"Kate, you're sure you don't mind Marsha staying over? It's an imposition, I know," he asked in the van.

"Not really. In an emergency anything goes, and this snow is an emergency."

He laughed, but sounded tired. "I still have a pile of dictating at home, but I think I'll put it off until tomorrow. There's nothing much doing at the office anyhow—most of the staff couldn't get there today." When they came back, he asked, "If it's okay I'll just drop you off at the door and not come in."

She went in the back way to shake off the accumulated snow from her coat on the service porch. The house was silent, so at least the kids were still in bed.

When she went through the dining room, Marsha was standing at the dining-room table, leafing through all the homeschooling material. She looked up, her violet eyes filled with alarm, anger, resentment. "What in the world is all this?" she demanded. "What are you two planning to do?"

Chapter Four

Oh, no, Marsha. Why can't you just go away?

Kate was so tired when she came in that she wanted nothing so much as to crawl into her bed, which she couldn't do because Marsha would be sleeping in it.

"It's nothing to worry about," she heard herself saying calmly, going over to the dining-room table. "Raymond is going to be privately tutored for a while. Ian is taking him out of the school he's in."

"For how long? When is Ian going to face facts that he's a single parent—*and I'm not?*"

The words sent a chill through Kate. Should she call Ian? No, he had left exhausted, as well. Marsha was right. Ian *was* a single parent, away most of the time, and Marsha was married with, as she had said, this perfect little gem of a house in Georgetown. How would that look in court? Before a judge who knew nothing of the background?

Kate started gathering up the homeschooling material.

"Look, Kate, let's level with each other. You and Ian think you're going to educate Raymond—*my son*—here at your dining-room table with... *this?* Well, maybe that's all right with Ian, but it's not all right with me. Or with my *father*, once he learns of it. I mean no offense, Kate, you personally are a lovely woman, and you mean well, but I can't just ignore this. I'm going to *have* to follow through on it. You must understand that. Raymond is my only son, and when it's time for college I want to see him accepted at a prestigious university, but he won't be if he's schooled at home.''

''That's not necessarily true. Raymond is a very intelligent boy,'' Kate said steadily. ''He is also a very sensitive boy. Ian talked this over with the pediatrician, Dr. Madison, and Dr. Madison was in favor of it. And I'm quite sure Raymond will be ready for a good university when the time comes.''

Marsha stood frowning, watching with troubled eyes as Kate put everything back into Pastor Ledbetter's old briefcase and stowed it in the bottom cupboard of the sideboard.

''I don't like it,'' Marsha said uncertainly. ''I'll have to discuss it with Chet. And with Daddy, of course. You do understand that, don't you, Kate?''

''Discuss it with anyone you want to,'' Kate said. ''You certainly have that right.'' She'd have to remember to tell Ian tomorrow, so that he could talk to Colonel Greer about it before Marsha got to him.

After Marsha had wandered back into Kate's bedroom and gone to bed again, Kate sat down in the big fireplace chair. She really should make down the couch and go to bed. She looked at her watch. Was it only ten forty-five? Jill would still be up. She and her husband, Greg, always had an unwinding interval after their three kids were down for the night. Kate, you're going off the deep end here, she thought. Deep end or not, she got up and went to the little phone table with its spindly little side chair. When Jill answered, she got right to the point. They knew each other so well that sometimes words were not necessary.

Kate, two years older than Jill, had abdicated her big-sister role early in their relationship. Jill was brighter, more assertive and seemed to have been born "in charge." It had taken Mom a while to stop saying, "Look after Jill, Kate" when they went out to play. Eventually Mom had "got it" that her baby was the leader and her older child seemed content to follow. Dad had always known, of course.

It was the same now and, Kate thought, a rather comfortable arrangement. She could always depend on Jill, and it had long ago ceased to bother her that Jill was the beautiful sister, with Mother's dark hair and eyes. Jill, who had a large share of the family guts, had made the hard decision to put her career as a successful restaurant owner on hold until their three children were raised.

"Jill," Kate said, "I've been thinking today how awful I look. I don't even want a mirror in the house anymore. I didn't used to look this awful. Claude thought I was pretty. I *was* kind of pretty, at least in my wedding picture I was. But, you know, I don't really keep myself up the way you do. It just doesn't seem to be in my nature. You would die before you wore your hair in a skinned-back ponytail fastened with a rubber band, wouldn't you?"

"Ah…yes, I would. Kate, what are you building up to? It's almost eleven o'clock and you are fretting about your ponytail? There's got to be a reason."

"Yes, there is. I want to *look* better. I mean all the time. And, uh, a couple of times you've mentioned that you wished I'd let you give me a makeover."

"A makeover," Jill said thoughtfully. "Kate, does this have something to do with Ian McAllister?"

Trust Jill to read between the lines.

"Yes. But I don't feel like talking about it right now."

"Right. Well, let me think a minute. We can't do much until the snow goes. And the weatherman just said we're stuck for at least three more days. But I think this is wonderful news. You don't *have to* look like a little peeled onion. I agree, your hair isn't the greatest color, but we can fix that..."

Kate started to object, but Jill cut her short. "No, not dyeing it. Just a few little highlights here and there. And Mom and I would love to see you in a short cut. But you know, a makeover isn't just from the neck up."

"Well, I'm not overweight anymore. I know I was getting a little chubby, which I can't afford to at my height, and I got that exercise video. Tommy and I do that every morning, and it's trimmed me down several pounds."

"I don't mean your body. Your body is okay for someone only five feet tall. I mean your wardrobe. Kate, if you are thinking about what I think you are thinking about, you're going to have to get rid of those faded denim skirts and tacky cotton blouses."

"I...I don't want to spend too much money," Kate said cautiously. Pinching pennies had become a life work since Claude's death, when her income had become so limited. On the other hand, she had more money now. Ian was paying her too generously for Raymond's care and Mom always insisted on paying top dollar for the homemade baked goods for the B and B.

"Kate? Are you there? Or did you go into shock about the wardrobe makeover? Thrift shops are out, Kate. Out. Are you hearing me?"

"Loud and clear," Kate said, suddenly laughing. Imagine that. Not shopping in thrift shops anymore. She really was going off the deep end, but somehow it didn't seem to matter. She looked down and saw the faded denim skirt and faded tacky cotton blouse, and remembered that Jill always changed her clothes in the middle of the afternoon, after her housekeeping was finished, so that she always looked lovely when Greg came home. Suddenly anything was possible.

As soon as the rains come back," Jill was saying, "we'll get together." Then, miraculously, Kate didn't feel tired any more and she and Jill settled down to a good gossip. She gave Jill an update on Raymond's condition. She told Jill about Marsha's arrival and the home-schooling decision. She told Jill about Mom's three-meals-a-day guests, until somehow it was almost midnight before they rang off.

The next morning about ten o'clock Kate saw Ian's sport van drive into the McAllister driveway and Ian, in jeans, boots and heavy windbreaker, walk through knee-high snow to her back door. She was at the back door to open it for him. He took off the knit cap he was wearing.

"I saw everybody out in front," he said, smiling. "They all seem to be having a great time."

"Yes, they are," Kate said, taking the cap. "Come on in. I was about to have a coffee break. Would you like some?"

All three children and Marsha, dressed in one of Claude's old ski outfits, were out in front rebuilding the snowman, who had suffered some damage during the night's storm. Marsha had said nothing more about the homeschooling or about Raymond's custody. She had been up early, had eaten breakfast with them, and seized the opportunity to join in the snow fun out front. Kate had observed her from the front window and knew that she was actually having as much fun as the children were. And they, like children everywhere, accepted a new playmate without question.

Kate did tell Ian that Marsha knew about the homeschooling idea. "I'm sorry," she said. "I should have cleared the stuff off the dining-room table."

"No problem," Ian said easily, sitting down at the kitchen table. "It's a done deal, anyhow. I called your Pastor Ledbetter early this morning. He's a great old guy, isn't he? He volunteered to go with me over to Raymond's school to see the principal. And we did. I think the principal didn't want to refuse a sudden request from a man of the cloth, and I think Ledbetter knew it, because he offered to make the call and ask for an appointment. Anyhow, we went over."

"And what happened?" Kate asked, pouring them each a cup of coffee. "Would you like some muffins with that?"

"Yes. Thanks. Orange and nut if you have any of those left. What happened was the principal already knew about the gang activity. The school bus driver had already not only reported it to him, she identified the kids involved. So that part's taken care of. Raymond doesn't even have to go down and appear or anything. He's a nice guy, the principal. Name of Donald Chan. Ledbetter and Chan got along great. Both are educators at heart. Did you know that Ledbetter started out as a teacher? Ledbetter's dream is that some day he can add a school to his church."

"But what did he say about Raymond?" Kate asked as she put some muffins in the microwave.

"He disagrees with homeschooling on principle, but he did agree that until this gang threat is resolved Raymond is better off out of that school. He talked with three of Raymond's teachers on the phone and they all told him that Ray is smart enough to probably get by with homeschooling until June and pass on into eighth grade on the basis of exams. Then he wants to talk to me about it again. Ray's English teacher says Ray owes an English paper, but beyond that he's up-to-date with everything.''

"Well, I can take care of that," Kate said decisively. "He didn't tell me he owed an English paper."

"Chan says he'd like a note from Dr. Madison about the extent of Ray's injuries, just for the record. So I'll get that for him. There was only one little hang-up.''

"What was that?' Kate asked, taking the muffins out of the microwave and putting a small plate of them with a pat of butter in front of Ian.

"First thing he asked was am I a single parent? And I had to say I was. But Ledbetter helped out there. He explained that Raymond had a full-time caretaker in you and he gave you high marks in parenting skills. Marsha is right. The single-parent thing is a handicap.'' Ian bit into his muffin.

Kate remembered suddenly, and very vividly, the opening lines of one of the Jane Austen novels she and Jill had loved. If ever a man was in want of a wife, Ian was. *Oh, Jill, think makeover.*

"So, anyhow, Chan is not going to make a fuss about the homeschooling in Raymond's case. Until he can quash that gang nonsense, he thinks it might be a good solution. Besides, it's perfectly legal in this state, so there is really nothing he can do about it.''

Kate sat down and took a sip of coffee. The die was cast, then. And she must make it work, for all their sakes.

Marsha stayed three days, until Seattle's dependable rains came pouring down and washed away the drifts of snow and the city came alive again. Kate observed Marsha's conduct with Raymond with mingled irritation and sympathetic understanding. Marsha was doing her best to behave in a motherly and attentive manner to Raymond. She gave him enormous amounts of affection. He had only to express a desire for something and Marsha ordered it sent to him. Deliveries of these goodies would begin after the snow melted. Thus Raymond became the owner of a new CD player and numerous records, and he almost got a moped, but Ian objected that he was too young for any motor-driven vehicle. So Raymond settled for two new skateboards, and Kate suspected that as soon as Marsha left, he would give one to Tommy.

Raymond, always hungry for love, responded to Marsha with cautious eagerness. It tore at Kate's heart. Marsha was, after all, his mother and, in her own way, she did love Raymond.

When Sea-Tac was again functioning as an airport Marsha took the first plane out that she could get for Alexandria, Virginia, where the Burgess family home was. Kate drove her to the airport, because Ian had had to leave earlier on another business trip. All three children insisted on going, too, as they all liked the excitement of the crowded airport, and Marsha had become their good friend because she had been such fun playing in the snow.

Marsha impulsively kissed Kate goodbye. "You've been such a doll," she said, "taking me in like that. I hope I wasn't too much in the way. And you're such a terrific cook I've probably gained ten pounds. I'll be in touch." Then she kissed all the children and they stood at the wide window waving at the plane as it took off.

That night when Kate listened to the children's prayers she was surprised that Raymond prayed for his mother.

"And please help Marsha, God. She doesn't mean to be like that. She really means well. It's just that, uh, she can't always make it as a mother. Uh...I guess that's all. Amen. G'night, Mom."

Children had their own wisdom, Kate thought sadly.

Ian's business trip was a short one this time, and he came back the same day Jill had set for Kate's makeover. She had talked to their mother about it, and so Beth came over to Kate's. Beth had brought them two early Easter gifts, mother-and-daughter dresses for Kate and Joy.

"What a nice idea, Mom," Kate said. "But why did you do it?" The dresses were pale blue challis with a Laura Ashley look, nice enough to wear to church in summer.

"Ask Jill," Beth said, smiling her lovely smile. Mom was so beautiful. She had come to terms with Dad's death more than a year ago and seemed more lighthearted than she had been in some time. All but one of her stranded B and B guests had gone. He had asked to stay on for a few more days, she said.

Jill had brought along her three children, and they all were now out in the backyard together. Mom would watch the children until Jill and Kate returned.

"I'll catch up on my bookkeeping," Beth said, putting a couple of ledgers on the kitchen table along with a brown envelope stuffed with papers.

"Well," Jill said, "I thought it looked rather too obvious for you to suddenly become adorable just as Ian needs a wife, so I thought a good cover might be this mother-daughter thing. We're going to restyle Joy's hair, too, unless you don't want her in short hair."

Kate had to laugh. There was no such thing as a secret in this family. They all knew each other too well.

"Short hair is fine for Joy unless she wants to keep it long. Summer is coming."

Joy was called in from the backyard and was elated at the makeover idea. On the way to the hairdresser, Jill spoke from her secure position of sister-plus-best-friend.

"What exactly do you want from this makeover, Kate?"

"I want to be beautiful," Kate said, half in fun.

"Forget beautiful, Kate. Beautiful is out. With a perfectly round face, round eyes, a short nose and five feet tall, you've got to settle for cute."

"Cute's fine, Mommy," Joy said from the back seat.

Kate grimaced. "I'll settle for what I can get," she conceded as they parked in front of the hairdresser's.

Two hours later she knew the makeover was going to be a success. "I'm afraid I am cute," she said with satisfaction, more pleased than she would admit, as she gazed in fascination at her highlighted light brown hair cut in a carefree, tousled style with little feathers of pointed bangs. "This is certainly an improvement."

"I think I got beautiful," Joy said, gazing at her own image. Kate, looking at her, silently agreed. This child had inherited Claude's dark hair and brilliant blue eyes. She felt a warm glow of pride.

Jill also insisted they shop, and Kate spent more money than she had intended. They first made a brief stop at the makeup counter. Although Kate rarely wore makeup—and bought cosmetics at the drugstore—Jill insisted she try some good moisturizer, a light foundation and lipstick in a fashionable color. Kate allowed the salesclerk to show her what she needed and was pleased with the results. It was amazing what a dab of lipstick could do for a person.

Next came clothes. The denim skirts and tacky cotton tops soon became history. She bought several casual daytime outfits in muted colors and a rather dressy evening suit in pearl gray with a slit skirt.

"I've never worn a slit skirt before," Kate said doubtfully.

"Slit skirts are fine if you have good legs," Jill said firmly. "And we both have good legs, even if yours are shorter."

Kate, fascinated with her improved appearance, had sneaked looks at herself every time they passed a mirror or any reflecting surface in the department stores and shops. Eat your heart out, Marsha, she thought. And I'm a terrific cook, too.

They stopped at a nice restaurant for lunch and only decided to go home when Joy started to droop with weariness. Kate, too, had suddenly had enough of shopping. She wanted to get home and change out of her brown suit. Before today it had been her "best," but it was one of the last things she had worn during her working years and was more than twelve years old. She had thought of it as "best" for too long. Today, in comparison with the new garments she had bought, she was acutely aware of the sprung seat of the skirt and the sag in the jacket pockets. The brown suit had to go the way of the denim skirts and cotton tops. It had served its time.

When they got home, she found Ian in the kitchen talking to Mom. They were discussing home burglar alarms and security systems. Last year during the slack season Mom and Laura, Jill's mother-in-law, had taken a two-week holiday in Hawaii and if it had not been for an alert neighbor, Mom's B and B would have been burgled. Mom was studying a brochure thoughtfully at the kitchen table.

"Think about it," Ian was saying. "If you leave the house empty again, this would be the minimum that I'd advise. I think—" He stopped, doing a quick double take as Kate, Jill and Joy came in.

"Wow," he said. "What have you done? I almost didn't recognize you. And Joy! Come here, Joy, let me look at you."

"Oh, girls! That's just lovely," Mom said, dropping the brochure. "It's marvelous!"

"I gotta show the other kids," Joy said delightedly and rushed out into the backyard, shouting, "Look at me! Look at me!"

Tommy and Raymond, plus Jill's three—Laurie, Ben and little Megan—all crowded around Joy, who turned this way and that, preening.

"You should see Mom," she said. "Come in and see Mom!" This prompted a pell-mell rush into the house to see Mom and, suddenly filled with awe at the change they saw in Mom, all the children stood staring, trying to take it in.

"All right," Kate said, embarrassment coloring her cheeks. "I have a new hairdo. I was sick of that ponytail. Let's not make a big deal of it."

Raymond was the first to find his voice. "Well, it wasn't what you call a great hairdo. I have to admit it. I never wanted to say anything because of, you know, respect and all, but that ponytail was the pits."

"Mommy, you're beautiful," Tommy said soberly. "I never knew you were beautiful."

Jill's eldest, Laurie, spoke up. "Well, you know, it's like a princess. You don't know the princess is beautiful until this magic charm happens, and then you know."

"We bought a zillion things," Joy announced exuberantly. "You should see the stuff Mom bought. Aunt Jill says her denim skirts and old blouses—"

"That's enough," Kate said in sudden panic. How many of the adults' comments had Joy picked up from the back seat?

"I'd love to see what you bought," Mom said, getting up from the kitchen table. "Why don't you give us a fashion show?" And blandly ignoring Kate's warning look, continued. "Let's go into the living room. There isn't enough room in here."

And Jill was no help when Kate turned to her. Ignoring Kate's signals, Jill said brightly. "What a great idea! We got some wonderful bargains."

Kate had to count to ten three times to keep her temper. She was very family oriented, a great believer in the family system, but now and then, to borrow a phrase from Raymond, it was the pits. Just a hint from her to Jill and then Jill and Mom both were throwing her in Ian's face. *I can manage my own life, thank you,* she thought as Mom was saying to Ian, "You come, too, Ian. We may need a man's viewpoint on some of these things.

"Don't look so grim," Jill said in Kate's bedroom. "You're supposed to smile as you model clothes. Here, let's hike that up a bit at the waist. You'll need to take up the hem on all of them, of course."

"I wish you hadn't told Mom," Kate grumbled.

"I didn't *have* to tell Mom. She *knew.* This light spring green is a good color on you. Not everybody can wear green. Mom has never stopped being Mom, Kate. She's had Ian pegged for you from a long time ago."

"You've *talked* about it!" Kate said, scandalized.

"Of course we've *talked* about it," Jill said, imitating Kate's outraged tone. "We *care* about you. And we feel, we both feel, and Greg agrees, that you and Ian would be a great couple.''

''You talked to *Greg*—''

''Relax. Smile,'' Jill commanded. ''Come on. You're holding up the fashion show. They're tired of looking at Joy in blue challis by now.''

Somehow Kate made the best of it and got through. The children's presence helped. Their ohs and ahs at each new garment made it possible for her to pretend she didn't notice Ian, politely admiring. Surely he must know she was blatantly being thrown in his face. As an attractive single male he must have coped with this sort of thing for a long time. He probably had all his defenses in place.

It was a relief when the day was over and she could put the children to bed. She always listened first to Tommy's prayers in the boys' room. He played hard after school and was a child who fell asleep as soon as his head touched the pillow. On the other hand, Raymond was a child who had to have what he called an ''unwinding'' time, and he always read for about an hour.

Tonight his prayers were rather perfunctory and hurried. As soon as he said his *amen,* he scrambled up from his knees and caught her arm as she started to leave.

''Can you wait a minute?'' he asked, keeping his voice low because of Tommy asleep in the other twin bed.

''Why? What?'' Kate asked as she sat down again on the side of the bed.

Raymond pulled over a stool and sat down in front of her. He was going to need new pajamas soon. He was outgrowing these. He would grow as tall as Ian. The pants were up above his thin ankles.

''Put your slippers on,'' she said automatically. ''I've turned down the heat.''

"I was thinking today," he said as he got his slippers and slid his feet into them, "about the future. I think I might as well just say it. Would you be interested in marrying my dad?"

Kate felt her face flame. "Raymond! Really—"

"I mean that seriously. You're single. He's single. He's a nice guy. You're a super mom. You guys get along. What's wrong with that kind of deal?"

"Raymond, this is really—"

"Okay. I apologize for invading your privacy, or whatever. But I'm like walking a tightrope, see. All the time. Dad could fall for any dumb little twit from his office any day. I got to give him credit. He's pretty good at not getting involved. We had a couple of young housekeepers before he wised up and told the agency to send only old ladies. But I'm not deaf, dumb and blind, see. I know a lot about life that people don't know I know and—well, I think you and he would be a great pair. And I got a lot riding on this because now Marsha and this Chet guy are after me. It'll be years and years before I'm old enough to tell everybody to take a hike." He paused for breath, his eyes, so like Ian's, troubled and anxious.

Kate looked at his earnest face, still bruised from the battering he had taken at school. He deserved her honesty. She chose her words carefully.

"This must be kept absolutely confidential," she began.

He nodded soberly. "I'm like a clam when I wanna be."

"I...have learned to care a great deal for your father. And...if it happened that he learned to care for me I'd be more than willing to marry him. But these things sometimes happen, and sometimes they don't. If this…doesn't happen, you can never say anything about it. Do you understand what I'm saying?''

"Yes. Yes, I do. I'm not stupid. I would never say anything. Especially to my dad I wouldn't say anything. But I think my dad is smart enough to pick up on this. Getting rid of that ponytail was a great idea. You owe Aunt Jill a big one.''

Kate started Raymond's homeschooling with the missing English paper. He wrote a rather good one on the poet Robert Frost, which earned him a B+ from his former English teacher. The English teacher sent Raymond a kind little note wishing him well, and a rather different note to Kate, which enclosed an article copied from a teacher's publication outlining the evils and risks of homeschooling your children. Kate set it aside to pass on to Pastor Ledbetter.

She and Raymond settled down at the dining-room table for the supervised study and work period every morning.

Following Pastor Ledbetter's advice, she didn't insist on too firm a structure, but let Raymond go at his own pace. It soon became clear that, left to his own choices, he would have skipped all math and science and concentrated on reading and history, which was new to him and which he found fascinating. She soon decided to use a workbook series for eighth-grade math, which included algebra. Raymond agreed that it would be best to do the math workbook sheets first thing, to get those finished and out of the way. Next he did the prescribed lessons in social studies, because it was another subject he would need to pass an exam in. About twice a week they made trips to the Pacific Science Center for its wealth of activities and exhibits. Ian kept close track of how he was doing and Kate kept him up-to-date on Raymond's progress.

"Pastor Ledbetter got some secondhand eighth-grade history texts used in some private schools. He says public schools skimp on history in favor of a broader social studies approach. And it turns out that Raymond loves history, along with reading, of course. He's reading at high school level, I think. We're working on some spelling drills, since his spelling is sometimes pretty original."

It had been a chill and windy March day and Kate had made a fire in the fireplace. She was wearing one of her new daytime outfits, a softly tailored brown jumper, hemmed just above her knees, with a cream-colored turtleneck underneath. Her brown tights and suede slip-on shoes gave the outfit a stylish, relaxed look.

"You can't know how much I appreciate this, Kate," Ian said, leaning forward and resting his arms on his knees. She could see only part of his face because he was looking down, but the firelight gleamed on his fair hair.

"I think I'm enjoying it as much as Raymond," Kate replied. "He's flourishing, and that's a real satisfaction. He's sleeping better and he isn't so nervous. He doesn't fidget so much now when he's supposed to be still.... You look tired," she couldn't help adding.

"I am." He leaned back in the chair. "I'm not prone to self-pity. At least, I hope I'm not, but...somehow...I've got myself onto a real treadmill. On the flight home this time, we were in this holding pattern over Sea-Tac for forty minutes, going around and around in circles, and it seemed the story of my life. Kate, I haven't had a date—I mean a real fun date, like a show and dinner and somebody to laugh with—for...oh, I can't remember when. And as I was circling around above Seattle this afternoon reading someone's discarded *Seattle Post-Intelligencer* for the second or third time, I saw that the Fifth Avenue Theater is reviving some of those old loud happy musicals. Like *Cats*. And *Evita*. and even *Hello, Dolly!* Look here, it's a series." He took a torn sheet of newsprint out of his jacket pocket. "Did you like those old musicals?"

"I loved them." Was this what she thought it was? *Oh, thank you, God.*

"Would you…could you…Kate, why don't you and I go out and have a night on the town? I'm not sure I'd remember how, but I'd be willing to give it a try."

She laughed in a sudden burst of pure joy. "I'll try, too. I'm sure together we'll remember enough to get by."

His laughter joined hers. "I'll get us season tickets, how's that? Can you arrange for the baby-sitting—I'll pay, of course."

"I don't think pay is necessary. My mother loves to baby-sit. I'll call her in the morning." Kate spoke with complete confidence. Sometimes families were a royal pain, but sometimes they were indispensable, and the pearl-gray dinner suit was waiting in the closet.

Chapter Five

Ian bought season tickets to the classic musical series at the Fifth Avenue Theater, and after the first show they lingered in the car in front of her house, laughing together, saying things like, "Remember when he..." and "What about the time she said..." as they relived the laughter they had enjoyed during the performance.

"I love the sound of your laugh," Ian said suddenly, and Kate sensed a new awareness between them. Her laugh dwindled, and she was looking up into his face *knowing* he was going to kiss her. She felt oddly tentative, hesitant. She had been locked in her widowhood for so long. *God, please let this be right. This has to be right.* And she went into his arms.

She was deeply shaken by his kiss, and he must have sensed it, because he drew back slightly. "Kate? Shouldn't...I have done that?" His voice was gentle and husky.

"Yes," Kate whispered when she could. "You should have. I love you. I love you so much," and she buried her face against him, and instantly his arms tightened about her. She heard him sigh as he continued to hold her closely, and kissed her again.

"Kate…do you love me enough to…marry me?" He held her away from him to see her face and Kate, breathless, filled with astonished wonder, looked up at him, cherishing the lines and planes of his face, the serious hazel eyes, the thick fair hair. *Can this be happening to me? Oh, dear God, thank you. Thank you.*

"Yes," she whispered. "Oh, yes. I do want to marry you. Didn't you ever guess?" And somehow she had started to cry. "I'll be a good wife, Ian," she said. "You'll never be sorry."

His arms tightened around her and he held her close again. "I know that," he said. "I just hope that I…" The sentence was never completed, because Kate took his face between her hands and kissed him again.

"When?" she asked. "When do you think—"

"Soon," he said firmly. "I'd say as soon as we can. No point in putting it off. We're not a couple of kids…"

"No. No, of course not." Kate was filled with wild excitement. "I'll tell Mom and Jill and call Pastor Ledbetter. Oh, and we must tell the children!" She felt the sting of tears again, remembering Raymond's desperate plea. *Would you be interested in marrying my dad?* "What about the wedding itself? What do you think?"

Ian had taken his handkerchief out and was gently blotting her cheeks. "I didn't intend to make you cry," he said softly.

"I always cry when I'm happy," Kate said. "Don't pay any attention to me."

"Oh, I intend to pay a lot of attention to you," Ian said. "I don't want you to…ever be sorry you married me."

"Sorry! How could I ever be sorry? Oh, Ian, there's so much to do, so many plans to make...."

"Yes. I want things to be exactly as you want them, Kate. However you want the wedding, then that's the way it will be." There was an oddly firm, no-nonsense tone to his voice.

"Oh, very simple," Kate said quickly. "I mean, since it's a second marriage for both of us. I think...just family? Would that be all right with you, just family?"

"Of course. And there isn't much family on my side. I have a married older sister, Denise. She and her husband, Chuck, live in Montana. He's a rancher. They'll want to come. And...would it bother you to have Raymond's grandparents? If it would, we'll skip them."

"No, of course not. I've met Mrs. Greer. She's a lovely woman. Yes, let's ask them. They're really still your relatives because of Raymond. Oh, Ian, I can hardly believe this."

"Believe it," he said quietly. "It's happening. And Kate..."

"Yes?"

"You won't be sorry. I promise. You'll never be sorry."

"Ian, you dear, dear, precious idiot. How could I ever be sorry?"

As they lingered, Kate talked in excited bursts, wondering if she had any sense at all, but did it really matter? She was going to be Ian's wife.

Finally, in her house, with Ian gone back to his house next door, she wanted to sing, dance, turn cartwheels. Her mother, who had been child-sitting, didn't need to be told.

"It happened, Mom," Kate said, her eyes brimming with tears.

"Oh, my dear baby. I'm so happy for you."

They had to talk about it, at least for a little while, regardless of the time. "Ian and I have a lot to decide yet...but, yes, we'll move over to his house next door...I don't know. I can rent or sell this one.... It's mine because Claude's insurance paid off the mortgage...I've got to call Pastor Ledbetter tomorrow...I really don't want a wedding dress, it's going to be so simple. You may think this is crazy, but I wonder if Jill still has that dressy ivory satin suit with the little seed pearls on the jacket lapels...we thought maybe we'd go away for a weekend at least...there really is so much to decide."

When Kate was finally in bed she slept only in small snatches, waking up repeatedly to think of just one more thing. When real sleep finally came it was a sleep of exhaustion and she didn't hear her morning alarm.

"Mommy! Mommy! It's time to get up! There isn't any breakfast made and we'll be late for school!" Joy was pulling at her shoulder.

Kate stumbled out of bed. Tommy and Raymond were in the kitchen engaged in a mild squabble about which cold cereal to eat.

"How come you're sleeping till noon?" Tommy demanded, clutching a box of cornflakes to his chest. "There isn't any oats cooked."

"Aren't any oats cooked," Kate said. "I'm sorry, but you know that Ian and I went to a show last night. We got in late and I overslept. Now, it isn't the end of the world. You can eat cold cereal for one day in the year."

"You know," Raymond said, "there's such a thing as instant oatmeal. Maybe we should get some for emergencies like this."

Somehow, in her nightgown and bathrobe, she got her two fed, Joy's hair combed the way she wanted it, dressed and out the door in time to get their school bus. She would have to wait until later to tell them the great news.

When they had gone she sat down at the breakfast table with Raymond for a cup of coffee.

"So, how'd it go last night?" Raymond asked. "Any progress to report?" He was looking at her anxiously.

Kate couldn't help laughing in pure joy. "Yes. I can safely say progress was made. You get your wish. Your dad and I are going to be married."

"Oh, wow!" His spoon hit the bowl with enough force to almost crack it. "You'd better not be kidding me. That would be too mean, Mom. That would be child abuse!"

"No. It's real. And it'll be soon. And simple. And—I don't know—we agreed on a couple of things. Let me think a minute. We'll move into the bigger house next door and— What's the matter?"

His face, which had been bright with happiness, suddenly became serious.

"You mean we have to leave home?"

"We won't be leaving home, Raymond. It would be pretty crowded here. Your dad wouldn't have a study. You know he does a lot of work at home. You would have your own private bedroom back, you wouldn't be sharing with Tommy anymore. You know you and he often squabble about space."

"Yeah, but..." He looked off into the distance. "This house was always, you know, the place I could come to. When things got bad over there. Whenever I came over here you never said Raymond go away. You always said, hi Raymond, come on in."

"I...don't understand," Kate said softly.

Raymond gave a gusty sigh. "Aw, don't pay any attention to me. I get nutty ideas. I'm almost an adolescent, you know. But that house over there was so, I mean, Dad and Marsha were always yelling at each other, fighting about something, having rows all the time. And then, after she walked out, there were those housekeepers. When I came over here it was like whatyacallit, my sanctuary. I could *always* come over here. You know, that Robert Frost, that poet guy, he said it. He said that home is where, when you go there, they have to let you in. And you did. See? You always did."

Kate felt a lump in her throat. "Raymond," she said gently, "the *family* in the house makes it the home. We're a *family*. So *anywhere* we live together, that's home. No matter where it is."

"Okay," he said, his eyes suddenly filling with tears, "if you say so." And then, embarrassed at crying, he got up and darted from the room.

You're safe now, Raymond. You're off the tightrope. It's going to be all right for you. And Kate hugged this certainty to her heart.

Her happy reverie was interrupted by a sound at the back door.

Ian.

Without thought, she hurried through the service porch to open the door for him.

"I guess I got here too early," he said, smiling, and Kate realized that she was in her ten-year-old bathrobe, which, many washes ago, had been bright blue. She hugged it around her. *Jill, we have to go shopping again!*

"You look terrific," Ian said, reaching for her, and she went into his arms. "With your hair all tousled and your morning-fresh face." He bent to kiss her.

"Come in," she said when she could speak. "Have you had breakfast yet? Let me fix you something." Taking his hand, she led him into the kitchen.

"Have you told the kids?"

"I told Raymond. I overslept and there wasn't time to tell Tommy and Joy. I told Mom, of course. Last night."

"How'd she take it?"

"Delighted. You know she's been throwing me at you since—"

"I know. I didn't miss that. I thought it was…nice." He didn't sit down at the table. "How'd Raymond take it?"

"Relieved, I think. But he started to cry, so he rushed off. At twelve it's hard not to be a child when you want to be. He's probably in the boys' room. Why don't you go talk to him while I make your breakfast? What would you like?"

"If you cook it, anything. I'll be right back."

While he was with Raymond, Kate rushed around the kitchen, her heart singing. She was cooking breakfast for Ian! First she would give him sliced strawberries, frozen from her garden in the summer. Then scrambled eggs, and he liked them a little soft and runny. Toast? No, she'd make those light, fluffy biscuits. *Settle down, Kate!* She leaned against the sink, laughing at herself. She was over thirty with two children, actually three now, and she was behaving like a giddy teenager. But, yes, she *would* bake the biscuits.

Ian came back, his arm around Raymond, whose eyes were red but whose face was bland.

"Sit down," Kate said. "It's almost ready. Raymond, would you like to eat again? Or were those cornflakes enough?"

"Yes. I think I would," he said, sitting down.

"You might say thank you," Ian reminded him.

Raymond grinned weakly at Kate. "Okay. Thank you."

She set places for three, and Raymond ate as heartily as Ian, which pleased Kate because he was so thin. She could sense the relief in the boy.

Finishing his third cup of coffee, Ian said, "You've never seen all of my house, Kate. Can you come over now and I'll give you a walk through? Maybe you'll want to change things."

"Yes, thank you," Kate said, feeling an odd hesitation. Marsha's house. Well, she would have to deal with it sometime. It was the house that Raymond really didn't want to go back to. She would have to make it home, their home. "Give me a couple of minutes to dress," she said, "and we'll go."

Raymond tagged along, reaching silently for her hand as Ian opened the back door and held it for them to go in.

"Well, this is the kitchen, of course," Ian said, and Kate, who had only glimpsed it before, looked around at the state-of-the-art kitchen, with shining wood surfaces and copper pots hanging on wrought-iron hooks.

"Nobody cooks in those," Raymond commented. "Some pots are in the cupboards, but mostly it's the microwave."

The rest of the house was much the same. "We bought the place four years ago," Ian said. "And Marsha took care of the furnishing and so on."

"The decorator, actually," Raymond murmured. "Always reminds me of a furniture store. Nothing's like, you know, lived in."

"Well," Ian said, "your mother did her best, Raymond. She didn't care much for the house in the first place, so you can't put too much blame on her for the motel look. At least she got it all furnished."

"Yeah, well."

"With three kids living here I expect it will get the lived-in look fairly soon," Kate said, feeling she must smooth it over somehow. She had worried for nothing. The house had no imprint of Marsha's personality. All the furniture was very good, and the appliances top of the line. There was a lot she could do to make it more homelike. And there were four very large bedrooms. Perfect. Plus a study where Ian did a lot of his work at home. And a large unfinished attic, which could add at least two more rooms later... *if. I want Ian's child.* The thought was there, suddenly, in her mind. She could have another child now. Joy might at last get a sister. But how would Ian feel about that? Would he agree? Or not?

They were all three in the attic. Raymond had opened the back window and was leaning out looking down into the backyard.

"Plenty of storage space," Ian said, indicating the collection of boxes placed haphazardly here and there. There was a plastic-wrapped mattress, which looked almost new, leaning against a wall. Scattered about were Ian's fishing tackle and an assortment of discarded toys and games Raymond had no longer wanted. The autumn rummage sale at church was going to be unusually blessed this year.

"Don't lean out too far, Ray," Ian warned, and then turned to look at her. "Kate? What is it?"

"Nothing." Her mind had flown back again to the idea of another child, hers and Ian's, and it must have shown in her face. She shouldn't bring it up while Raymond was here, but she couldn't resist asking, "Have you ever thought of adding a couple more rooms up here...if they were needed?"

"Not really," Ian said to Kate. "Do you have something in mind for this space?" And even as he said it, he caught Kate's meaning and, without pausing, he added firmly, "That's your decision. I told you last night that we would do things the way you want them done. Okay?"

"Okay," she said softly, hoping she wouldn't cry. The creation of another human being was such a holy thing. She had never felt closer to God than during her pregnancies.

"Are you two going to talk mushy?" Raymond said, closing down the widow.

"Nope. We're not going to talk about much of anything," Ian said. "I've got to get out of here and get to the office. I'll leave the keys with you, Kate, so you can come over later if you want to."

After Ian had left for work and she and Raymond had come back to the small house, the phone rang. It had to be Jill. Mom would have called her. Kate picked up the phone.

"Hi, Jill," she said, and heard Jill's quick laugh.

"Congratulations! Mom was on the phone at the crack of dawn. What's the program today? We *have* to get together! Today!"

"Yes. Absolutely," Kate agreed. "There's so much to decide."

"Okay, here's the plan. Mom and I will both come over to your place, and we'll work it all out. Kate, I'm so happy for you."

"What about the children?"

"Well, Megan is the only one here all day. Laurie is in school until two-thirty. Ben comes home from kindergarten at noon. But one of my group will come over, so that's all taken care of." Jill was part of a congenial church support group of formerly working mothers who had put their careers on hold until the children grew up.

These stay-at-home moms helped each other out whenever it was necessary.

"And your two are in school until midafternoon. You've only got Raymond at home. Maybe he'd like a holiday."

Kate turned to Raymond. "Would you like to skip study today and take a holiday?"

His face lit up "Yes! I can finish my book! And I *need* a holiday. This getting married is gonna be pretty frantic." He started toward his bedroom, suddenly stopped and turned.

"Look, don't decide who gets what bedroom yet over there until you see me, okay? I don't wanna be in the same room I was before." He grinned engagingly. "Got it?"

"Got it," Kate said.

With Mom and Jill with her, the hours flew by and, somehow, things were all falling into place. She and Ian would get their license from the city tomorrow. The wedding itself would be in two weeks. That would give them time to get in touch with the few invited guests. Mom offered her B and B for the out-of-town people. She would have plenty of space, because this was the slack season. She wouldn't take any reservations for that time, and there was only the one leftover guest, Douglas Colby, an artist who had stayed over during the snowstorm, then persuaded her to take him as a lodger while he painted his landscapes in the Northwest.

"I wonder if we could have the actual ceremony at your place," Kate asked. "With so few people coming, I don't think I want all those empty church pews behind us. I think the church would be too big."

"Of course," Mom agreed. "But check with Pastor Ledbetter first."

So they made the first of several calls to him. He was delighted to be interrupted for such a reason, and spoke warmly to Kate. Her eyes were misty when she hung up the receiver. He had been so good after her father's death more than a year ago, and they had become closer. He had understood how difficult her father's death had been for her. She only let herself speak one time about Dad during their hectic planning.

"I just wish...Dad could be here." She was sorry she had said it, because Mom's face, so happy the moment before, became suddenly closed and blank. *Don't think about it, Kate. Dad's at peace. And when he was here, the one thing he wanted above all else was to see his womenfolk happy.*

Mom and Jill were talking about the wedding dress.

"You know," Kate said, "you may think this is silly but, Jill, do you still have that ivory satin dinner suit? I loved that suit. At a wedding you're supposed to have something old, something new, something borrowed and something blue. If you still have it, and if I can wear it, we could combine both the 'old' and 'borrowed' in one."

"You bet I've still got it," Jill said. "I haven't worn it in a while, but I'll get it cleaned right away. That was the last really expensive garment I bought for myself before I gave up the restaurant. It's the one thing I can't ever give away. It's still there in the back of my half of the closet. We'll have to take up the hem, but the rest would be okay. So we cross off wedding gown." And Jill dashed a line through that item on their growing list.

Somehow in the days that followed everything came out beautifully, as they phoned one another or rushed to each other's homes, and back and forth to the airport as people came. There were new people for Kate to meet, happy people, coming with smiles and good wishes, and because they were staying at Mom's B and B there was the quick congeniality among them that people on a journey together enjoy.

Ian's in-laws, Colonel and Lydia Greer, were happy and relieved that Ian had found someone. And Ian's sister, Denise, tanned, athletic, tall, with sun-bleached blond hair, came with her husband, Chuck, quiet, good-humored about all the fuss and wearing a Stetson hat and tooled leather boots that fascinated Tommy. Denise was considerably older than Ian, and their two sons were away at college.

And somehow, an older man named Douglas Colby became a permanent part of the wedding arrangements, *part* of things. He was a large man, but fit-looking, probably in his late fifties, retired. He had salt-and-pepper hair and the rugged looks of someone who had climbed mountains, or could any day, with ease. Her mom's artist-in-residence, who had come to the Northwest to paint his landscapes. He was there, at Mom's beck and call, for unexpected errands, airport meetings, or any heavy lifting.

During one pause, when Kate and Jill had a moment alone together, Kate asked, "Just *who* is this Douglas Colby? How did he come into this? He's just a B-and-B guest, isn't he?"

"I wouldn't say just a guest, actually," Jill said. "He's besotted with Mom, for one thing."

"Besotted with *Mom!*" Kate gasped. *"Mom!"*

"Mom is still a beautiful woman, Katie. With that dark hair and eyes, and her slim willowy shape and that cameo face."

Kate was astounded.

"Katie," Jill said gently, "sometimes...when this is

all over and we have some time, we'll talk about it. But…life goes on.''

Kate stared at her, and Jill reached over and patted her cheek. ''I think the main thing is that Dad devoted his life to making Mom happy. If she had a chance at happiness again, well then…''

''Yes,'' Kate said slowly. ''I see. Yes.'' But it left a vestige of sadness in her heart.

Of course it wasn't possible to limit the guest list to just family. It soon became just family and Kate's neighbors next door on the other side. This was a relief to Ian, because he really wanted to invite two special friends from his office. Then Kate included a woman she liked so well from the food bank. Kate always gave excess vegetables from her garden to the food bank and worked there two mornings a month. Then there was a deputy police chief from a midsized Texas town who felt very beholden to Ian because Ian had persuaded the chief to supply his men with much more protective bullet-proof vests—and lighter, too—than they had had before. He was going to be in Seattle on the actual day and wanted to look Ian up. One by one the list kept growing.

They thought they had managed to round it off at eleven nonfamily, until it came out that Tommy, in a burst of goodwill and without so much as a by-your-leave, had given an invitation to his Sunday school teacher, who was delighted to accept. This move mandated at least three other invitations to church members. Mom kept saying she would manage all right—the B and B living room *was* huge—and they'd already decided that they would need to rent chairs.

The wedding took place on a Saturday in Mom's lovely old home on the hill overlooking the beautiful Sound. And, Mom being Mom, with a pure genius for homemaking, had made the great living room a bower. So beautiful, so beautiful, Kate thought. She knew she would remember this day for the rest of her life, every precious moment of it.

And Ian was everywhere—helping, organizing—and in those moments they had together he would say, "Are you happy, Kate?" Or, "Is this what you want, Kate?" Or, "I want this to be perfect for you, Kate." She felt like a princess, he was so considerate.

And the children were all beautiful. Tommy in a new suit he hadn't grown out of, Joy a perfect delight in another new dress and Raymond looking almost elegant in his new suit, plus Jill's three attractive children, looking their best.

Because bride and groom each had a house completely furnished, wedding gifts had to be original creations. Jill's mother-in-law, Laura, gave them her Honolulu condo for a week. Ian's in-laws, the Greers, supplied the airline tickets. Ian's sister and brother-in-law announced they were hiring the movers to transfer Kate's family possessions over to Ian's house while they were gone. Mom and Jill would handle the organizing of this. And Jill's husband, Greg, a CPA, added Ian to his list of relatives for whom he did the income tax returns gratis.

So Kate would leave her old house and return to her new one ready to start a new life. And Mom and Jill would juggle the child care between them for the week that Kate and Ian would be in Hawaii. There was such an uprush of kindness, so much reaching out, so much love.

This is a dream. It's got to be a dream. I don't want to wake up, Kate thought. For Kate, her wedding day was a series of little vignettes, small treasures she could remember in years to come.

The sacred moment when, in the late afternoon, standing before the arch of flowers and her pastor, she said "I do," with all her heart, starting a whole new life as Ian's wife. Then the wonderful endless laughter of the wedding supper. Mom had outdone herself. Then the little vignette of kindly Mr. Colby handing Mom his handkerchief. And Ian's brother-in-law, Chuck, talking to Tommy about the horses on his ranch. Cyrus Ledbetter, with tears in his eyes, saying, "Be happy, Katie, you're entitled." And as they left for the airport in the limo provided by that deputy chief from the midsized Texas town, Raymond clinging to her for an instant. "I'm off the tightrope now. I owe ya."

Kate had never been out of the continental United States before and everything about travel was new and exciting. The bustling airport at Honolulu, where the Hawaiians rushed to place leis around your neck and kissed you on both cheeks. The elegant little condo that was their tiny home for seven days.

Ian and I.

The warm golden beach and the beautiful sea, blue, green or lavender, wherever you looked. And Ian so thoughtful, so considerate, so loving.

"Here, Katie, put this lotion on. You're not used to this much sun." Or, "Where would you like to go tomorrow?" Or, "Forget about the phone bill. Talk to the kids as long as you want to. It's the first time you've been away from them." Or, "Buy anything you like, Katie. This is once in a lifetime," in the shops as she delightedly bought gifts for everybody back home.

Then finally there were only two days left. Then only one. And, loaded with tote bags, hung with sweet-smelling flowers, sunburned, they flew home again. Jill met them at the airport in her van because of all the packages.

Ian's relatives had gone home, of course, and on the way into Seattle from Sea-Tac Jill brought them up-to-date.

"We got everything of yours moved over to the big house. We had a few questions, but thought they could wait for you. Joy borrowed Laurie's skates and took a bad fall, skinned both her knees badly, so she walks a bit stiffly. Please sympathize with her, because she was a little trouper about it. And Raymond wanted me to tell you first thing that he has kept at working on the math work sheets. Greg had to help him a little, but not much. And after we got your stuff out of your house and got it in order again, we showed it to an elderly couple who might want to rent it, if that's what you decide to do with it. But they weren't sure about keeping up such a large backyard with garden and all."

"Oh, dear, my asparagus bed," Kate said. "It takes about three years to get asparagus really established, and it's doing so well."

Ian laughed. "I guess the honeymoon is over when the daily problems surface again. Why don't you rent them just the house and retain custody of the asparagus bed?"

"Actually," Jill said, "you may want to sell it. A Realtor came by. It's a seller's market now in Seattle, she said, and she gave me her card. Here, put this in your pocket." Jill handed her the card, which had been waiting on the dashboard. "Tommy got lonesome and cried twice but I managed to comfort him. I think he's more emotionally dependent on you than Joy is. And Raymond said to tell you he'll be home about three. He's down at the library. Mom begged off coming down, because she was bushed with so much child care, I think. And I want to talk to you more about Douglas Colby. He's off in the Cascades now, painting something, but he'll be back. Your kids are riding the school bus today, so they'll be back home at their regular time, about two-thirty. I gave them careful instructions. I hope you like the way we arranged things. Most of your stuff is pretty old, Kate. You may want to just donate it to the annual rummage sale. It's in the attic. A lot of mail has accumulated. I've left yours on that hall table, and Ian, I put yours on your desk in the study.''

Kate thought, I'm moving back into real life, bit by bit. As Jill brought them up-to-date, Kate reached over and touched Ian's shoulder, and he turned and smiled at her. The days in the warm Hawaiian sun had relaxed him. He seemed at ease, not tense or worried about Raymond anymore. *I take thee, Ian, to be my wedded husband, to have and to hold, from this day forward.*

"Okay, here we are. Welcome home!" Jill said, turning the van into Ian's driveway, and suddenly Ian laughed.

"Did the kids do that?" He pointed to a gaudy banner on the front door. It said in large colorful letters, Welcome Home. It's About Time.

Jill laughed, too. "Yes. They all worked on it. Raymond blocked out the letters in outline, and all the kids colored them with different colors. When you get closer you will see little pictures of flowers, animals and so on, scattered here and there. Each kid did his or her own thing. You should really keep it, Kate."

"Oh, I will. I will."

After the luggage and all the packages and the wilting flower leis were inside and Jill had gone, Kate and Ian had an interval of quiet together.

"Let's just rest a minute," Kate said, sitting down in

one of the living-room chairs and looking around. She couldn't see anything of Marsha in the room. Marsha's decorator furniture was solid and comfortable in muted shades of beige and brown, but here and there were things she recognized. Mom and Jill had tried. She recognized her own two small orange throw pillows on the big couch. And there was the cut-glass vase Claude's aunt had given her years ago, now filled with bright spring flowers. And in front of the fireplace was her own antique brass screen. I'm home. I'm home, she thought.

She looked at Ian. He had stopped in his study to pick up his stack of mail. He sat down on the couch behind the coffee table. His fair head was bowed as he looked at each envelope and began tossing them into two stacks on the table in front of him. Then, sighing, he leaned his head back against the couch, one envelope still in his hand.

"Aren't you going to open any?" Kate asked.

"In a minute," he said, sounding oddly tired. Kate sat up straighter, suddenly alert and anxious when there was nothing to be anxious about. Was there?

"Ian?"

He sat up straight with an effort. "We're not quite out of the woods yet on Ray's custody, Kate. I've put off telling you, but…I was notified…" He seemed to be dragging the words out. "I was notified…about a month ago that Marsha and Burgess are going to fight for permanent custody."

"You mean they…they're going *to court* about it?" Kate said in disbelief.

"Yes…they were, but…" He paused.

"What is that? In your hand? Is that from them?"

"No." Again the tiredness. "This is from my own attorney. I'm pretty sure I know what it says. I… You see, when I was served with papers last month, I...I told my attorney to file for a summary judgment.''

''What does that mean?'' Kate asked, and felt an immediate uneasy sense that she didn't want to know.

''It's a motion to dismiss their case. I think this letter is simply telling me that he's done it.'' He ripped open the envelope and scanned what appeared to be a brief letter. ''Yes, this is the date of the hearing. We'll...need to attend. It will be a formality only now, you see.''

''No. I don't see.'' *Oh, dear God, what is this? What is happening here?* ''You'd better explain it.''

''Well, their case was based on the fact that I'm—I *was* a single parent. But I...told my attorney that I was going to marry again, so that nullifies their case. The fact that I'm now *married.* I have a *wife.*'' There was a hint of grimness in his tone as he said it. He looked up at her, meeting her eyes. ''Kate, please try to understand. I *could not* let them destroy Ray.''

Kate felt strangely distanced from herself, as if she were on the outside somehow, looking at the scene.

''When did you tell your attorney you were going to marry?'' she heard herself asking.

''I can't lie to you, Kate. You're too good, too decent. I told him...when they first filed their case. Try to understand.''

''I'm afraid I do understand. You were in want of a wife and I was...available.'' Again there was the feeling of looking on two strangers from some outside place. She got up rather stiffly from the couch. The lovely clock, chosen by Marsha's decorator, in the front hall tolled twice, so it must be two o'clock. In less than an hour Raymond, who was off his tightrope, and Tommy, who had cried for her twice while she was gone, and Joy with badly skinned knees would come trooping in the door, demanding their presents from Hawaii. Mom, lovely Mom, was elated at her marriage. And Jill, who had worked so hard at the move to this house, and Cyrus Ledbetter who had said, "Be happy, Katie," were all so pleased at her marriage to Ian. *From this day forward... Oh, God, please help me now.*

"Kate?" Ian was standing behind her. He placed his hands on her shoulders hesitantly. "Please listen. What could I do? If I had offered you a—what they call—a marriage of convenience, would you have accepted?"

"No."

"What...are you going to do?"

"I thought," she said carefully, "that I'd unpack the luggage and put things in the laundry."

"Katie, we're a good team. We can make it work." His voice was unsteady, pleading. "We *are* making it work."

"Yes," she said remotely, trying to sound polite. "Yes." *You're a good friend, Kate.*

"Ian, would you mind...just leaving me alone for a while?" She heard his whispered, "Sure, Katie" as she walked carefully out of the living room. Think about the luggage. I must unpack the luggage, she thought. And put things in the laundry. And, soon now, the children will come home.

Mindlessly she went about the tasks she had set herself. And I must find the Realtor's card Jill gave me, she thought. I must tear it up. I can't sell my little house now. And I must keep all old furniture. I can leave it in Ian's attic. Because at some point Ian won't need this marriage anymore.

Small, odd things registered in her thoughts. Someone had left an empty detergent bottle in the corner of the service porch. She must put it in the trash. The pocket on her yellow Hawaiian skirt was ripped. Now, how had that happened? And there was leftover sand embedded in Ian's blue polo shirt. She could feel the grit of it against her palms.

"Mommy! Mommy! Mommy! Where are you!"

Kate turned from the washer, straightened her back and, walking as tall as she could, went into Ian's beautiful kitchen.

"I'm here," she said steadily. "I'm here."

Chapter Six

The beautiful hall clock chimed the half hour as Kate sat down in the empty living room. The children, sated with the excitement of the homecoming, the many presents, settling into the new house, had finally gone to bed. And Ian, who had followed her lead in pretending everything was fine, had joined her in focusing on the children all evening answering questions about Hawaii and listening to their endless chatter about the past week.

Sitting on the living-room couch, Kate resisted the temptation to stretch out and just fall asleep. Suddenly she was unbearably tired. From her side vision she was aware that Ian came and stood hesitantly in the doorway. She couldn't—wouldn't—look at him. The anger, embarrassment, bitterness, despair she had held off for hours came flooding back, filling her with shame. *What a fool I am. How could I have let myself be deluded into thinking this man could fall in love with me? Dad, I have to tell you something. I've blown it again. Help me. Comfort me. Tell me it's okay to be always second-best.*

She refused to acknowledge Ian's presence, and was

aware when he turned and went silently up the stairs. She heard the opening of their bedroom door. Was it boring to make love to me, Ian? Plain little old Kate from next door—or maybe it didn't make that much difference to you.

Kate shut her eyes, remembering her father clearly, intensely, for a long moment. They had been together in the grape arbor at what was now Mom's bed-and-breakfast place. It was the end of summer and she was about to start her senior year at high school and dreading it. Overhead were the last of the purple grapes, with a few lazy bees humming around the remaining clusters.

"Well, I'm not going to try for the Senior Prom. The Junior Prom was bad enough. I learned my lesson. Jill won't have that problem." In her mind she could hear her young voice, bitter and angry. Then her father's words, slow, kind, incredibly understanding.

"I know, Katie. In a world that sets so much store on physical beauty it's hard to be one of the...not-beautiful. And you have to remember, your sister can't help being pretty. Any more than your mother can help being beautiful." There had been for a moment in his voice such a deep loneliness that she had been startled out of her own self-absorption and had turned to look at him. A bee had come down and hovered about his thinning hair. She'd reached out and brushed it away, seeing very clearly the lines in his homely face, the heavy stocky body, and she knew, with no words passing between them, that Mom, lovely Mom, didn't really love Dad as he loved her, but was—what? Kind to him? And Kate knew that it wasn't enough. Love given needed to be returned, or the giver suffered loss, a kind of inward maiming, a slow breaking of the heart.

"You need to make your peace with it, Katie. God

gives us all different gifts. You take what is given and you make the best of it. Life consists of many things and can still be good, even if you don't have everything.''

Then, possibly because he had realized that she understood more than he had intended to reveal, he'd added, *''I have a good life, Kate. To the starving man, half a loaf is far, far better than no loaf at all.''*

I don't think so, Dad, and, startled, she glanced around the empty room, not sure she hadn't spoken aloud. She pushed the old memory aside.

After a while she became aware that slow tears were rolling down her face. Where had she seen a box of tissues here? She got up from the couch and wandered back toward the kitchen. Paper towels were good enough. She tore one off the roll and blotted her face. She must get some sleep. She went back, turning off lights as she went. Had the alarm been set? She stood in the hall looking at it blankly for a long moment. Yes, Ian had set it. She'd have to get used to that. There was no alarm system in her little house next door.

No! Half a loaf is not enough! Not nearly enough! She turned and started up the long stairway, pulling herself up by the polished banister. Tired. Tired. Tired. The bedroom door stood open and the light was on. She went in and shut the door behind her. Ian was still in the casual clothes he had changed into for the evening, jeans and a tan sweater top, with a Scandinavian pattern knitted into it around the shoulders. He was packing a bag. It was the big folding two-suiter with the little pockets and spaces for everything else. He turned as he heard her enter.

''Kate?'' he said tentatively as she stood just inside the door, looking at him.

''Don't ask me what I'm going to do,'' she said harshly. ''Because I don't know yet.'' She felt an uprush of sheer rage, wanting to hit him, hurt him. Striving for control, she gripped her hands into fists behind her back.

"Please," Ian said, "try to understand. I was desperate. I didn't know what to do. I...couldn't let them destroy my kid. I...I do care for you, Kate."

"I know. I'm a good friend," she said grimly.

"Please...don't do this. We can make it work. We were—"

"Ian, *do you love me?* The truth!" She must lower her voice. The children might hear.

"I think you are a...wonderful woman," he said.

"Love, Ian. Say it. Tell me I'm the love of your life. Do you love me the way you loved Marsha? Do you still love Marsha?" She was shaking now, and her voice rose in spite of herself. *Don't do this. Remember the children.* But she couldn't stop. "Do you?" she fairly screamed.

"Kate, please. Be sensible. People have married for hundreds of years for practical reasons other than romantic attachment. Good marriages. All marriages aren't based on romance and wine and roses. You mention Marsha. We—she and I—started out with wine and roses and it turned out to be the worst mistake either of us had ever made. Listen to me." He spoke with intensity. "We can make this marriage work. We're the same kind of people. We believe in the same things. We live in the same world. We have the same values."

"No! We don't have the same values! I would *never* have done this to you! Not good friend Kate! I would never have lied to you!"

"Kate, I didn't lie," he said desperately. "Not...not exactly. I did what I thought I had to do. And your life is the better for it. Try to think of that. Please. Put aside your anger and just think it through. We've salvaged Ray. Isn't that important to you? If Marsha and Chet got custody and he was stashed in some military school he'd be a mental basket case in a year. And he'd resort to any escape hatch he could. He's not too young to get into drugs or anything else that offered temporary respite. And think about Tommy and Joy. They are both far more financially secure now than if you were still alone. Tommy and Joy will finish university without college loans hanging over their heads. They'll get a clean, easy start in life. Aren't these things important, too?''

"Oh, I see. It's not a marriage. It's a bargain. Is that it?'' She could no longer stand still, but started pacing about the room. *I mustn't do this. I'm tired. I can't think.* "I, Kate, give you my love, my heart and soul and you, Ian, pay my children's way through college, give me pretty flowers and make love to me. Is that what it is? Is that our bargain? Well, I don't like that bargain. It's not enough. Not nearly enough.'' *I must not cry. I will not cry.* She took a deep breath, seeing him so clearly next to the bed beside the half-packed travel case, loving everything about him, but hating him, too.

"Why are you packing?'' she demanded. "We just got back.'' She was dimly surprised that her voice sounded, if not calm, at least steady, but still far too loud.

"I'm...I have to leave. This trip was scheduled before we went to Hawaii. I've left my itinerary down on the desk. If...you need to get in touch with me. I'll be back...I think in four or five days. Not longer.''

"Don't hurry back on my account. Good old friend Kate will keep the home fires burning and take care of everything here. When are you leaving?''

He sighed and turned back to his packing, pushing some socks and briefs into the bag. "As soon as I finish this. It's an early departure and I'd best be down at the airport. I'll get a few hours' sleep in one of the airport motels."

"Fine." She paced around the room like a restless cat until he finished. Her back was turned to him when she heard him zip the case closed.

"Goodbye, Kate. I'll see you in a few days. Call me...if you need to. Any time."

This time she didn't answer and wouldn't turn around but held her breath, listening intently as he went out, quietly shutting the door behind him.

Tiredly, her hands fumbling, she pulled off her clothes and dropped them where she stood and somehow or other she was in her nightgown standing beside the bed.

Oh, Ian. Ian.

Miserably, she crawled into bed. *What shall I do? What can I do? I must think. I must think what's best.* And while she was trying to think she fell into the troubled sleep of exhaustion. She was dreaming about the children squabbling. She could hear Raymond's furious voice from far off. "Comb your own hair! Mom didn't comb your hair all week and you didn't die!" He was squabbling with Joy then, who always needed help with her hair in the morning. Then there was Joy's voice from far away, angry and strident. "Last week Aunt Jill fixed my hair! Somebody's gotta fix my hair!" This was a wail of desperation. Kate struggled against the dream. Raymond's voice again. "Give me the comb, you little jerk! I'll comb your hair." Sounds of a struggle, something crashing to the floor. "No! You can't comb my hair. You're just a stupid boy. I'm gonna wake up Mom." The sound of running feet.

Kate was suddenly wide awake. It wasn't a dream. The kids were fighting. It was morning. She stumbled out of bed, grappling for her robe, and was out in the hallway just as Raymond caught up with Joy halfway up the stairs.

"All right. All right," she said. "I'm up. I guess I overslept. It's okay, Raymond. I can do it. Come here, Joy. Come in here."

At the sight of Kate, Joy started to cry. "He *pulled* my hair—he pulled it out by the *roots!* He can't comb hair. He's a stupid dummy."

"All right. Calm down," Kate said and, turning to Raymond, who looked stricken, she added, "It's okay, Raymond. No harm done."

"It's not okay," Joy shouted. "How can it be okay when he pulled my hair? He—"

"Never mind. Come in here." Kate pulled Joy into the bedroom and over to the dressing table she had never yet used for herself. She half turned to Raymond, who hovered by the door. "Be a good guy, Raymond. Go down and make the coffee will you? I'll be down in a few minutes."

"I already did that," he said diffidently. "And I made some oats in one of the middle-sized pans. I woulda got 'em both off to school okay if Joy didn't freak out over her hairdo every morning. She's obsessed."

"I'm not obsessed," Joy snapped back. "What's obsessed?"

"Forget obsessed," Kate said. "Calm down. Count to twenty. Right now. Count to twenty."

Sullenly, Joy began to count.

Raymond still lingered at the door. "I made orange juice. Is it too soon to take it out of the fridge and pour yours?"

"No. The timing is fine. I'll be down in a couple of minutes. You go ahead. How's Tommy doing?" she added as an afterthought.

Raymond answered with heavy sarcasm. "*Tommy's* doing fine. He's practically ready for *school*. He's looking over his homework. And *Tommy* combed his *own hair* without calling in the marines. I'll go down and get your orange juice."

A few minutes later, with both the younger children out the door and heading for their school bus stop, Kate went to the kitchen. Raymond had set two places for them. Tommy's and Joy's dishes were rinsed and in the open dishwasher.

"You *have* been busy," Kate said. "I really slept late. I'm sorry. Maybe I had jet lag or something." She picked up her glass of orange juice and sipped it.

"Could you eat some oats today? I think I made too much, and I know you hate to waste things."

"Oats will be fine. And thank you. If you hadn't taken over they'd have been late for school. You did a good job."

Silently Raymond filled two bowls with oatmeal and brought them to the table. He slid into his chair, looking glum.

"This is good," Kate said cheerfully, sensing his depressed mood. "Oatmeal gives me a nice back-home feeling. All last week your dad and I were eating pretty exotic stuff for breakfast. Mangoes. Papaya. Fresh pineapple. And banana pancakes with coconut syrup. It's a delicious combination. I brought home the banana pancake recipe and we got several cans of the coconut syrup. Raymond? What's the matter?" She put down her spoon and looked at him in consternation. He had ducked his head down and was trying not to cry.

"I'm back on the tightrope, right?" he muttered. "I heard you and Dad last night. Fighting just the way Marsha and Dad did."

"Oh, Raymond." She was filled with remorse and shame. "No. No, you're not back on the tightrope. We just had a…had a disagreement. People do. We'll…work it out."

"Listen, I'm not dumb. He married you to get *me* off the hook, right? So it's *my fault.* You'd do better to give Dad the heave-ho and write me off. Forget about me. I'm jinxed." His hopelessness chilled her. He had run away from home once.

She pushed aside her bowl and got up, going around the table to put her arms about his shoulders, but before she could speak he went on.

"What I think I'll do is try to make a deal with Marsha and Chet. See if I can talk them out of a military school and just settle for a plain old boarding school."

"No. Don't even consider that. I've…I've decided what I'm going to do. I was angry at your father last night, certainly. But people…disagree sometimes. I won't leave, Raymond. We're still family." *I cannot abandon this child. I'll have to work it out somehow. I have to.*

"But I don't wanna push you into anything you don't want," he said in a muffled voice.

"You're not. It's not your fault, anyhow. Nothing's your fault. Don't ever think that. Your dad and I have a misunderstanding to clear up. I'm going to talk to Pastor Ledbetter today. He can usually help me think things through."

"You think he can help?" Raymond asked hopefully.

"Yes. He has before."

"Boy, I sure hope so." He pushed away his bowl of oatmeal. "Look, I really don't feel hungry for this. I just didn't wanna waste it."

"That's okay," Kate said, smoothing back his hair.

"At least you got the other kids fed. I don't feel much like eating, either. Do you want anything at all?"

Raymond thought a moment, smudging tears from his eyes. "I hate to be such a wimp. It's like I got a water faucet in my head and I spend half my life wantin' to cry." He paused a moment, then continued. "Yeah. You know, maybe we could eat some of those chocolate-covered macadamia nuts you and Dad brought back. There's a whole other can." He got up and went to the cupboard.

"Fine. Let's go into the living room where it's more comfortable." Kate wrapped her robe about herself and tightened the belt. I must talk to him, reassure him, she thought. He had been doing so well with the lessons, and had been so happy about the marriage, to be part of a whole family at last.

Sitting companionably on the couch in the living room, they talked and munched the chocolate-covered macadamia nuts, and gradually Raymond's tension lessened. Kate steered the conversation to the future. A job fair was coming up at the Seattle Center and she had planned to take Raymond there. It would broaden his knowledge of what kinds of careers were open to him when he finished schooling. He became interested, and seemed to throw off his depression.

"I've thought about doing what Dad does," he said, swallowing and licking chocolate off his fingers. "I guess I won't eat any more of those. We gotta save some for the other kids. Dad's is a good line of work, getting stuff to the good guys to help protect themselves from the bad guys. But I don't know if I want to travel that much. Dad's always complainin' about living out of a suitcase."

Kate had just started to answer when the hall clock

began chiming, but there was another sound, too, which it almost drowned out.

"Was that the doorbell?" she asked, straining to hear as the clock continued to chime the hour of eleven.

"Yeah. It was. I'll get it," Raymond said, getting up.

"Thanks. I'm still in my bathrobe at eleven. We've lost almost half the day." She got up, but paused because she could hear Raymond with someone in the hall. Good grief. He was bringing someone in. And there was no way to escape.

He came in smiling. He had the same smile Ian had, lighting up his whole face. He seemed deeply pleased.

"Guess what! This is Miz Lundy. You remember. I told you about Miz Lundy, my English teacher when I was at school." He was almost beaming.

And Mrs. Lundy, middle-aged, getting a little stout, with a pleasant face and untidy flyaway hair, stepped forward, holding out her hand.

"Yes, I was Raymond's English teacher. We haven't met, but I sent you a note and an article a while back?" She ended on a questioning note.

"Yes, of course," Kate said. "I remember. I read it. And thank you. Won't you sit down. Please forgive the way I look, but we've just returned from a trip. Raymond's father and I were just married." She could feel herself flushing.

"How lovely. My congratulations." Mrs. Lundy sat down. "I went next door, but the house seemed empty so I just took a chance and came on over here." She was putting her purse and a book on the floor beside her chair, glancing around the room. "I have an early lunch break this term, so I just thought I'd check up to see how Ray was doing. We do miss him in English class. I've really enjoyed his book reports. He has such a good mind."

"Yes," Kate agreed. "He has. Mrs. Lundy, I feel I should explain. I'm not usually sitting around in my bathrobe at eleven o'clock, but Mr. McAllister and I just got back from Hawaii yesterday and I was trying to—"

"Please. You don't need to explain. There's always an unwinding period after a trip. And I had no business to pop in unannounced like this. I really came to see how Raymond is doing with the homeschooling."

"Really great," Raymond said quickly. "I like it a lot." Kate began to relax a little.

Mrs. Lundy tilted her head to one side. "You don't think you'd like to come back to school for another try?" she asked.

"No way," Raymond said firmly. "Mom and I are doing great. And we're not skipping the hard stuff. I do math and all that first, before the stuff I like. And I'm gonna pass all the exams, too. You'll see."

"Oh, I'm sure you will," Mrs. Lundy said comfortably. "I did like your paper on Robert Frost. The only thing that brought your grade down from an A was the spelling. Are you doing anything for that?"

"Yep. Sure am," Raymond said, smiling.

Kate observed Mrs. Lundy. Really this woman had no right to come in like this and question Raymond, but she did genuinely like him, was concerned about him. That was clear in her friendly, open manner.

Mrs. Lundy turned to Kate. "Teachers can't help but be interested in their pupils' progress. Raymond shows such promise. I don't mean to offend you, Mrs. McAllister, but I was, I mean I am, worried about homeschooling."

"I know," Kate said quietly. "I read the article you sent, but we have to agree to differ. Raymond's father and I decided that this would be the best course at this time. We'll know whether it is a success or not when he takes the exams."

Mrs. Lundy sighed. "True, and he may well pass them, but have you considered what he may be missing? The companionship of his peers? The group fun-things the students have in a school situation? The glee club? The various sports teams? The school play? The satisfaction of graduating with all the others when the time comes? Are you sure he's not missing too much?"

Raymond spoke before Kate could. "Miz Lundy, I'm not such a great team type. I'm kind of a loner. I don't miss the peer stuff, trust me, I don't miss it."

"I know," she said softly. "You had a bad time, but our principal, Mr. Chan, is taking a strong stand on that sort of thing now. I'm not suggesting you drop this idea immediately, but what I am suggesting is that you think about coming back next term. Just think about it, will you?" She sounded cajoling, persuasive, and Kate thought she must be a good teacher, with a lot of quiet influence with her students. The dowdy, grandmotherly appearance, the kindly and very real interest in the child. Kate could see her being "my favorite teacher" in the minds of many of her students.

"What are you studying now?" she asked Raymond, and he began to tell her. Kate sat back, listening. Raymond spoke well when he got going and he told Mrs. Lundy with considerable enthusiasm about his present lesson schedule and field trips.

"That does sound great," Mrs. Lundy said when he finished. "Can I just take a peek at some of the work?"

Kate sat forward. This was a bit much, but she held her peace as Raymond got up eagerly, saying, "Yeah, I'll get—" Then he stopped in confusion.

"Criminy. I didn't bring my stuff back from Aunt

Jill's, did I?'' He looked at Kate blankly. Yesterday had been such a frantic hassle after the homecoming.

"I don't know, Raymond. You keep everything in your desk. They certainly moved your desk over, didn't they?''

"Yeah, yeah, yeah," he said, suddenly nervous. "But I didn't use the desk here in this house yet. Over at Aunt Jill's I had everything in the backpack—''

"Never mind," Mrs. Lundy interposed. "It doesn't matter. I don't have that much time, anyhow. I'm just on my lunch break. Maybe next time." She was standing up, picking up her purse and book. "It was good seeing you again, Raymond. And Mrs. McAllister, again my good wishes to you and Mr. McAllister. And thank you so much for seeing me." She bustled toward the front hallway. Raymond and Kate followed.

"Thank you for coming," Kate said at the door, and she and Raymond stood in the doorway, watching Mrs. Lundy get into her car, wave cheerily out the window and drive away.

"She's really nice," Raymond said with some satisfaction. "Not all teachers really like the kids, but she likes kids, she really does."

"Yes, I could tell that," Kate said, shutting the door.

"I remember now," Raymond said. "I did leave my backpack over there. I'll just go over and get it."

"That's a pretty long bike ride," Kate said. "Maybe I'd better run you over in the car. Let me get dressed." Kate felt vaguely disturbed by Mrs. Lundy's visit.

"No," Raymond was saying. "You don't hafta do that. I'll go by bus. I know the transfers and all. And you were gonna talk to Pastor Ledbetter, remember?'' He was looking at her anxiously.

He was almost as tall as she was now. Kate reached

over and smoothed back his hair fondly. He was such a dear child.

"You're right. I do need to talk to him. If he's got some time." She turned and started up the stairway. Better get into the day. Where was Ian now? She hadn't even asked his destination. He was out there, working hard at his job. *Oh, Ian.* She would have to come to terms with this. There was no way she could just take Tommy and Joy and leave. *For better or worse.* she felt a hot flush of humiliation. How could she ever tell Mom? Or Jill? How could she face them? It was the high school Junior Prom all over again. Nobody really wanted Katie.

She would take a quick shower and get dressed. First she would call the church and see if Pastor Ledbetter was available.

She heard Raymond's "Bye, Mom. I'm going" as he slammed out the door to catch the first bus to Jill's house on the other side of the wide city.

Pastor Ledbetter was at a meeting, but Bessie, the church secretary, said she would try to reach him on his cell phone with Kate's message. Not that it mattered that much, Kate thought. She'd already made up her mind. Or had it made up for her. There was too much at stake. She had to chat with Bessie for a while, about the trip to Hawaii. She did her best to sound upbeat, but was glad when the call was over. Tiredly, she took her shower and dressed.

She had been downstairs but a few minutes when the doorbell chimed again. When she opened the door she was so glad to see Cyrus Ledbetter's aging face with his big smile that she almost fell into his arms.

"Oh, come in. Come in," she said, opening the door wide.

When they were seated in the living room, and he had

commented on the house, he got right to the point. "What's up, Kate? Bessie said you sounded a bit distracted on the phone."

"I guess I was." She paused. How could she tell him, or tell anybody. But even as she thought it, the words came tumbling out, her humiliation, her anger and resentment, and when she wound down he was silent for a long time. Then he surprised her.

"How do you think he's feeling?"

"Who?" she asked blankly.

"Ian. Think a minute, Kate. In the past couple of weeks I've gotten to know him a little better. On the whole, I see him as an honorable man. How much did it bother him to violate his own sense of integrity to con you into a marriage of necessity? And the *why* of it. If Tommy or Joy were to be threatened in some way, to what lengths would you go to protect them?"

Kate quelled a sudden flare of resentment.

"I suppose…to any length," she admitted slowly. "I shouldn't have bothered you, anyhow. I've already, not exactly made up my mind, but realized I have no choice but to stay with marriage. I can't let Raymond down. I'm…his only chance."

"I'm glad you know that. He's twelve, almost thirteen, a very vulnerable age, adolescence. It's during this period that a child can make wild decisions, crazy choices that they have to live with the rest of their lives. With this boy's deep sense of insecurity, if he were put out of the family situation now, he would very probably seek whatever escape he could, just as Ian had feared. The adolescent can't see beyond today. His whole life could disintegrate. Whatever potential he has might never be realized. He could throw it away in an attempt to escape from a temporary despair."

"I know," Kate said soberly.

They were silent for a time, then he added, "What about Kate?"

"What do you mean?" she asked with an edge of bitterness. "Good old Kate will come through."

He was looking at her, his wise old eyes thoughtful. "Why do you think Kate resents this so much?"

She had started to brace herself. From past talks with him she could sense what was coming. When he started referring to "Kate" in the third person, he was going to be bluntly honest. She felt a wry half smile twist her lips.

"Maybe Kate's ego has taken a beating," she admitted.

"And we all know that's not easy," he said gently. "That's why pride is listed as one of the seven deadlies."

Kate sighed. "I shouldn't have bothered you. I know what I'm going to do. I'm going to make the best of it."

"Maybe it would help if you know *why* you will make the best of it," he said after a moment.

"What do you mean? I guess I'm compromising because I...I've been in love with him for quite a while. It never dawned on me that I would...ever be his wife. I guess I'm saying I'll hang on because, even if he doesn't love me as I thought he did, I'll take him on any terms. I guess it's that part that's the real ego buster."

He reached over and took her small hand in his. "Katie, there's more to it than that. Think a minute. Give yourself credit. Part of it is that you took a *vow* before God's altar to be his wife. For better or worse. You can't erase that."

"No. I can't," she said slowly. "That is part of it."

"Another part is that—and this is an old-fashioned word you almost never hear anymore—there is a *duty* here. Don't forget that two thousand years ago He said,

'When you do it for the least of these, you do it for Me.' And Raymond was that unhappy, at-risk little kid next door. You *could* do something about it. You saw a duty there and you fulfilled it. If you see a need, and you are able to help, you must.''

Kate's vision blurred with tears. ''Are you trying to be kind to me?''

''No. I'm trying to help you sort out some confusion. Your personal disappointment is getting in the way. Part of why Ian did what *he* did was also duty. Think about that—it might make it easier. He had a duty to protect his child, and he was fulfilling it the only way he could think of. Ponder that one a minute.''

She clung to his gnarled old hand as she had after Claude had died when she had been filled with unresolved anger at God, demanding why, why, why. Together they had sorted it out until she could accept—never understanding, but accepting. His words spoken then came back to her now. *Katie, don't expect to understand the vast mind of God. He gave us our instructions and they are all we need. For now. Later we will understand.*

Kate felt a half smile tug at her lips. ''Okay. I've pondered, and I'm coming up empty. What do you suggest?''

''Ian was selfish and self-serving, for whatever good motive. He needed you. And he used you. You *have* the answer. You say it every day when you pray. 'Forgive us our trespasses as we forgive those who trespass against us.' *Forgiveness*, Kate. Blessed forgiveness. Can you do that?''

Chapter Seven

Thank God for work. In the days that followed her talk with Cyrus, Kate filled her days with a much heavier schedule as she began the process of settling into her new life. There was plenty to do. She and Raymond resumed their schooling schedule. Raymond worked harder than he had before and, sadly, Kate knew why. He couldn't help but worry about the upcoming custody suit.

Tommy and Joy were settling into the new house well. Now and then she sent up a silent prayer of thanks for Tommy. He was a sturdy, easygoing, loving little boy who was never a problem. She thought, and hoped, that he would grow up to be the same type of man her father had been.

Two days before Ian's return from his trip, Kate took time to go next door. She must do something about the little house she and Claude had bought and which had been her home until a few days ago. She unlocked the front door and went in. All her well-worn furniture was stored in Ian's attic, and the unfurnished rooms looked small and drab. Everything had been done in such a rush during the honeymoon in Hawaii that Jill hadn't done anything about getting the place cleaned, and Kate took a sad pleasure in that. *I will clean my house.*

She stood looking around the living room. The floors needed sanding, but perhaps that could wait. She had no idea what it might cost. The bookcases flanking the small fireplace were empty and dust covered. Dad and Claude had built those bookcases. For the first time she wondered where the books were, hers and Tommy's and Joy's and some leftover from Claude. Perhaps they filled some of those boxes now in Ian's attic. There were well-filled bookcases in Ian's study, but none anywhere else in the house. She must have some built in the living room. With Dad having been a librarian, she didn't feel at home unless there were books about.

She wandered on through the small house, taking note of this and that. She knew for a fact now that she would not sell. This would be the safe haven if—at some time—Ian didn't need their marriage any longer. Or, and this thought made her catch her breath, if Ian some day found some woman he could love as he'd loved Marsha. *Don't think about that. Think about this house. Concentrate. What's to be done here?*

Firmly, she noted that Tommy's posters, now in his bedroom next door, had left pale squares on the wallpaper in what had been his bedroom. In the bedroom she had used there was a crack in the window glass that hadn't been there before. And the linoleum on the kitchen floor was broken and cracked in front of the sink. She had covered it with a small braided rag rug she had made. The new tenant might want new floor covering. How much would that cost?

And the vegetable garden? She stood looking out over the sink. That garden had provided so much food for so many people. Could she give it up? Suddenly in the empty house the phone started to ring. Nobody had thought to disconnect it. Where was it? She had just seen it somewhere. The dining room? She went back into that room and saw the phone sitting on the floor in a corner. She hurried to answer it.

"Mrs. McAllister?" The voice sounded old and somewhat tired.

"Yes?"

"I'm Mrs. Hyslop. Adelaide Hyslop. I don't know if your sister mentioned it or not, but I—I mean Mr. Hyslop and I—looked at your house a few days ago."

"Yes. She mentioned it," Kate answered.

"She didn't know if you were going to sell it or rent it, but I, Mr. Hyslop and I, have been looking for a small cottage and we wondered..."

"I have decided to rent it," Kate said firmly. "On a month-to-month basis, no lease." It was clear in her mind now. She would simply rent and put the money aside in a savings account. She might well need it some time in the future. And she felt somehow drawn to the thin elderly voice on the phone—the way the woman had introduced herself, the formal way she referred to her husband as "Mr. Hyslop." There was an old-fashioned dignity to it that appealed to Kate.

"Oh, I'm so relieved. It did look promising." There was a lessening of tension in the old voice. "Your sister was so kind. She was awfully busy, but she stopped long enough to let us take a quick walk through. When would it be a convenient time for the house to be shown?"

"Any time," Kate said. "Your convenience. I'm going to start cleaning up and I'm right next door."

She heard a quavery sigh. "We have only two weeks left in this place. They are turning our apartment house into condos, and Mr. Hyslop and I can't—that is, we're not interested in buying a place at our age. We're both elderly."

"No, of course not," Kate agreed. "There is a lot of hassle to owning. Sometimes it's easier to just rent."

"We think so. Mrs. McAllister, you are in the house now? Would it be all right if I came over? I have some-one to…I mean, Mr. Hyslop is occupied and I have a bit of free time."

"Of course. I'll probably be here the rest of the after-noon. If I'm not, I'll be next door, so just walk in."

"Thank you. Thank you so much."

Kate hung up and went next door for cleaning mate-rials. She was mopping the kitchen floor when Mrs. Hys-lop rang the doorbell. Kate put the mop in the bucket of sudsy water and tiptoed across the wet kitchen floor.

Mrs. Hyslop was a thin sparrow of a woman, probably in her seventies. She was wearing a light spring coat in faded navy-blue and a navy straw hat that had seen many summers.

"I'm Mrs. Richard Hyslop," she said with the same formal dignity Kate had heard on the phone. Old, obvi-ously poor, she seemed to hold about her the aura of better days gone by. Kate sensed that at some time, in the long ago, her words *I'm Mrs. Richard Hyslop,* had commanded respect.

"Come in. Forgive the way I look. I'm mopping the kitchen."

Mrs. Hyslop smiled. "Housework can be messy."

Kate began to show her through the empty and par-tially cleaned house. "It's supposed to be two bedrooms and den, but I changed the little den into a small bedroom for myself after the children's father died. I wanted my little girl to have a room to herself. My boy had his own room. I think my sister mentioned that you and Mr. Hyslop are just a couple. Do you need this much room?"

"Yes," Mrs. Hyslop said. She paused at the kitchen doorway, looking into it but not really seeing it. "I need the extra space," she finally added, and paused as if deciding to say more. Then she turned to Kate, slight color rising into her thin cheeks. "Mr. Hyslop is…unwell," she said finally. The words came slowly, reluctantly. "Mr. Hyslop has Alzheimer's disease. His…his mental faculties are not what they were. His care is sometimes difficult for me. I have reached the time when I really need to employ a live-in aide. I've been advised to hire a college student, and if I can offer both a bedroom and study, it might be an inducement."

Kate's heart went out to her as she remembered the long days and nights of caring for Claude during his illness. "I understand," she said. "The children's father, my first husband, was an invalid for a time before he passed away. It can be exhausting."

"Yes," Mrs. Hyslop said in a soft faraway voice. "Mr. Hyslop had such a very fine mind.…" Her voice trailed off and she lifted her head in a gesture of remembered pride. "What a nice roomy kitchen," she added in a falsely bright voice.

And I was so sorry for myself, Kate thought. Shame. "The place needs some work, of course. I guess I didn't notice how worn-out things were. I don't know how long it will take to fix things up a bit. Did you say you needed a place in two weeks?"

"Yes, I did." The old lady paused a moment, then, coloring again, said, "Actually, Mr. Hyslop and I are living on somewhat limited means. Would you consider renting the place just as is, at a lesser figure? I could put a little rug over the worn places." And Kate wondered how difficult it had been for Mrs. Hyslop to admit this, but she agreed instantly.

"Of course. That might be simpler all around, if you don't mind." She recalled the figure Jill had quoted for a possible rent and cut about one-fourth off it. Repairs and upgrading would have cost a lot, she assured herself.

"We'll take it," Mrs. Hyslop said quickly, almost before Kate had finished speaking. "And thank you. Thank you so much."

"Fine," Kate answered briskly. "I'll be finished with the cleaning by tomorrow, then I thought I'd do some painting and repairs. It should be done by next week and you can move in any time after that. Do you have someone who can move you?"

"Yes. That is simple to arrange."

One by one things were falling into place, and she was getting started into her new life. It wasn't what she had so ecstatically imagined, but she had no cause to complain. Good things were happening. She would keep her mind on these things.

Mom came over the next day with a large painting.

"I want you to see this," she said, her lovely face glowing and eager. "Just look!" She turned it around and Kate recognized it immediately. It was the back garden at Mom's B and B, with the end of the white grape arbor showing.

"Mom," she gasped. "It's lovely. It's so real. I feel I can just walk into it and be in our old back garden." She saw the old birdbath, with the surround of green grass and white benches. She saw the row of bright petunias against the back fence. She saw the white table where they had sometimes eaten in summer, under its faded umbrella. The artist had painted the table in use, with a scatter of dishes, a crumpled napkin and one of the chairs pushed back as if someone had just got up and walked away. It was beautifully done.

"My guest, Douglas Colby, painted it," Mom was saying, and Kate's attention was suddenly drawn out of the picture back to the present.

"He's giving it to me?" Kate asked in astonishment.

"Not exactly," Mom said happily. "I'm giving it to you. Here, help me with this chair. We can take down that impressionistic thing you said you didn't like. Ian said you could change anything you wanted."

"Wait a minute. Let me get the step stool. Don't stand on the chair. You might fall."

Together they took down Marsha's decorator picture and hung the one of the garden. "You see," Mom was saying as she straightened it. "Stand back. See if this is even. This is one of Doug's discards. He's such a perfectionist. He always throws pictures away, or paints over them. But I've been taking them. They're just too good to discard. I'm saving them for the church fall bazaar. I've got four in the garage. Three now, since I'm giving this one to you. The craft guild at church is going to frame them. Cyrus is donating the money for the framing. They'll sell better if they are already framed. And the church always needs money."

When the picture was up, they stood in front of it, admiring it. "How long is Doug going to stay?" Kate asked, remembering what Jill had told her. How odd it would seem if Mom fell in love. Surely not. She observed her mother, looking up at the picture, her eyes shining. *Life goes on,* Jill had said.

"I don't know. I told him he could stay as long as he needed to. His work is getting so good. Jill said one of Greg's accounting clients is an art gallery. Greg's going to ask the man to look at Doug's work. Maybe he can get a showing. Are you sure you like it? Doug was afraid you'd think you had to take it. You don't, you know. If you don't like it.''

"I love it," Kate said. "It...it takes me back. Tell him that. Tell him thank you."

Ian arrived back home from his trip a bit after noon. Kate wondered if he had planned it that way so they could have some time alone. Her children were at school and he knew that Raymond took off right after lunch on Thursdays to the library. Dad would have loved Raymond. He'd had an affinity for book-loving kids. Kate was putting the dishes from Raymond's and her lunch into the dishwasher when she heard Ian's car come into the driveway. Her heart stopped a moment and her resolution failed.

Come on, Kate. You promised Cyrus.

She went to the back door to open it. He came in somewhat diffidently, carrying the big two-suiter. He looked tired.

"Leave that on the porch," Kate said. "I'll want to put things into the laundry, so I'll unpack it." And seeing his questioning look, she added matter-of-factly, "I'm over my tantrum. Come on in."

"All the kids out?" he asked, putting the two-suiter down and following her into the kitchen.

"Yes. Have you had lunch? I can fix you something if you're hungry?"

"I did, thanks. On the plane." In the living room he noticed the new painting right away. "Where'd we get that? Isn't that your mother's back garden? I like it. It's good. I like trees that look like trees."

"Yes, I do, too." And in telling him about the picture she felt the tension ease between them.

"I'm glad to see the last of the other one. What'd you do with it?"

"It's stored in the attic for the time being."

"You could have tossed it for all I care. Ray always said it looked like chocolate and peach ice cream being stirred with an invisible spoon. Actually, it kind of did."

Kate had to laugh, remembering the brown-and-peach swirls on the large canvas. "I thought it might be worth something," she said. "Raymond said Marsha paid a bundle for it. I'm quoting now." She had sat down across from him, and a little silence fell between them.

"Kate...is...are things okay between us? Can you...be happy?"

She looked at his serious eyes, his strong face, and spoke carefully. "I had a long talk with Pastor Ledbetter. He's helped me sort out things before. I...our marriage isn't what I expected, but...I'm not *un*happy, now that I've had time to think about things. Maybe you're right. Maybe we can still be a good...team. I won't lie to you. You didn't lie to me. I'm disappointed, but I think I was foolishly expecting too much. I can put aside disappointment. Everybody has disappointments. They're part of life. I prayed about it. We took the vows, Ian. Both of us. For better or worse. If it isn't exactly as I thought it was, that's...all right. Other people have bigger problems than I have. We're going to have a new neighbor next door. I rented my house." And she told him about the frail, valiant old woman next door whose heart must break anew every time she looked at her husband, a relic of the man he must have one time been.

Ian pushed an ottoman across the space between them and came to sit on it before her. "That's rotten luck for anybody," he said, taking her hands. "We've got it better than that." His voice was husky. "We can make it, Katie."

And Kate answered carefully, "Yes, we can make it." She wondered how much he might be missing Marsha, and made herself add, "Will you promise me one thing?"

"Yes. Of course."

"If you ever change your mind, will you tell me? I don't want you to stay tied to a marriage you don't want." Despite her best effort, her voice was unsteady as she said it.

"This is for keeps, Kate. But, yes, if that should ever happen, I would tell you. I probably wouldn't have to tell you. You'd probably already know. But I'm way past the hearts-and-flowers-falling-in-love stage. Been there. Done that. It didn't stand the test of time when the bloom was off. I wanted a marriage with someone I could admire and respect and...trust. And I'm grateful to you, Kate. So grateful, you'll never know how much."

But I don't want your gratitude. I want you to love me, love me to distraction, the way I love you. "I understand," Kate said gravely, withdrawing her hands. *So be it. Half a loaf is better than no loaf at all.* "I took some phone messages for you while you were gone. They're on your desk in the study."

"Okay, thanks," he said. He seemed to sense her withdrawal. "I guess I'd better catch up on a few things." And for the rest of the afternoon, whenever Kate passed the study door she could hear the murmur of his voice on the phone, or the steady tapping on his computer keyboard. She didn't see him again until she was in the kitchen preparing their evening meal. He came to stand beside her, looking out the window into the backyard, where their children and some friends were playing.

"One of those letters was from our attorney," he said. "We have a court date for our hearing to dismiss the custody suit."

"When?" She turned from the sink, unable to keep the alarm from her voice.

"April fifteenth. Eight in the morning. It'll be just a formality. They haven't got a case now. There was one thing. In that exchange-of-evidence thing attorneys do, Rick says they have a deposition from a teacher, a Mrs. Lundy. Do you know anything about that? I hate to ask Ray. He gets so upset."

"Yes. She sent me a letter sometime just after we took Raymond out of school. She also sent me an article against homeschooling. Then she stopped in one day to see Raymond. She's a pleasant sort. I could tell she was fond of Raymond."

"I wonder what she was deposed about. The home-schooling, I guess. I'll give Rick a call tomorrow. As soon as we get the case dismissed, we'll be in the clear."

Thanks to good friend Kate standing in, she thought, and was immediately ashamed of herself. He'd been in a trap and he had got out as best he could. She'd learn to live with it.

The vegetable garden helped. It was past time to plant. She should have done that two weeks ago, to take full advantage of Seattle's short summer.

The backyard in the new house was a well-used play-ground for Raymond and his friends. In front was a lawn and formal flower beds here and there, all attended by a gardening service. She had no idea how much Ian paid for it. She had watched the gardening crew of three come once a week to cut, trim, pull up and replant. From time to time they planted masses or rows of bright flowers. In due course they came to pull them out and plant others as the seasons passed. She had grown to know them, for on very hot days she had given them iced tea and on chill fall days she had given them hot coffee.

But *her* garden, as she thought of the space behind her small house, was the *real* garden, which had fed so many people so much food. Very early she had interested Tommy and Joy in gardening. Then Raymond had become involved, too. Somewhere she had read that if you garden in childhood you garden in age, and this was something of value she could pass on for lifetime comfort and satisfaction.

The children had become quite good at weeding, watering, planting and harvesting. They had all picked, trimmed and washed fresh vegetables, for home and neighbor use. She had taken them with her on trips to the food bank, and to the Millionaire's Club, which served countless meals, day after day, to Seattle's large homeless population. Let them learn responsibility. Let them learn life wasn't easy for everybody.

A couple of new rules were put into place when the Hyslops moved in next door. One, they should keep their voices down when Mr. Hyslop was taking his afternoon rest. Two, they mustn't laugh or comment when Mr. Hyslop got confused and said something that didn't make sense when he sometimes wandered around outside. All three children showed considerable sensitivity about this, which gladdened Kate's heart.

Mr. Hyslop was a tall, thin man with white hair and a look of timid confusion in his pale blue eyes. He sometimes came to sit, gazing vaguely about, in the back of the vegetable garden on a wooden bench Kate had left there. But when he was outside Mrs. Hyslop was close by to see that he didn't wander off and become lost.

Kate found that church work also helped in the process of accepting her new life. Ian had always had a cleaning service come in twice a month for work like vacuuming, mopping and window cleaning. He insisted on continuing this, so Kate had more free time for parish work. It came at a good time for the church, as she filled in when the secretary, Bessie, took a spring vacation. Kate could work in the church office mornings to take care of routine clerical tasks. She set up a small table in the corner of the church office for Raymond to complete his morning studies, so these were not interrupted.

April fifteenth came all too soon, Ian repeating that it was just a formality. The custody case would be dismissed without fail. They discussed it one early evening.

"I'm coming with you," Raymond said as Kate was arranging for the children to spend the night of the fourteenth at Jill's house.

"No," Ian said. "That's not a good idea, Ray. It's only a dismissal hearing. Just a couple of lawyers arguing in front of the judge. You've been upset enough about this."

"I know, but I gotta see it happen, Dad. Give in on this. So I won't go bananas waiting around. I gotta see the judge bang down the gavel and say, 'Case dismissed. Everybody take a hike.' I'm *involved,* see. This is my *future* we're talking about."

Ian laughed. "Okay," he said, "but you have to keep quiet."

"Won't I be called as a witness or something?"

"No witnesses at this. It's just a hearing. Just the lawyers arguing. I've made a declaration that our guy will read, stating my reasons the case should be dismissed and all. Our attorneys will present our case, read that, and then I guess the judge will think it over a minute and deny their motion.''

"He better," Raymond muttered, then, "Dad, what if he doesn't?''

"Why wouldn't he?" Kate interposed. "They want you to have a two-parent family. You've got one now, so where's the case? Don't worry about it.''

"Okay, but I sure hope you and Dad are right. I'm gonna go for a bike ride. See you later.''

"Come back before dark," Kate cautioned automatically.

After Raymond had gone Ian looked doubtful for the first time. "I hope I'm right. The attorneys seem confident enough. I'd like to see the last of this. Marsha's welcome to visit Ray any time she wants to. That's part of our original understanding. But they mustn't get custody. I don't think Ray could take that.''

On the evening of the fourteenth Kate drove Tommy and Joy over to Jill's house. She had never yet told Jill or her mother that her marriage hadn't turned out to be what she wanted, but somehow, as happens in families, they seemed to know. It was comforting and somewhat irritating at the same time.

Jill was going to drive Tommy and Joy to school in the morning and they would come home as usual on their regular school bus. Since the hearing started so early, she knew that she would be home long before school let out.

The next day she, Ian and Raymond arrived at the old courthouse in congested downtown Seattle, with its dirty gray facade and dusty gray-and-white marble floors. They had to pass singly through the metal detector just inside the doorway. Kate passed through without incident, but when Raymond came through behind her the alarm sounded. Then, as Ian passed through, the guard took Raymond aside and he stood, arms outstretched, while the guard passed the wand over and around him. The difficulty turned out to be a metal bicycle clamp Raymond had around one ankle.

"It's not like I'm armed and dangerous," he muttered to Kate in the elevator and Kate laughed, knowing that he was secretly delighted at the small sensation he had caused. For some reason she was suddenly nervous. None of this seemed real. They were all going into some strange room and some man in a black robe would make a decision affecting their lives.

The courtroom itself seemed too small. Kate wasn't sure what she had expected, as she had never before been in a courtroom. There were rows of seats, of very old wood, somewhat like church pews. The carpeting was faded and worn. There was the expected railing between where the spectators sat and where the hearing took place. There was the expected jury box, although there would be no jury for this. There was the judge's place, at a somewhat higher level with a little fenced-in space where, she supposed, the court reporter sat. She had watched enough TV courtroom dramas to know in general what to expect. Everything had an old and shabby look. They slid into the front-row seats. Neither Marsha nor Chester Burgess was there, which was a relief.

"Please rise." Some male voice spoke loudly. She wasn't sure from where, as there were two or three people near the judge's bench. Then the judge, a middle-aged woman in a black robe, entered and took her place. "Judge Mary Howell presiding. Be seated, please," the unidentified voice said.

Judge Howell took her place, tapped with the gavel on the desk and began the proceedings. It seemed each side had two attorneys for some reason Kate didn't understand. She should have talked this over more with Ian. As if sensing her confusion, he leaned over to whisper to her. "Our guys are at this end of that long table. Their names are Rick Hersey and John Wilson, of the firm Hagaman, Matthews and Wheeler."

It appeared that Rick Hersey was the lead attorney. He stood up, rustled some papers and began to speak. He was presenting their argument for dismissal. He seemed about Ian's age, but shorter with a more stocky build. He spoke in a positive and unhurried manner, pausing now and then to turn over a page in a folder he had left on the table before him. When he read from Ian's declaration it sounded like something Ian would say. Kate began to feel more confident. Marsha and her Chet really didn't have any reason to sue for custody. Raymond was fine just as things were. He was where he needed to be. He was doing well.

Judge Howell listened intently to what Rick Hersey said, and then, all of a sudden, Hersey was finished and sat down at the long table.

A man and a woman were representing Marsha and Chet. The elderly, gray-haired man stood up and began their statement, which was, Kate realized wryly, a very sugarcoated description of Marsha's motherhood, a version of a very loving and dedicated mother temporarily leaving her son with her former husband as she, for reasons beyond her control, could not care for him at that time. At one point Raymond moved restlessly and Kate saw Ian's hand clamp firmly on his arm and heard Ian say softly and distinctly, "Cool it." So Raymond subsided. The gray-haired man paused for a moment, seeming to be finished. He put down some papers and picked up some more.

"If the court pleases, I would like to read into the record a deposition taken in our offices nine days ago, from a former teacher of the child, Raymond McAllister."

Kate heard Raymond sniff in disgust as the judge said, "To what purpose?"

"It pertains to the situation in which the boy now lives, Your Honor. We believe his present situation is open to question. The boy is no longer attending any school, although he is only twelve years old. The present Mrs. McAllister is purportedly teaching him at home. The boy's mother, Mrs. Burgess, is deeply concerned about this."

"Read it," the judge said, leaning back.

"Thank you." The attorney nodded his head and began. "This is a deposition taken in the offices of Bancroft, McPhail, Crandall and Woods, on April sixth of this year from Mrs. Jean Lundy. The deposing attorney is Melvin Dodd." He paused and turned a page.

"Dodd: 'Please state your name.'

"Lundy: 'My name is Jean Marie Lundy.'

"Dodd: 'Mrs. Lundy, are you making this statement of your own free will, and have been subject to no influence or coercion?'

"Lundy: 'Yes.'

"Dodd: 'What is your profession or occupation?'

"Lundy: 'I teach seventh-and eighth-grade English at West Middle School here in Seattle.'

"Dodd: 'Did you have Raymond McAllister among your students?'

"Lundy: 'Yes, a lovely boy.'

"Dodd: 'Is Raymond McAllister one of your students now?'

"Lundy: 'No.'

"Dodd: 'Were you advised why?'

"Lundy: 'Yes. Mr. Chan, the principal at West Middle School, notified me that Raymond's father was going to have him taught at home.'

"Dodd: 'Mrs. Lundy, have you had occasion to see Raymond McAllister since that time?'

"Lundy: 'Yes. I stopped by the McAllister house one day on my lunch break.'

"Dodd: 'Did you see the boy, Raymond McAllister?'

"Lundy: 'Yes, I did. And with Mrs. McAllister, too.'"

Kate, listening intently was suddenly suffused with anxiety. The attorney's voice droned unhurriedly on.

"Dodd: 'Can you give us the gist of your conversation with the boy and Mrs. McAllister?'

"Lundy: 'Yes. Well, Raymond was glad to see me. As I said, he's a lovely boy. Mrs. McAllister seemed a little put out. Maybe not put out exactly, but surprised. You see, I had just stopped in, without any call first or anything.'

"Dodd: 'And what time of day was this?'

"Lundy: 'I think about eleven-thirty. I was taking an early lunch break.'

"Dodd: 'Do you know why Mrs. McAllister seemed to be put out?'

"Lundy: 'She seemed embarrassed because she was still in her bathrobe, I think. She tried to be nice about it.'

"Dodd: 'But the boy was glad to see you. Did you discuss his schoolwork?'

"Lundy: 'Yes. We did, a little. He seemed enthusiastic about it. He said he was doing fine. He seemed satisfied with it. I asked to see some of it, just to get an idea of what he was actually studying.'

"Dodd: 'And what did you think of it?'

"Lundy: 'Well, I didn't actually see any of his work. He didn't know where any of it was. He'd forgotten where he had put it.'" The attorney paused for several seconds, then went on.

"Dodd: 'You called at the McAllister home at eleven-thirty on a weekday morning. Mrs. McAllister was still in her bathrobe and the boy, Raymond, couldn't recall where he had put his schoolwork? Is that right?'

"Lundy: 'Well, yes, but they had just—'

"Dodd: 'Thank you, Mrs. Lundy. That will be all. This ends the deposition.'"

The attorney put the sheaf of papers down on the table and approached the bench. Rick Hersey got up at the same time and came over to the railing. He leaned over and spoke quickly to Kate. "Is that the way you recall that incident?"

"Yes," Kate said, her face flaming. "But we had just got back from Hawaii and had just moved into Ian's house from mine, next door. Raymond had been staying with my sister. He'd left his work over there."

"Thanks," he said, and swung back to stride over to the bench, as Kate heard the last of what the other attorney was saying.

"...ask that Your Honor consider this unusual arrangement for the boy's education. Is this in the child's best long-term interest? What other unusual arrangements are there? Since this has been revealed, we submit that the custody hearing should go forward as planned as in the best interests of the child, so that the situation in all its complexities may be clear. We ask that the defendant's motion to dismiss be denied. Thank you." He turned with grave dignity and went back to the table.

"Your Honor," Rick Hersey said. "To clarify, Mrs. McAllister has informed me that they had just returned from…'' He went on, attempting to repair the damage, and seemed to be doing a good job. Then he, too, turned and went back to the table.

''Thank you, Counselor,'' the judge said. ''However, this is an unusual arrangement, although I am aware that homeschooling is legal in Washington State. And it is the court's opinion that the interests of the boy, Raymond, are paramount here.'' She went on, meticulously reviewing what each attorney had said, summing up the arguments on both sides.

Kate felt Raymond stiffen beside her and gave his arm a reassuring pat. The judge was turning over sheets of paper on which she had written notes during the presentations.

''A later court may well decide that Mr. McAllister's present arrangements are in the best interests of the boy, Raymond, and must stand. But in view of the objections raised by the boy's natural mother, Mrs. Burgess, this court believes that the custody hearing should go forward as scheduled.''

The judge pushed aside the papers and picked up her gavel. She was looking directly at Ian and sounded regretful. ''Therefore, this court must deny the defendant's motion to dismiss. Motion denied.''

Chapter Eight

Kate sat stunned, aware that Raymond, who seemed to be shrinking down beside her, was trying to make himself smaller. She saw Ian stand up and go over to the rail to shake hands with his attorneys. There was the sound of people moving about, getting ready to leave. The judge was gone now. When had she gone, and where? Some male voice from somewhere had said, "Court is adjourned."

It's my fault.

She could feel her face flushing with embarrassment as Ian and his attorneys separated and Ian turned back.

"Dad?" Raymond's voice was unsteady. He stood up, staying close to Kate. Ian's face was grim. Kate knew he was avoiding her eyes. "I'm sorry, buddy." He touched Raymond's shoulder. "We lost that round, but only that one. It'll all be sorted out in the custody suit. Don't worry about it."

Raymond caught at Ian's arm. "But it's my fault," he whispered tensely. "I caused it."

"Nonsense," Ian said briskly. "Look, let's get out of here."

Wordlessly, Kate moved toward the door when they did. Raymond was clinging to Ian's arm. "Dad, wait up. I gotta talk to you. I gotta explain."

"In the car, Ray," Ian said, almost shortly. "Right now priority one is to get out of here." He was deeply angry and trying not to show it.

They couldn't get into the first elevator because it was full, so had to wait. More people were coming up, probably for the next case. She hoped they would have better luck, whoever they were. Ian was standing close to his attorneys again, as they had now come out into the hall. They were talking in low tones. Probably about his dumb wife who sat around in her bathrobe all morning and his son who couldn't recall where he had left his schoolwork.

Eventually they were out onto Seattle's crowded downtown street. It was an overcast gray day. They had come so early that Ian had found street parking a block down. They walked toward it now, making what progress they could along the crowded sidewalk. She was walking beside Ian now, but conversation was impossible because of the noise of the bumper-to-bumper traffic, creeping along. They skirted a vagrant digging desperately into a trash can. The skyscrapers soared around her, making her feel closed in and stifled. Ian caught her arm to pull her out of the way of the staggering panhandler. A bike messenger swerved up onto the sidewalk and off again to avoid a taxi in his frantic haste to deliver his basket of messages. Rush. Rush. Rush. She avoided downtown Seattle whenever she could, and now she breathed a sigh of relief when they reached Ian's car, although it took a while to wait for traffic to thin for him to get into the driver's side.

As Ian eased the car out into the line of cars, Raymond, in the back seat exploded angrily, "Okay, we're in the car now. Will you listen to me, Dad! It's not Mom's fault. I did it. I opened the door when Mrs. Lundy came. I *invited* her in! I *knew* we weren't into the day yet. I knew it. I'm stupid! You got a stupid son!"

Ian spoke quietly. "Nobody is at fault, Ray. Sometimes you win. Sometimes you don't. I picked up from the woman's deposition that it was the first day back from Hawaii. She started to say that and the attorney stopped her. It's just bad luck, that's all." Either his anger had cooled or he was controlling it better.

"Raymond," Kate said, "don't blame yourself for this. You did the natural thing. Mrs. Lundy was interested in you as her student. You like each other. What else would you do but invite her in when she came? Forget it. It's all right."

"Yeah," he muttered. "But I didn't know she was a traitor. I didn't know she'd gone over to the enemy."

Kate knew she should say something, tell him that his mother wasn't the "enemy," but she couldn't think of anything to say. Ian was inching his way through Seattle's congested traffic toward getting onto the West Seattle Freeway. "Kate, I'll drop you two off at home and head back to my office. That all happened so fast that I can still get in a good day's work, and things have kind of stacked up, as usual."

"Don't drive us clear home," she said. "You're within blocks of your office now. Let us off. We'll take a bus. Really."

"Sure, Dad. I know the bus system by heart. Let us off anywhere along here."

"Well, if you're sure," he said doubtfully, but pulled the car over to the curbside the first chance he got. "And don't worry about today. It's a minor setback, sure, but not the end of the world.'' But even as he said it he couldn't hide his worry.

Kate felt guilty, knowing that he blamed her. After all, he had married her because he thought he was getting someone to mother his child and take care of the home problems. Well, she had failed in this for sure. If only she had thought to call Raymond back. If only she had known in advance that Mrs. Lundy was coming. If. If. If. She got out of the car and waited while Raymond scrambled out of the back seat.

''Don't worry about it, Kate,'' Ian was saying, leaning over to look out the window. ''We'll talk about it tonight if you want to. I can see you're upset.''

She wished again that he would stop treating her with such deference, but was rescued from having to reply by the man in the car behind Ian's who beeped politely on his horn, so Ian drove on.

''Guess what,'' Raymond said with one of his sudden angelic smiles.

''What?''

''Dad let us off in front of McDonald's. It's fate. You think my math work sheets can wait another ten minutes? We didn't eat much breakfast.''

She had to smile. ''Okay. Why not?''

They both felt better after a quick muffin breakfast and in midmorning the swaying bus wasn't crowded, so they could sit together going home.

''I'm really gonna hit the math and hard stuff now,'' Raymond said. ''I gotta be prepared for anything. When will the custody thing come up again?''

''Your dad said early November for the actual custody hearing.''

''They sure take their time, which I guess is good.''

"It's because the court calendar is so crowded."

"So we got till November to prove that our way is best?"

"Something like that," Kate answered, trying not to sound as troubled as she felt. Was this way *really* best? Maybe now that Ian wasn't paying alimony to Marsha, they could afford a private day school. What did Seattle have to offer? She would have to find out. Ian was spending too much on household expenses. Why did they need a cleaning service? Why a gardening service? He should let her handle the household expenses instead of trying to treat her like a princess because he felt guilty about the marriage. After all, if anyone in the world knew how to economize, she did.

Remembered words from Pastor Ledbetter came back to her. *Concentrate on your wifehood, Kate. Your vows, made to God, not Ian, remember that. If Ian stumbles and doesn't fulfill his vows as well as he should, that's between Ian and God. But for Kate, for Kate's self-respect, for Kate's integrity, for Kate's honor, look to Kate's vows.* She stared out the bus window not seeing the houses, the trees, the people. What could she do that she was not doing now?

"Come on, Mom." Raymond was getting up. "It's our stop." The bus was swaying over to the curbside with a swoosh of air brakes and there was the muffled sound of the folding door slamming open.

At home, Raymond went right to his desk in his room, where he studied now, and attacked the daily math sheets.

"Let me know when you finish," Kate said, "and we'll go over them. I want to get the phone messages." She knew that both Mom and Jill would have called.

She was right. Both wanted to be called back as soon as she got home. She sighed, picking up the phone to call Mom first. Yes, their motion to dismiss had been denied. Yes, there would now be a custody hearing in November. She listened to both remonstrating that it certainly *was not* her fault, though neither tried to explain whose fault it might be. She made a small bet with herself that as soon as they talked to each other, both would call back. She was with Raymond, going over his math, when his extension rang.

"I think this is for me," she said, answering it. It was Jill.

"I made two of those slow-bake cheesecakes from your recipe yesterday," she began, getting right to the point. "We haven't had a family visit for a while. Is it okay if Greg and I come over tonight? I'll bring one of the cheesecakes. I mean after dinner, sometime maybe around eight. We can have cake and coffee. I think I've got it right this time, but I'd like your opinion. And Mom could come, too."

Kate had to smile, and felt a quick sting of tears. The *family,* God love them, rallying around in time of stress.

"Sure, why not?" she said. "Sounds like a good idea."

"I'll see if I can get Daphne to baby-sit my kids."

"No," Kate said quickly. "Bring them. Raymond's grandmother has sent him a couple of new videos. The kids can watch those, and it will force Raymond to write his thank-you note. He can't watch the videos until he does, and he knows it." She could hear the relief in Jill's voice when she agreed. Kate hung up the phone feeling better. If they were going to have a family summit, they might as well have Laurie and Ben and little Megan. The cousins always enjoyed getting together.

She had to concentrate on Raymond's lessons, and

later she went over a book report he had written. It was good.

"For a boy who does so well on book reports it seems odd he has so much trouble writing thank-you letters," she commented, and saw his abashed grin.

"I told you. I'm gonna do it today because I wanna see the videos."

"Good," she said absently. An idea had half formed in her mind and she had to keep pushing it aside until she finished with Raymond.

"Well, that's it for today, then," he said finally with a gusty sigh of relief. "I gotta get outta here. I gotta have a break." He usually took off on his bike or skateboard as soon as lessons were over. "I'll write the letter later," he assured her.

Ian called about five to tell her he might work late and to go ahead and have dinner with the children. "Or were we supposed to do something social tonight?"

"Actually yes, but it just came up this morning. Both Jill and Mom are coming over. Jill's bringing dessert." She felt a bit apologetic. Ian's family wasn't as close as hers. He might be uncomfortable. "I think they're going to commiserate with us," she warned.

There was a pause at the other end. "Then I'd better cut this short and get home earlier. It's...it's nice of them," he added awkwardly.

She wasn't sure whether he was pleased or merely felt he had some obligation. It didn't matter. She was glad he was coming home. Her idea was taking shape and it was a little frightening. She couldn't do it alone. She'd need some cooperation. She wanted some quiet time to talk with him.

Raymond timed his return to be just in time to meet the school bus that brought Tommy and Joy home. Kate could hear snatches of their conversation as they came noisily into the house, heading for the kitchen. Kate hugged them all.

"Your snacks are ready," she said as they clustered around the kitchen table. Kids always seemed hungry, and she had put out glasses of milk and graham crackers today.

"I'm going to be phoning in the study," she told them. "Try to keep the noise level down if you stay inside, will you? And rinse your milk glasses out and put them in the dishwasher."

Closed in Ian's study, Kate looked up Seattle's list of private schools in the Yellow Pages. She called seven schools within reasonable distance from home and asked her list of questions. Is the school accredited? Is it church-connected, and if so, which church? Is it coed? How much is the tuition? Does the school supply transportation? She could hear the children's voices in the background. They must be in Raymond's room. From long practice she could tune out their noise, and she kept adding to her notes, smiling as she did. Maybe it was motherhood or something, but she had learned long ago that she could tune out the children's noise until it signaled a real crisis. *That* came through loud and clear, and she could spring into action. *Thank you, God, for whatever it is You give to mothers' hearing.*

Ian didn't make it home to dinner, but said he would be home by eight. Just before she and the children sat down for dinner all three rushed out to mail Raymond's thank-you note to his grandmother.

"So you finally got down to writing your letter," Kate said, almost laughing, before they went.

"Yes!" Raymond said, flourishing a letter, and Joy was seized with a fit of uncontrollable giggling as she ran after the two boys heading for the corner mailbox. Now what were they up to?

Ian got home just moments before Jill and Mom were to arrive. "Do you want me to fix you something to eat?" Kate asked. "There are plenty of leftovers."

"No, thanks, I'm okay. I had a sandwich from the vending machine, but I'll have some of Jill's cheesecake when she comes."

A stale sandwich from a machine. Kate sighed, and was about to protest when the doorbell rang. It was the first of their evening's guests. Mom had never looked better. Never happier. She was going to age beautifully. She was wearing gray culottes, topped by a hand-knitted lavender sweater. Her cheeks were flushed and little wisps of her dark hair had escaped from her usually perfect hairdo. She had brought her lodger, Doug Colby, with her. Was Doug the reason she looked so happy these days? What would happen when Doug decided to move on? She pushed the idea away and greeted them.

As she invited them in they were greeted by Ian, and Kate observed Doug Colby closely for a moment. What did Mom find so attractive? He *was* nice-looking in a rugged, rather outdoorsy way. And he was about Mom's age. He had dark eyes and a warm friendly smile. It was difficult to picture him as an artist. She knew that the landscape painting had begun after his retirement from some sort of business career. He had a kind of old-world courtesy and deference to Mom that pleased Kate, but now and then, when his face was in repose, there seemed a sadness, as if he had some private sorrow he was too polite to mention. Well, who didn't, after all? She was glad he had come, because she had wanted to tell him how much she loved his painting of the back garden at home.

"We went walking down at the waterfront," Mom was saying. "We were talking this morning at breakfast. We don't get enough exercise, and we decided to reform our lives. Get into fitness."

Ian was laughing with them. It was good that he honestly liked her family. "Kate tells me Jill is bringing cheesecake," he said, and Mom groaned.

Kate felt a glow of pleasure and was just going to mention Doug's painting when there were sounds of Jill's children clambering up the front steps and then the doorbell sounded again.

There ensued a period of noisy confusion as Kate and Jill sorted things out. They had to admire Laurie's new hairstyle. She had talked Jill into the same short, feathery cut that Joy had. Things were just getting organized when Kate realized that Jill's little boy, Ben, had been saying soberly several times, "I really don't like cheesecake." So she got cookies for both Ben and Megan, and the children were finally settled in Raymond's room to watch one of the videos.

Jill had taken over in the kitchen and was making coffee, so Kate sat down with a pleasurable sense of well-being and security. She could always count on family. Vintage Mom, protecting her chick. Jill's husband, Greg, tall, blond, so dependable. She and Greg had always had good rapport. Jill, pretty, brisk, efficient, who had hugged her briefly in the kitchen. And even this Doug. Since all his help at her wedding he seemed almost like family. If Mom was thinking of taking the plunge into September love, this big, quiet, gentle man might be a good choice.

After they had eaten Jill's cheesecake and pronounced it delicious and were drinking second cups of coffee, Ian explained to them about the dismissal of their motion.

"It only means," he said, "that there *will* be a custody

battle. I had hoped to avoid it, but that's life. Kate and Ray are both blaming themselves, but there's no blame. It was just an unlucky break.''

They all commiserated, each maintaining firmly that there was no blame for anybody, and it was just a minor setback. It was Greg who finally had the courage to say what they were all avoiding.

"What happens if you lose the custody battle?" he asked quietly.

"I...don't like to think about that," Ian said, his face coloring slightly. Kate saw his hand tighten on his coffee mug.

"You may *have* to think about it," Greg said. "Have you got a Plan B? Just in case?"

Kate sat forward. "I...I was thinking today. Maybe I've got a sort of a Plan B." She could feel herself flushing. She felt uncertain, uneasy. All her life she had been the dutiful little follower. She had lived surrounded by good, strong people, always willing to help little Katie. She had only coped with everyday things like stretching the budget, nursing a sick husband, filling in at the church office, packing up groceries in bags at the food bank. Other people did the deep thinking. Suddenly her idea seemed idiotic. If the idea had any real value, somebody else would have thought of it. And here they all were, silent, waiting for her to go on, looking at her expectantly. It was Ian who sensed her plummeting self-confidence.

"Let's have it, Kate. It could be a beginning, and so far we have zero Plan B."

She swallowed hard. "I called some private schools today. I haven't had a chance to talk to you about it yet, but..." She cast him an apologetic glance. "Since the only thing really against Raymond staying here is the homeschooling thing, I thought..."

"A private day school?" Ian asked. "I wouldn't want him away nights."

"Yes. I called several and got their fees and if they're coed and if they have van transport and such. It's pretty expensive."

"Maybe that would be an answer," Jill said. "If you could afford it. Day schools have got to be cheaper than boarding schools."

"I was going to talk to Ian tonight about how we might...I mean, there are economies I could make that we aren't making now." She went on hurriedly as she saw Ian's frown. He was still paying off his guilt. *Are you happy, Kate? Is this what you want, Kate?* He'd have to give that up. As Raymond would say, "Get real."

"I wasn't thinking of one of those schools," she said firmly. "I was just getting an idea of private school fees and services. Pastor Ledbetter had always wanted to have a school at the church. How difficult would it be to start our own private school? He would know all about getting it accredited, about how much it would cost to begin and all that. Ian, you talked to him about it when you both visited Mr. Chan at Raymond's old school. Has he ever really tried to do it?"

"Yeah. He has," Ian said thoughtfully. "That is, he had done a lot of the preliminary work. I think the main problem might have been money, start-up costs, before the school began paying for itself. When he got to talking money, I was a little out of my depth. In my work I don't deal with the financial end, except in a minimal way."

They all glanced at Greg, who was the family's source of financial information.

"Maybe I could talk to him," Greg said. "We could

at least inquire, see how far he had gone with the idea. Jill and I haven't got around to talking about it yet, but I'd feel better if our kids were in private school, at least after primary grades. Most certainly by the time they get to middle school.''

Mom said, frowning, ''Coming clear over to our church school, if we should get a church school, would be a long commute for your kids—way on the other side of Seattle.''

''All private schools have vans,'' Jill said, and she and Greg turned to look at each other, in one of those husband-and-wife looks, in which some silent message is sent and responded to.

''Yeah,'' Greg said. ''We've still got Jill's old van, and it's in good condition. When I got the VP spot at my firm, I got a company car and we've still got my old car, which Jill could use instead of the van.''

Doug Colby smiled slightly. ''And I could paint the school logo on the side of the van,'' he added, and they all laughed.

Kate felt a sudden leap of hope. Anything is possible, she thought. They were all taking it seriously. Maybe it was a good idea, a great idea, not a daydream. Maybe she had invented Plan B. It was impossible not to smile, and smile, and smile as the excited talk swirled about her.

''Look Doug,'' Mom said. ''What about those other paintings you've got stashed in the garage cupboard?'' She turned to the others. ''Doug's got about a dozen paintings that he thinks are good enough to keep. But he has this thing about *selling* them.''

Doug shifted in his chair. ''I spent my work life grubbing for money,'' he said slowly, and the strange look of fleeting sadness came and went. ''When I retired and indulged myself in painting beautiful places, I didn't want to commercialize it. But for something like a school for kids who need one...well, that's another matter. I get my pleasure, my satisfaction...from painting them. Once that's done I certainly can't keep them all. If they're really worth anything and if they can help the children, well, then..." His voice dwindled off.

"I was going to talk to my client Jim Halloran of the Halloran Gallery," Greg said, "but I hadn't got around to it. Now I will. He can look at your work. See what he thinks."

Ian looked over to Kate. "We'll need to talk with Pastor Ledbetter. Maybe he's given up the idea. Will you be seeing him soon? Do you have time?"

"I'll see him tomorrow. I'll make time," Kate said firmly. How wonderful it would be if they could start their own school. But even if they didn't, she could— must—convince Ian that they should budget for the real priorities.

After the others had left, she broached it to Ian. They were in the kitchen putting the cake plates and coffee mugs into the dishwasher.

"Ian, there's something I need to discuss with you."

"Isn't everything all right?" he asked, frowning. "Don't you have everything you need?" Poor Ian. He sounded almost panicky.

"Actually no," she said bluntly. "I'm accustomed to running my own home."

"Kate, this is your home."

"I mean I'm accustomed to running it, making it all work."

"You're doing great. You're—"

"Listen to me. When I say 'running my home' I mean household *management.* I'm used to budgeting. Homemaking. I think you're spending too much money on house expenses. We don't need a number of things you routinely write checks for every month. If we are successful in getting a private school started at the church, well and good. But if we aren't, Raymond will have to be sent to another one, soon, as early as this September. The homeschooling is doing fine, but if it isn't acceptable to the court in the custody hearing—you see what I mean. I know you must make a good salary. This house tells me that. But we're going to need to factor in more expense for Raymond, if we intend to keep him."

He sat down at the kitchen table. "I...I guess I don't think much about money. Since the divorce, I know in a vague kind of way that I seem to have more—" He stopped himself before he said anything disparaging about Marsha. "What are you proposing?"

She sat down opposite him. "I would like to handle the household management. I would like to pool our resources. I have a modest income from the insurance Claude left. I think for future expenses, we'd better start planning now." She took a deep breath. "And I would like to handle the money. I'm accustomed to setting priorities, planning for specific things. I got pretty good at it, Ian." She left it there.

He had the same sudden lovely smile that Raymond did. "I don't doubt that for one nanosecond," he said. "But I...our situation is such that I...I don't want to burden you. When you agreed to marry me I promised myself..."

Kate sighed deeply and closed her eyes. Would she ever be free of Ian's guilt trip?

"It might be a hardship, with all the other stuff you have to do. I mean, would you want to handle the whole ball of wax?"

"The whole ball of wax," she said firmly.

He was silent for a long moment, and she wondered if she had gone too far. Often men wanted to handle the money, whether they knew how or not.

"You see, Ian, you've been treating me like the princess and the pea. And that's not my role. I'm not comfortable with that. If you want me to be as happy as I can be in this marriage, we're going to have to get rid of the princess and the pea."

"The princess and the what?" he asked, his eyes suddenly glinting with amusement.

"Didn't you read that fairy tale when you were a child? The one where the princess had to prove she was a princess? And she did it by not sleeping comfortably on the seventeen mattresses because she could feel the pea under the bottom one."

"You lost me."

"Well, she said she was the princess, but they tested her, to see how delicately she was bred, how luxuriously she had lived. They put the pea under the bottom mattress and she felt it. So that proved she was the princess."

He laughed. "I guess I missed that one. As I recall, I wasn't that much into fairy tales. I was more into cops and robbers."

"Well, setting aside the princess, may I take care of the finances from now on?" She waited for his reply a moment then added, "You do want to keep me happy."

He grinned. "Okay, if that's what you want. Just let me have enough lunch money and you're in charge. I'll call the bank tomorrow and have them do the paperwork to get you on my checking account, okay?" Then he added, "Kate, if it gets to be a burden, promise me you'll tell me. If you change your mind, for Pete's sake, say so."

She suppressed a sigh. Back to the princess and the pea again. "Of course I'll tell you," she said seriously, since that was what he wanted to hear.

The next day, when Raymond's lessons were finished, she gave him enough money for another visit to the Imax Theater at Seattle Center for a film he wanted to see. Partly, she knew, because he liked to mingle with the other kids his age. He might welcome going back to school, if it was the right kind of school.

She had called for an appointment to see Pastor Ledbetter at three, so as soon as Tommy and Joy came home from school they could leave. Both of them arrived on schedule, and after a quick snack she took them with her down to the church. For some reason they both rather enjoyed the church on a weekday. There were toys in the basement Sunday school rooms. There was also the big empty yard at the parsonage next door. And once when she had been talking to Pastor Ledbetter and had gone to find them, Tommy had been standing on a box behind the pulpit in the empty church itself, giving a sermon in a fairly good imitation of the pastor.

"I was sorry about the court defeat," Cyrus said. "It means a long time of uncertainty for Raymond, and for the rest of you."

"Yes. I've about come around to thinking that Raymond should perhaps be in a real school. He's doing fine at home, but if it doesn't pass muster with the court..." She paused.

"Yes, of course."

"Ian said you once wanted to start a school here, in connection with our church."

He leaned back in his chair, put his hands behind his head and looked dreamily at the ceiling. "Yes, I did."

"Why didn't you go on with it?"

"Money. I couldn't figure out how to get enough for the start-up costs. Building a school reputation takes time and, well, I guess I was afraid to venture. Look here." He straightened up and went over to his closet where he kept an enormous amount of papers, books, pamphlets, boxes and files, but could always find anything he wanted. Bessie had always marveled at this.

"I even had the uniforms picked out." He showed her an old catalog from a school uniform company. "Page fifteen." He was smiling with just a touch of sadness.

Kate turned to page fifteen. She saw a picture of a small girl with blond curls, dressed in a green-and-gray-plaid skirt, topped with a white blouse and dark green sweater.

Kate put aside the catalog. "My family got together last night. It was kind of a sympathy thing, because we lost at the hearing. We...have you given up the idea completely? I mean, if *enough* parishioners helped? Couldn't you go on with it now?"

He was looking at her intently. "Are you suggesting what I think you are?"

"We kind of made a beginning last night. I think it's doable. If enough people got involved. This is a fairly big parish, lots of families with children. Why couldn't we start a school here now? We're going to have to send Raymond to a school before the custody hearing in November. I'd like it to be here...if we could do it."

A dull flush rose in his wrinkled face, and his eyes filmed over.

"Last night," Kate continued firmly, "my mother's lodger, Doug Colby—you know Doug—said he is willing to donate any money he gets for his paintings. And they're good! You've seen the one in my living room. And my sister, Jill, will donate her van. And Greg, her husband, is a CPA. He would help us with the financing if we needed it. We could also donate *work*. I know my mother would undoubtedly set up the school library. If enough parishioners who were qualified could give their time—don't you see? We might just do it."

He was staring at her in fascination. "We might," he said softly. "We just might." His gnarled hands began moving things about on his desk in suppressed excitement.

Kate asked, "When you were planning, were you planning to use the rec room, or the Sunday school rooms, or build another building, or what?"

"No. No, the parsonage. We are one of the few churches left that still has an old-fashioned parsonage next door. Kate, that's a ten-room house. I've been rattling around in there alone ever since my wife passed away and my kids went off to live their own lives. All I need is a little apartment. We could use the parsonage. The elders would agree, I'm sure."

Kate was euphoric, and they began to discuss it in excited half sentences. Greg could get a showing in a gallery for Doug's paintings. Maybe a school-supply house would have secondhand desks they wanted to recycle. They could sell off all the furniture now in the parsonage and use that money. Maybe the church ladies could be persuaded to donate the proceeds from the spring rummage sale and the fall bazaar for a couple of years. There were three retired teachers among the parishioners. They might be interested in part-time teaching. And how many parishioners had school-age children who might want a good private school? Time flew by.

The desk phone rang twice before either heard it.

"Has Bessie gone home?" Cyrus asked, picking up the phone. Kate glanced at the wall clock. Good grief. It was ten after five. She'd better collect her kids and go home. Raymond would have been there for some time alone.

"It's for you," Cyrus said, handing her the phone.

"Hello?"

"It's me, Raymond. When are you coming home?" His voice sounded strained.

"Right away. I got to talking with Pastor Ledbetter and forgot the time. Are you okay?"

"Well, kind of. But can you hurry it up?" Now he was keeping his voice low and guarded, which made her uneasy.

"Why? What's the matter?"

"Uh...well, we got company. Uh...Marsha and Chet are here and they wanna talk about where I'm gonna spend the summer, like I'm not gonna spend it here. You better come."

Chapter Nine

Before Kate left the church to go home, she called Ian's office and spoke to his secretary. "Yes, Mrs. McAllister, his son called, but he's in a meeting. I can slip a note in front of him if you want me to."

"Would you please?" Kate asked. "And thank you." It would have to do. She knew that the custody arrangement was that Marsha could come and see Raymond any time she chose, but he lived year-round with his father. These were the terms dictated by Marsha herself at the time of the divorce because she felt she could not care for Raymond alone, or it wasn't convenient to do so.

Kate primed her children going home.

"This is going to be grown-up stuff," she said, "so after I introduce you to Marsha's husband, you just politely fade out. Go out and play or something."

"I'd rather stay and see what's going on," Tommy said. "I don't want Raymond to go away."

And Joy said, "Besides, I like Marsha. Marsha is fun."

"Of course you like Marsha. You remember the snow and all the fun you had, but this is different."

Tommy must have caught the desperation in her tone. He turned to Joy. "Look, Joy, we can go over and pull some weeds next door. Okay?" And Joy was placated. She liked to work in the garden but wasn't allowed to pull weeds by herself, as she sometimes pulled up plants instead. Kate reached over and gave Tommy an approving pat. More and more he reminded her of her father. He might well go through life as Dad had, with other people depending upon him, and content to have it so.

When they entered the living room, a quick glance told her that Raymond had done his best, although he looked very uncomfortable. He had served them cups of coffee and he was sipping from a cold drink, still in the can, without apparent pleasure.

"Kate, this is my husband, Chet," Marsha said. He had risen as Kate entered, and she had a quick impression of several things she would have to sort out later. Elegant tailoring. Immaculate grooming. The best health money could buy. Pale, assessing eyes. Carefully styled hair frosted with silver. Control. And barrier. He was behind an invisible wall and he would come out, or not, as he chose.

"How do you do," he said. "I'm so glad to meet you at last. It was so good of you to take Marsha in during that winter snowstorm." His voice was pleasant and low. And Kate thought, why wouldn't it be low? He had probably never had to raise it to get the complete attention of everyone around him. *Old money,* Marsha had said.

"I was glad to do it," Kate answered. "It was a good visit for everyone. There isn't much choice of what to do when you're snowed in. Please sit down. I see Raymond has given you coffee. I called Ian and left a message that you were here."

Marsha spoke hurriedly, sounding nervous. "I hope

you aren't angry about the custody suit, but Ian simply doesn't understand. Now that I am *able* to have Raymond with me, I'm entitled. I'm certainly—''

Raymond looked sullen, and Chet Burgess made the slightest possible motion to silence her. Marsha turned to him. ''You don't know Ian like I do.'' She sounded petulant.

''The custody matter is in the future,'' Chet began quietly, and again Kate got the impression he was accustomed to dictating the terms and fully expected to do so in this. Ian might surprise him. She didn't look forward to their meeting, and felt her tension increasing.

''We just stopped in today,'' he continued in his unhurried manner, ''to talk about the boy's summer plans.''

He isn't the boy. He has a name. His name is Raymond.

''...while our Georgetown house is being redone, we decided to spend the summer weeks at my family's farm not far from Alexandria, Virginia. My mother has made something of a name for herself raising horses. Marsha says the boy doesn't ride. He could have riding lessons and...''

Kate cast Raymond a quelling glance as he rolled his eyes in horror. She was recalling Ian's failed effort to introduce his son to the joys of nature. She couldn't imagine Raymond riding a horse. Tommy, yes. Raymond no. She brought herself back to Chet's pleasant, assured voice. ''...let him get acquainted with the Burgess family. It could be a lot of fun for him...''

Oh, Chet, you don't know Raymond, she thought.

Then, suddenly, Chet had her full attention. ''...whichever way the custody agreement is settled, the child of divorced parents has two families. This can be harmful to the child, or positive, depending on how it is handled, don't you agree, Kate?" How reasonable he sounded.

"I can agree in principle," Kate said carefully, "but it's Ian you'll need to convince. I'm not..." *Oh, Ian, come home.*

"How wise of you to realize this," Chet was saying. "You are not Raymond's mother. Marsha is."

Raymond erupted out of his chair, his face taut, but Kate forestalled him with a gesture. "Raymond, why don't you go help in the garden or ride your bike?"

"I don't wanna help in the garden," he said sullenly, and sat down again, obviously miserable. *Change the subject, Kate.*

"Were you in Seattle yesterday?" she asked brightly. "We didn't see you at the hearing to dismiss."

"Because we weren't at the hearing," Chet said, with just the hint of a smile. "There was no need."

Marsha said suddenly, looking puzzled, "Why weren't we there? We were bored out of our skulls at the hotel."

"If I hadn't been confident that the attorneys could handle it I wouldn't have engaged them," he said, sounding patient. "And I wasn't bored. As you recall, I was on the phone most of the morning."

Marsha sighed and slumped back in her chair. "Yes, you were."

Chet turned to Raymond. "Seriously, don't you think you'd enjoy the farm? Wouldn't you like learning to ride? Your mother thought you'd be delighted." The pale, assessing eyes were on Raymond, weighing him, deciding something.

Raymond heaved a deep sigh. "Which, no disrespect intended to anybody, shows you how much Marsha knows about me. *Seriously,* no, I would not enjoy spending the summer on a farm. I'm a city kid. *Seriously,* I would not enjoy learning to ride. To say it flat out, getting on top of some big animal and steering it around is not something I ever intend to do. No offense.''

Chet's small smile widened. ''Have you ever tried getting on a big animal and steering it around?''

''Well, no.''

''Then how do you know you wouldn't enjoy it?'' Again there was the note of pure reason. Kate waited for Raymond's reply.

''Look, Chet,'' Raymond said patiently, ''there are some things you just *know*, see. Like I *know* I wouldn't like choking myself to death. You don't have to try it. You just *know*.''

Chet laughed, a very pleasant sound.

''You see,'' Raymond continued, ''my dad's been that route. That's why we have this big sports van in the garage. He already tried with the father-and-son deal, taking me fishing. That didn't work. I never got the connection between having fun and watching a semi-dead fish flopping around. It was a total turnoff as far as I was concerned.''

''Well, what *do* you want to do this summer?'' Chet asked, amusement sounding in his voice.

''What I really wanna do this summer is just stay put. I wanna stay here. I got my routine all set.''

Chet turned and looked questioningly at Marsha.

''That's ridiculous,'' she snapped. ''Of course you want to spend the summer with your mother. I thought you loved me.'' She looked hurt.

Not fair, Marsha. Not the wounded mother act, thought Kate.

Raymond looked more uncomfortable, but whatever he started to say was drowned out by the resounding slam of the back door and the sound of Tommy's feet pounding through the house.

"Mom," he said breathlessly. "Oh, 'scuse me," he added in a breathless aside to the others, "but we got a crisis. Mom, Mr. Hyslop's gone. We gotta help find him."

"Oh, no," Kate said, getting up.

"When! How long ago!" Raymond demanded, also getting up.

Kate turned to Marsha and Chet. "I'm sorry. We have an elderly couple living next door. Mr. and Mrs. Hyslop. He has Alzheimer's disease and...and... Tommy, how do you know this?"

"Joy and I went over to pull weeds out of the garden and Mrs. Hyslop was asleep in that garden chair, the one with the headrest. Then we went ahead because pulling weeds is quiet. We thought Mr. Hyslop was inside, see. Then Mrs. Hyslop woke up. She didn't mean to go to sleep. She thought Mr. Hyslop was sitting on the bench, you know, but he wasn't anymore. He was gone."

"Well, call the police," Marsha said. "Don't the police take care of things like this?"

"Where's Joy?" Kate said.

"Still over there. She's trying to help Mrs. Hyslop because she's crying—Mrs. Hyslop is."

Chet had stood up when Kate did. "Can't I help?" he asked.

"No, really. I'm sorry, but I'll have to go over there."

"Kate, just call 911. They'll help," Marsha objected. "We really must talk. We can't let this—"

"No," Chet said. "They're Kate's neighbors. She knows them. What do you want to do?" he asked Kate.

"Well, not call the police. That would be Mrs. Hyslop's decision. You see..." How could she explain Mrs.

Hyslop's holding on to vestiges of their past, keeping up a front? "I'll explain later," she said. "I'll have to help find him. Please excuse me. Ian will be home any minute. Just stay and wait for him, please."

She hurried toward the back, followed by Tommy and knowing that Raymond was behind him. The children were all rather fond of Mr. Hyslop and she had seen them, now and then, talking with him. Sometimes he was lucid, sometimes confused, but they seemed to take these changes in stride. She didn't know that Chet had followed them until she was next door.

"Oh, Mrs. McAllister, thank you for coming," Mrs. Hyslop said in a shaking voice. "I just dozed off for a moment, and Tommy said he was only pulling weeds for just a little while, but Mr. Hyslop…"

"He can't be far," Kate said with more confidence than she felt.

"We could fan out," Raymond said. "Each go a different way. Tommy and I could bike it. That'd be faster."

"Good idea," Kate said, giving quick instructions. She sent Mrs. Hyslop and Joy down to the mom-and-pop store a few blocks away, in a small neighborhood business district. She knew that the Hyslops sometimes used that store. She sent off the boys in different directions on their bikes, telling everybody to come back in about half an hour.

"Kate," Chet said, "in case he's wandered farther away, why don't we take my rental car and circle the neighborhoods? I'll drive and you can look into yards and bushes and cul-de-sacs. Finding your place, I learned that Seattle has lots of winding streets and dead ends because of the hills."

"Thank you," she said. "That's a good idea." Maybe

there was more to this Chet than she had thought. The invisible wall seemed to be gone.

Kate sat tensely beside him in the luxurious car as he circled slowly around the nearby neighborhoods, following her directions.

"I just have a hunch," Kate said after a while, "that he may have gone down to The Corner Store, that little mom-and-pop place. Sometimes Mrs. Hyslop shops there and he walks along beside her."

"Will they help him if he gets there?" Chet asked.

"Oh, yes. They're immigrants from Nigeria. An older couple. Very laid-back. Very gentle. They'll look after him if he's there. Lets check it out." She gave him directions.

"Is that him?" Chet asked as he pulled the car to a stop at the curb across the street from the small corner store.

"Yes," Kate said with a sigh of relief. "Look. They are okay." And they watched a moment as Mr. Balewa handed what appeared to be a sandal to Mrs. Hyslop, who took it with grave dignity. Mr. Hyslop, clad in his baggy tan slacks and worn sweater, looked pleased, a half smile on his face. And Joy stood beside them sucking on a red Popsicle. "Let me just check things out," Kate said, getting out of the car.

When she reached the group she saw that the sandal was Mr. Hyslop's, one of the pair he scuffed about the house in.

"Mrs. McAllister," Mr. Balewa said, bowing slightly, his dark face serious. "Mr. Hyslop asked me to repair the strap of his sandal. It was broken, you see, here. I affixed it with a staple. I think it will hold until Mrs. Hyslop gets it to the shoe repair shop."

"Yes, I'm sure it will." Kate felt a rush of gratitude

for his tact and kindness. She and Mr. Balewa steadied Mr. Hyslop while he slid his thin foot into the mended sandal, and Joy, Popsicle gripped between her teeth, squatted down to buckle it.

"Can we give you a lift home?" Kate asked Mrs. Hyslop, forestalling the pathetic thanks she saw coming.

"No, thank you," Mrs. Hyslop answered. "It's such a pretty day, we'll just walk back."

In the car with Chet again, Kate breathed a sigh of relief. "Thank goodness he hadn't gone too far away."

"Does he do this often?" Chet asked.

"No. Mrs. Hyslop usually watches him very closely. It's very tiring for her." They watched the little group, Mr. and Mrs. Hyslop, with Joy skipping alongside, walking back toward home.

"It must be quite a burden to her," Chet said, watching them, not starting the car as Kate expected him to. "Can we talk a minute?" he asked, turning to her.

"Talk? About what?" Kate asked. They should be getting back. Ian might have come home by now.

"About Raymond's future," Chet said quietly.

"I didn't miss what you said before," Kate said. "About the child of divorce having two families. It's a good point. I was lucky. I grew up in a solid, secure two-parent family." She was remembering Raymond at the kitchen table, clicking the saltcellar and crying and saying *I don't care,* when he *did* care, when he was being torn to pieces.

There was the faintest sigh from Chet. "I know McAllister is angry about the custody suit, but…frankly, I had to get his attention. I don't intend to let Marsha lose her son, if I can help it. I would rather do it in a more peaceful way if I can, but McAllister is adamant. May I ask you a very candid question?"

Kate's guard went up. "You can ask. I'm not sure I can answer," she said carefully. "My loyalties are with my husband and Raymond. You have to understand that."

"Fair enough." The faint smile touched his mouth. "My question is, do you think Raymond loves his mother at all? Or has she lost him?"

"I believe I can answer that. Raymond is very dear to me. And I know him pretty well. You have to know first that *I'm* his mother-figure. We—Raymond and I—established that quite a while ago. Before I started taking full care of him. Long before I married his father. To answer your question, yes, Raymond does love Marsha, but… cautiously. Do you understand what I mean?"

"Yes. And it was well put. I understand. Marsha hasn't been—how can I say it—the most attentive of mothers. Most women have that gift. Some don't. She tries and…she wants to salvage her relationship with Raymond. And I want to help her. Right now there's this impasse. I'm not asking you to be disloyal to McAllister, but there must be a better way than with a court battle. I ask that you think about it. Just think about it. Will you do that?"

"I'll…think about it," Kate said, feeling uneasy.

When they got back to the house, Tommy was sitting dolefully on the front porch step. "Did somebody find him? You said come back in about half an hour."

"Yes. He's found," Kate said. "And thanks, Tommy. He'd gone down to Mr. Balewa's. They're on their way back now. They're walking. Has Raymond come back yet?"

"Yeah. He's in there." He gestured with his thumb. "Better not go in yet, Mom. It's kinda…I mean…" He stopped, glancing at Chet Burgess.

"Then we'd better go in," Chet said, opening the door and holding it for Kate. And even as they entered the front hall they could hear Marsha, angry, strident. "You never understand anything!"

As they entered the living room Kate took in the scene. Marsha and Ian both standing, tense, angry at each other, and Raymond hunched over in his chair with his head down.

Ian turned and stiffened as he saw Burgess.

"McAllister," Burgess said, striding over with his hand extended. "Sorry to barge in on you folks like this, but we thought we'd better start some discussion about Raymond's summer."

Ian ignored the outstretched hand. "I thought you had decided to duke it out in court. Or has that master plan been changed?" he asked sarcastically.

"We'll duke it out in court if we have to," Chet said evenly, "but I was thinking there might be a better way."

"Such as?" Ian asked his tone flintlike.

"Chet, let's go," Marsha said angrily. "There's no point in staying here. He's turned Raymond completely against me. That much is clear." She was starting to cry.

Chet's cool gaze flicked over the tableau they all presented. "I'm sorry you're angry," he said, still speaking to Ian. "I'll take Marsha back to the hotel. She's obviously upset. We'll be there another day at least. Maybe if tempers cool a bit we can talk. It's the Sorrento." He turned to Kate. "Thank you for your hospitality."

Kate gratefully watched them go. She had never seen Ian so angry. His face had a grayish look and he kept clenching and unclenching his hands. He went over to Raymond. "It's okay, buddy. Don't worry."

Raymond looked up. He had been crying. "I will *not*

go to some dumb farm and ride some dumb horse. I will *not.*"

"You don't have to go anywhere you don't want to go," Ian said grimly, and Kate's heart sank. He shouldn't promise Raymond things he was not sure of. What if they lost the custody fight? What then? Tommy came in the front door as soon as the Burgesses left, and Kate heard Joy coming in the back door. When she wandered in, her mouth was stained pink from the red Popsicle.

Tommy looked at her. "You had a Popsicle," he said accusingly.

"Mr. Balewa gave it to me because I helped find Mr. Hyslop." She turned to Raymond. "You've been crying. Why were you crying?"

"Forget it. It's history," he snapped.

"Isn't it dinnertime?" Tommy asked. "I'm hungry."

"I don't know if I can eat anything now or not," Ian said.

"Maybe you'll be ready by the time I get something fixed," Kate said, trying to keep her voice calm. She didn't feel calm. What Chet had said disturbed her. Were they being unfair to Raymond, dividing his loyalties like this? *Should* Marsha have a bigger place in his life? Would he be happier if she did? Would Ian permit it? *Help me, God.*

Dinner wasn't too uncomfortable because the children kept a conversation going about Mr. Hyslop being lost and found again. They were hungry and ate quickly. Immediately after dinner Ian shut himself in his study. He was still there when Kate had finished clearing up in the kitchen.

She gave a smart rap on the study door and then went in. He wasn't working, but was seated at his desk, looking blankly into space.

"What?" he said, startled, getting up.

"Don't get up, Ian. I just wanted to talk to you a bit."

"Oh, okay," he said. He went over to the burgundy leather conversation grouping and sat down on the two-seater, while she took a chair. "What's up?"

"You're not going to like this, but Chester Burgess said something today that made me think."

"And what pearl of wisdom was that?"

"Ian, I know you don't like the man," Kate said placatingly.

"I hate his guts."

Kate shut out the sudden question of why. Was it because of Marsha?

"He did make a good point," she said steadily. *Forget jealousy, Kate. You're not entitled. You're just a convenience, like his microwave or his computer.*

"I can hardly wait." His hazel eyes were stormy, his jaw set.

"He said a child of divorced parents has two families. And...I think he said it could be good or bad for the child, depending on how the parents handled it."

"Psych 101. I know all about being a child of divorce. I don't need a secondhand lecture from Burgess. I *was* one. I was *there*. I know what Ray goes through. And I mean to protect him as much as I can, or die trying."

"I didn't know," Kate said softly. What did she really know of Ian, except how she loved him? What did she know of how and why he had become the man sitting across from her now? She felt hesitant, as if she were intruding into some private place.

"Well, now you do. I've developed a kind of...protective device, keeping things to myself. You don't know, for instance, that Denise and I are only half siblings. We had different fathers. Our mother was—how can I say this kindly—undiscerning in her relationships. That's as good a word as any, I guess. She had a real gift for picking men who were jerks as husbands. She wanted to uplift them, reform them in some way. It played hob with her kids' lives, I can tell you that. Counting Denise's father, there were four. It's ugly, Kate. Very ugly. You wouldn't want to know, coming from a family like yours."

Kate was stricken, murmuring a helpless "I'm so sorry."

"So am I," he said somberly, "So am I. One of the stepfathers was…abusive, directed mainly at me." He was quiet for a long moment. "You probably noticed that Denise and I are…not close. Our growing up was hard on Denise. She was older, and I guess she felt she had to look out for me, protect me. We were separated a lot of the time because of the custody arrangements. She ran away once…when she was staying with her father. She was worried about me, and she came to check it out."

Kate couldn't speak. She wanted to reach out, touch him, comfort him. But for the moment he seemed unaware of her, lost in some past misery, in some different time and place. An ugly place. He looked vulnerable now, and she felt a deep sense of shock because he was usually so confident, so sure of himself, so in charge. This was an Ian she had never seen before.

"You see," he resumed, "her stepmother of the moment went into a panic. Denise was picked up by the juvenile authorities. I don't know exactly what happened, because she never told me. But things changed after that. It sort of ended our relationship, such as it was. I think maybe, for survival purposes, she gave up thinking about me, worrying about me. She seemed to shut me out. She was just a teenager herself then. Maybe she figured out her life would be better if I wasn't cluttering it up." He lapsed into another silence.

"Then later, quite a long time later. I'd learned to be a survivor myself by that time. Our mother was long dead. I'd made it through college and graduate school on a patchwork of scholarships and student loans. I was doing well. And it was Christmas and I was...on my own. I knew vaguely where she was. She'd married this guy in Montana. I invited myself there for Christmas. I liked Chuck. Denise got a good deal there. They had two kids. But between Denise and me there's a wall. Too many memories, too much ugliness to forget...and I bring back the past. On the rare occasions when we meet now everything is fun and laughter, it looks okay, but the wall is there. I wish..." He seemed to pull himself back into the present. He was looking at her with a level gaze.

"So what did Burgess suggest?" Ian's tone was hard.

"Nothing specific," Kate said carefully. "I think he wants to patch things up better, do things more peacefully. They—or he, I'm not sure—seem to think that if Raymond visits them this summer..." Her voice dwindled away before his implacable face.

"In other words, start tossing the kid back and forth? That's what it would amount to. And where is Raymond's *home,* his *stability,* his *security?* Where's that, Kate? And what happens when Marsha gets tired of this marriage and walks out? Who does Raymond get for stepfather number two? Or three? That's not the way my son is going to grow up." The words fell like stones between them. "Whose side are you on, Kate?"

Chapter Ten

Kate's heart ached. She had to try twice before she could speak. "I'm on the same side you are—Raymond's side," she said gently, and she could see the collapse of his anger and resentment. He slumped over and put his head in his hands.

"Oh, Kate, where's it all going to end? I didn't mean that the way it sounded. You must know that. It's just that I...carry around so much old baggage from the bad times. Maybe everybody does. I don't know."

Oh, dear God, how fortunate she had been, growing up with Mom and Dad and Jill. How must it have been for Ian? Growing up with a series of stepfathers. Depending only on his big sister and suddenly not being able to any more. How much of a struggle had it been, that making it through college "on a patchwork of scholarships and student loans"? And he was right, we all carry along our old baggage, she thought. Somebody wise once said, "We are the sum total of all our days."

Chet's reasoning had seemed good about the child of divorce having two families. Chet was thinking of his marriage to Marsha as permanent, but what if Ian's fears were well-founded? What if Marsha tired of this marriage and left Chet for someone else?

But Chet and Marsha were carrying all their past days, too. Maybe that's why God was able to love everybody, because He would know the hidden burden everybody carried. What had Marsha said of Chet? *All the Burgess men serve the nation in some way.* Had Chet Burgess really *wanted* to serve the nation in some way? No one would ever know from his smooth demeanor. And what had Ian said of Marsha? That she had been an army brat, warehoused in some boarding school when the Greers couldn't have her with them in the faraway places. All these people in their present tangle, dragging with them the sum total of all their days. Even my own days, Kate thought, never being as pretty as Jill, losing Claude and having my life crash to pieces. Oh, yes, the days were inescapable. Kate was aware of thinking on two levels. The surface of her mind struggled with the anguishes of Ian and Raymond, and perhaps Marsha and Chet, too. But beneath the surface, in the bottom of her mind, like a faint drumbeat were words, in her own voice, saying her wedding vows. "...from this day forward, for better or worse..." Well, Kate, this is some of the worse, she thought. What can you do about it? What must you do about it? She was aware that Ian was speaking again.

"...Burgess has half the money on the planet. He can afford to keep me in court for the next twenty years and not feel the pinch."

"I know you don't like him, Ian. But try to set aside that for a few minutes. He'll be at the Sorrento for another day. Why don't *I* go down and talk to him?" *What am I saying? If only Jill could do this. She's so much brighter, so much more assertive.*

"Talk to him about what?"

"There may be more to Chet Burgess than you realize. He *did* try to help find Mr. Hyslop today."

"He did? Burgess *helped?*"

"Yes. That's why we came in together after you got home. He was driving me around the neighborhoods. It's easier for us to talk. You see, I'm not Raymond's mother and he's not Raymond's father. So maybe we can be more objective. We're not so emotionally tangled up in it."

"Well," Ian said slowly, "what could you talk to him *about?* Until this custody arrangement is overturned by some court, Raymond is in *my* custody. That includes summer. No way is he going to spend the summer away from me."

"I understand that. Maybe I could persuade him to...wait a while. Wait until the case is heard. Marsha *has* visitation rights, but if she's going to live in Washington, D.C. for the rest of her life, visiting her son could be a problem."

"Yeah, well, I guess so."

"Even if we win the custody hearing in November you may, of necessity, need to change the arrangement at some future time or Raymond will never see his mother again. This will mean Raymond visiting her where she is."

"Yeah, I see what you mean," he said somberly. "We're assuming, of course, that she stays married to Burgess." He got up and started to wander aimlessly around the study.

"Let's assume that for now. He seems confident of it," Kate said. She was feeling a little more sure of herself. He was at least listening.

"So was I," he said bitterly. He was looking away

from her, so she couldn't see his face. Forget that, Kate, she thought. Push it away.

She went on, dimly surprised at how calm and steady her voice was. "Why don't I just put it to him that this is not the summer Raymond could visit them, not ruling out time in the future—always provided that Raymond wants to go, is secure enough in this family situation to be comfortable leaving it for a visit someplace else." And suddenly remembering, she added, "Chet did ask me an interesting question, which I thought went right to the heart of the matter."

"Oh, what was that?" He turned, seeming more composed now, more like the Ian she knew.

"He asked if Raymond still loved Marsha, or if she had 'lost' him. I thought it was very discerning of him. He's certainly not a fool. He said something about some women having the gift of mothering, but some don't. So he apparently does understand that—for whatever reasons—Marsha wasn't really ready for motherhood when it came to her."

"Well, he got that right," Ian said bleakly. "Poor little Ray was not, shall we say, a lovable infant. I can't count the nights I spent walking the floor, holding that puny little guy. Any ailment that an infant can get, he got. And even now he's kind of skinny and...different from other kids...overly sensitive, not sure of himself. When I was little I was kind of rough-and-tumble, but Ray..."

"I cannot, for the life of me," Kate agreed, "see Raymond on a horse."

A reluctant grin tugged at Ian's mouth. "Amen to that. Even if Ray does ever visit their farm, they'll have to settle for him comfortably seated on the veranda or someplace reading a book."

"Do you have any objection to me talking with Chet?"

"No. If you think you can help, go ahead. It's a given that I can't keep my cool around the guy. I'd probably end up punching his face in. Go ahead. Give it a try...and thanks."

What are friends for? No, Kate, scratch that. Don't get testy.

The next morning, as soon as Tommy and Joy were off to school, Kate spoke to Raymond about it. He was helping her put the breakfast dishes into the dishwasher.

"Don't make any promises," he said in a panic.

"Of course not," Kate said, laughing. "Your dad and I agreed that you'd visit them only if you wanted to. Can't get any fairer than that. Let me ask you something." She shut the door of the dishwasher.

"Like what?"

"Do you love Marsha?" She watched his sensitive face as she asked it, and saw a flush rise to his cheeks.

"Uh, Dad's had such a time..."

"Forget the time your father has had. Just think about how *you* feel. You get upset when they quarrel, don't you? You enjoyed Marsha's visit last winter."

"Yeah, well, I guess," he said, seeming embarrassed. "But I feel, you know, Dad tries so hard and..."

Kate had the answer she wanted. Regardless of how lacking Marsha's mothering instincts were, Raymond couldn't help but love her. And if that was the case, at some point—not this summer, perhaps, but at some time—he must have a relationship with her. And who knew, maybe some day Marsha would surprise them all and grow up. Miracles did happen now and then.

"It's okay," she said. "While I'm gone you concentrate on the math work sheets, and as soon as I get back I'll tell you what happened, or didn't happen.''

Chet Burgess, when she called, had welcomed her visit and offered lunch, but she'd begged off, asking to meet with him at about ten. He had agreed immediately and, she thought, with some satisfaction. When she arrived she learned that they had been out late the night before and Marsha was still asleep. She sensed that they were both relieved to be able to talk one-on-one, without Marsha.

She had forgotten how grand the Sorrento was. Dad had taken the family there for an Easter breakfast years ago. The Burgesses had a suite, of course, so that without disturbing Marsha, snug in the bedroom, Chet could serve them coffee and miniature croissants in the sitting room.

''I'm so glad you came,'' he said cordially. ''I'm sorry that McAllister and I don't hit it off, but in the circumstances I suppose...'' He shrugged. ''Am I right in assuming that Raymond spending the summer with us is not an option?''

''I'm afraid so,'' Kate said, sipping delicious coffee from the delicate china cup. ''But that doesn't rule out some future time, even if the present custody arrangement is confirmed in November.''

''McAllister agreed to that?'' he asked in his quiet voice.

''Let's say he didn't disagree when I mentioned it. We talked about Raymond's relationship with Marsha. If the visitation arrangement holds, they can at least have some sort of relationship. Neither of them should be denied that.''

''I'm glad you agree.'' He sighed softly, perhaps not realizing that he had. ''It might be better another year. Raymond said it himself. He said he's a city kid. If it's another year, it would be in D.C. That's about the ultimate in cities. Before you came home he was telling us how he goes to all sorts of events here in Seattle, often on his own.''

"He does," Kate said eagerly. "And later, when he's ready, when he feels secure enough to leave, I can just imagine him spending days in the Smithsonian." She went on, explaining Raymond as best she could to this cool-eyed, intent man who had half the money on the planet. She told him about how good Raymond's book reports were, how hard he was working at the math, about his current passion for history, about his spending a couple of hours a day in front of Ian's computer surfing the Net, looking up all kinds of things, about how helpful he was with the younger children. About how he was feeling more and more secure in the family situation.

Now and then Chet would say, "Yes," or "I see."

It was almost eleven when she wound down, wondering if she had talked too much, wondering what he thought—it was impossible to tell. Feeling suddenly embarrassed, she stood up.

"I really must be going," she said. "Can I…can I tell Ian that…"

He stood up when she did. "Yes. I understand that this is not the summer Raymond will visit." He had a half smile when he said it. "Maybe another year." And again she had no idea what he was thinking. "I'll see you out," he said, and walked with her to the elevator.

Downstairs she breathed a sigh of relief that he hadn't come down with her to the street, as she had parked her rattly twelve-year-old car down the block, not having had the sheer nerve to park it among the cars of the Sorrento's guests. She couldn't wait to get home to tell Raymond. Now all they had to do was prepare for November. A small chill went through her even though it was one of

Seattle's brighter days. By November Raymond would have to be in some private school.

On the off chance of speaking with Pastor Ledbetter, Kate detoured on the way home to stop at the church, but Bessie told her that the pastor was out making hospital calls. She left a message and drove on home. Raymond would be wanting his lunch.

When she drove into the driveway she saw a woman turning away from the front door. It took a moment to recognize Mrs. Lundy, Raymond's former English teacher, she of the damaging deposition. What in the world would she want now? Kate jerked her car to a stop and got out.

"Oh, good morning. Or is it noon?" Mrs. Lundy said. She seemed nervous and upset as Kate approached her. Mrs. Lundy came down the two steps from the porch so she and Kate faced each other.

"I think it's still morning," Kate said cordially. "Were you about to ring the bell?"

"I did ring it several times, but you weren't there, of course. You...you do have a lovely garden."

"Thank you," Kate said. No point in telling Mrs. Lundy that the disappearing and reappearing flower beds were going to be replaced by masses of beautiful and easy-care perennials the Pacific Northwest was famous for.

"Well, Raymond should be at home. He's supposed to be working on his lessons." Oh, dear, maybe I shouldn't have said that, Kate thought. Would it go in some future deposition?

"Well, actually, it's you I need to talk to," Mrs. Lundy said. "I'm so sorry about everything."

Kate looked at Mrs. Lundy closely. Sorry about everything? She looked as if she might cry at any moment.

"All right," Kate said. "Let's go inside. I can't imagine where Raymond is, unless he didn't hear the bell. Or maybe he just ran out on a quick errand." She took out her key.

They went into the silent house and Kate called out for Raymond, but got no answer, so she led Mrs. Lundy into the living room.

"Please sit down. What seems to be the problem?"

"It's that deposition," Mrs. Lundy said. "Raymond's letter was so angry, so accusing. He sounded so terribly upset. I can't get it out of my mind. I certainly had no wish to…disturb things for your family. He's such a sensitive boy. He's—"

"Wait a minute," Kate interrupted. "What letter? I don't understand."

The teacher started rummaging in her large handbag. "It's here. It's right here," she was muttering. "I've read it a dozen times. I can't imagine…I mean…the last thing I would do is to hurt… Ah, here it is." She took out a limp envelope and handed it to Kate, and Kate recognized Raymond's handwriting immediately.

She took the envelope. What in the world had Raymond done?

"Open it," Mrs. Lundy said. "Please." Now she was taking a tissue from her handbag and blotting her eyes.

Raymond, I think you're in big trouble. Kate took the single sheet of paper out of the envelope and began to scan it. Oh, no! Surely she wasn't reading this. Not "Dear Mrs. Lundy. You are a cruel creep. You have probably ruined my life and you probably don't care." Kate felt her face go hot with embarrassment.

"Mrs. Lundy. I'm awfully sorry. I know he was angry and upset. We all were, at that deposition you gave the lawyer—"

"But I didn't realize how it would be used," Mrs. Lundy wailed desperately. "Read on to where he says he plans to run away if his mother and stepfather win custody."

"Nonsense," Kate said sharply. "In the first place I've talked with his stepfather, and he seems a very reasonable man. I have high hopes that things can be worked out. I'm so sorry Raymond did this."

"But he sounds so miserable," Mrs. Lundy said sadly.

Kate glanced down at the letter again. Raymond had outdone himself overdramatizing. Now she was recalling the incident. The night her family had gathered here to talk about forming a church school. Raymond and Tommy and Joy all in Raymond's room when he was presumably writing that thank-you note to his grandmother. There had been far too much giggling.

"Look," Kate said, sighing. "I'm awfully sorry about this. I do apologize for Raymond. And *he* will apologize as soon as he gets back from wherever he is."

"You see—" Mrs. Lundy was almost pleading "—I didn't realize how the deposition would be used. I was just worried about the homeschooling."

"It's all right," Kate said. "We'll probably drop the homeschooling soon anyhow and—"

"You mean you will send Raymond back to school?" Mrs. Lundy asked eagerly.

"Not that school," Kate said firmly. "His father and I were thinking of a private school. In fact—" And Kate found herself telling Mrs. Lundy about the idea of starting a school at her church. Mrs. Lundy, as a teacher, was very interested, and soon they were discussing curricula, discipline problems and the pros and cons of student uniforms.

"Look," Kate said suddenly, "it's almost one o'clock

and Raymond isn't back yet. Have you had lunch? Why can't we—"

"Oh, dear me, I had no idea how late it was. No, I'll need to get back. I'm late. Can we talk about this again? I'd like to talk with your pastor, too. Maybe I can help." She got up, flushed with pleasure now, and, grasping her big handbag, she managed to leave, still offering advice and asking questions as she went out.

Kate was thrilled as she shut the door. Pastor Ledbetter had worried because his teaching experience had been years ago, but here was Mrs. Lundy who was teaching now, and coping with all the now problems in the public schools. Problems they must avoid in a private school.

"I'm starving." Raymond's doleful voice came to her from behind the living-room couch as he crawled out.

"Raymond! What were you doing back there!"

"Well, obviously, I was *hiding,*" he said testily. "When a person does *not* answer the doorbell because he does *not* want to talk to the person ringing it, and *someone* actually *brings* that unwanted person *in,* the only thing the *first* person can do is *hide.*" He stood up, brushing dust from his skinny jeans. "And for your information, that cleaning service we have is the pits. There's dust under there that was there when the decorator delivered the couch. When can we eat? I am starving to death before your eyes."

Despite herself, Kate had to laugh. "Well, for one thing, you don't need to worry about the cleaning service, because they are getting the sack, because your dad and I agreed that I'd take over managing the family budget. But Raymond, you *must*—"

"I know. I heard it all. I'll apologize for the letter. I was so uptight I guess I got carried away. I guess she's not so bad really."

"Okay, but that's got to be the best apology you ever wrote in your life. Understand?"

He was nodding, shamefaced.

"And I want to see it *before* you send it. Is *that* understood?"

"Everything is understood," he said with a look of deep misery.

As she and Raymond put together a tuna-sandwich-and-fruit-salad lunch Kate told him about her talk with Chet Burgess.

"He bought it, huh? That I don't hafta go to some farm this summer?"

"Yes. I thought he seemed very reasonable," Kate said. Then she added carefully, "That doesn't rule out some future summer. Now, don't look like thunder. Maybe at thirteen or fourteen you'll feel differently than you do now. And don't forget they'll be living in Washington, D.C. They won't be living on the farm."

"Oh, yeah," he said thoughtfully. "Maybe I could tour the White House or something. That might be kind of fun. Maybe Tommy could go with me."

After lunch they worked later than usual with the schooling, but were finished before the younger children came home. After she had given them snacks and seen them all out the back door, she went into Ian's study to go over the household expenses, and was appalled at the amount of money Ian was spending.

She broke the news as kindly as she could to the cleaning service that they would not be needed after this month, and made an appointment with the gardening service to relandscape the front yard as soon as they could with easy-care perennials. She was so absorbed in planning all the money she would save for Raymond's schooling and other things that it was almost six o'clock, and Ian stuck his head in the door.

"Hi. Are you hungry yet?"

"Oh, good grief, what time is it? When did you get home?"

He laughed. "Not long ago, and you were so engrossed I didn't want to break your train of thought."

"But dinner," she said, getting up from the mass of papers spread out on his desk.

"All taken care of. It's such a nice day that the kids wanted to eat outside, so I fired up the barbecue. Ray found some burger patties in the freezer. We're all set for food. He wants to know if it's okay to invite the Hyslops next door?"

"Of course it is," she said. "I'll do something about a salad. We can't just have burgers. And I always freeze ahead on desserts." She hurried toward the kitchen.

"I think Beth has it under control. She and Doug came over."

And when Kate got to the kitchen she saw Mom had already started making the salad. "I had an ulterior motive in coming over tonight," Beth said as she washed lettuce. "The Pastor's Aid Group is trying to get some new members, and I was thinking of Mrs. Hyslop."

"I don't think she has time," Kate said, frowning slightly, "but it would be a godsend for her, if she could manage it. She's so exhausted all the time. People don't understand how wearing it is taking care of an invalid full-time, day after day, with no respite."

Beth shook water off her hands and hugged Kate briefly, both remembering Claude's last couple of years.

"She wanted to hire a live-in student but hasn't had any luck. If she could just get one afternoon off each week, it would help," Kate added.

The Pastor's Aid Group was composed of older women of the church with leisure time who could meet every Wednesday from noon until four to work together sewing, quilting and doing craft projects. It was this group that provided a steady supply of handmade crafts, knitted or crocheted afghans, homemade quilts, baby layettes, stuffed cuddle toys and all sorts of attractive merchandise for sale at the annual fall bazaar. Year after year their steady earnings went into the pastor's discretionary fund so that, when Pastor Ledbetter saw a need, he could fill it without going to the church elders for the money. Beth had joined the group as soon as Kate and Jill had left the nest. It was one of Beth's several "good works," as she called them. And after Dad's death, when she began her bed-and-breakfast business, she still found time to arrive at the church rec room every Wednesday at noon with her sack lunch to join her friends for a useful four hours.

"Well, I think that's taken care of," Beth said. "I got the idea from Tommy and Raymond."

"The boys?"

"Yes." Beth smiled her lovely smile. How can Mom still be so beautiful? Kate wondered. "The last time we were together they were both grousing because they didn't have enough pocket money. And I was thinking about how to get Mrs. Hyslop to join us and it all came together. The children—all of them—get along well with Mr. Hyslop." She paused, a look of sadness touching her eyes. "After all, Mr. Hyslop is something like a child himself now, isn't he?"

"Yes," Kate said slowly. "She needs a respite and..." Kate suddenly smiled. "Well, they'll have a bundle to spend come Christmas, because I've been working out a new chore list for gardening and housekeeping." And she told her mother with satisfaction how she was taking over the household finances.

After they had all enjoyed their slapdash barbecue in the long twilight, they worked it out how Mrs. Hyslop could join the Pastor's Aid Group. Beth had cleverly brought along attractive samples of their work—a rag doll with red yarn hair, an exquisitely hand-knitted baby cap of yellow and white and a pair of hand mitts for lifting hot things in the kitchen, which could be special-ordered in colors to match your kitchen's decor. Mrs. Hyslop was entranced with the idea of a whole afternoon a week of freedom. When she found out that Kate was not a member of the Pastor's Aid Group, and would be on hand on Wednesdays in case of an emergency, she agreed that the boys could handle it.

"I used to embroider," she said, faint color coming into her thin cheeks. "And tat. I used to tat. I've made yards and yards of tatting before…before…when I had more time."

Now it was Beth's turn to be enchanted. "Tatting! That's almost a lost art now. Maybe you could teach some of the rest of us."

"What in the world is tatting?" Ian asked, scraping out the barbecue.

"It's a narrow little lace edging. Very delicate. There are many different classic patterns. It's made with a single thread coming out of a little shuttle or bobbin. It used to be popular for baby clothes, or edging for ladies' hankies. Tatting! Imagine that!"

The boys worked out their schedule to stay with Mr. Hyslop. Raymond would go over at noon on Wednesdays with his sack lunch just before Mrs. Hyslop left, and would stay until Tommy came home from school. Then Tommy would take over. Everyone was pleased with the

plan, and Mr. Hyslop sat there among them with his be-
mused half smile on his thin face, and Kate wondered
with a feeling of sadness how much, if anything, he understood. When the party broke up, she watched Mrs.
Hyslop, thin, somewhat shabby, but with loving deference, guide Mr. Hyslop home. Kate felt a lump in her
throat. *When you think wedding vows, Kate, old girl,
think of that gentle tired old lady next door.*

"Why so pensive?" Ian asked and, startled, she turned
to him, and she realized that the evening had ended and
she was alone with him. The sun was almost set. Don't
talk to Ian about wedding vows, she thought. She
searched her mind for an answer to his question.

"I've worked out the household budget," she finally
said. "Do you want to go over it with me?"

"Sure. Why not?"

After she had got the children down and heard their
prayers, she joined him in his study. He pulled up a
straight chair for himself and gave the big swivel chair
behind the desk to her. She took it, trying to sit as straight
as she could so she might look bigger, and began to go
over her plans.

"Kate, you're a wonder. We could become indepen-
dently wealthy. I had no idea how the money slipped
away. Are you sure you can—"

"Positive. The kids have been griping about not having enough pocket money. Now they will have. They'll
jump at the chance, and it's good training for them—
having responsibilities. I've been through this with my
own two to some extent when we lived next door, but
we haven't gotten anything organized over here yet. Now
we will." She felt a warm glow at his praise.

"Let's sit over here," he said, getting up. "I want to
run something past you."

When they were seated across from each other on the comfortable leather furniture, he went on. "There are going to be some changes at my firm at the year's end. The sales manager's job is opening up. I'm going to ask for it."

"That would be quite a promotion, wouldn't it?" she asked.

"Not only that and more money, the best thing about it is that I would be the one assigning the travel to the other guys."

"You mean you'd work in Seattle all the time?" Her breath caught in her throat and a sudden uneasiness gathered in the bottom of her mind.

"Yes. You have no idea how tired I am of living out of that two-suiter. Of racing to catch a flight that has just been canceled. Of trying to write a report on my tray when the guy in the seat behind me won't stop talking. Of not getting home on weekends. It's a scientific fact that Sunday afternoon in a strange hotel in a strange town is the longest time span known to mankind. That's on record in Greenwich, that time place. Have you heard that?"

Kate laughed. "No. I hadn't heard that, but I believe it." He looked so dear with his hair kind of mussed, his hazel eyes full of laughter, his strong face. If he doesn't travel, will he need me so much? she thought.

He must have sensed her withdrawal, because he reached out and took her small sturdy hand in his. "Kate? What's wrong?"

"Nothing," she said briskly. "When…when will you be leaving again? What I mean is, will you still be here day after tomorrow? Pastor Ledbetter wants to talk to the elders about the school plan and he'd like us to be there. If you can't I'll go by myself."

"No. I can go with you," he said quietly, freeing her hand. "I'll be home all this week. We're in a series of in-house meetings. And I want to follow through with the school idea as much as I can. How's it coming, by the way?"

"Great," she said. "If the elders go along with the idea, we think they will contribute to the funding from the church annual budget. He's asked Jill and Greg to come, too, since they plan to help out, even if they live across town and go to another congregation. He plans on having quite a crowd."

The next day, after school, Kate held a meeting with the children, who were delighted with the new house rules. Tasks were assigned and the amounts to be paid for them figured out.

"We're rich!" Tommy exulted.

"Filthy rich," Raymond agreed, "when you also put in the money from Mrs. Hyslop for the Wednesday deal."

They couldn't stop talking about their good fortune. Kate could hear them huddled in Raymond's room, deciding how to spend their coming wealth.

The church elders met every other Thursday evening to conduct the church's business. There was indeed quite a crowd for this meeting, as the pastor had talked about the idea to a number of parents who might want to send their children to a church school.

When just the elders met, they used the pastor's office, around his painted kitchen table. But when members of the congregation also attended, they all met in the rec room. The elders sat behind one of the folding dining tables facing the members, who were seated on folding chairs arranged in wide circles, so everybody could see everybody.

As Kate and Ian entered the big rec room, Kate glanced around for her family. She saw Jill and Greg at once, and right behind them were Mom and Doug. The pastor was leaning over Greg saying something. He straightened up and came over to Kate and Ian. He gave Kate's hand a quick squeeze.

"Don't get your hopes up too much, Katie," he said softly just for her ears.

"Why?" she couldn't help asking, but someone came up and he couldn't answer.

There were no empty chairs near the family, so she and Ian sat in the back circle.

"What was that supposed to mean?" Ian asked.

Kate sighed. "He must have spoken to the elders. Maybe they don't want the church to have a school, or they don't want to help fund it. It could be anything." And then, recalling that Ian's church experience was limited, she added, being as tactful as she could, "Now and then there is such a thing as church politics. Very serious disagreements among the members happen. Sometimes congregations can split up over something. Cyrus says we come to church to worship and learn, and congregation infighting can be learning the hard way." She saw a grin tug at Ian's mouth, and she added, "He says it turns a lot of people off going to church at all. The outsiders, the newcomers, the unchurched, come in timidly looking for God and all they find is people."

"That could be a jolt, all right," Ian murmured. "How did Cyrus get up to that table so fast?"

As the pastor reached the elders' table, they stood up and Cyrus bowed his head. There was the rustle of movement as they all stood, and Ian whispered, "I think he's going to make us pray before the infighting. Good idea."

Chapter Eleven

"It just means we'll have to work harder raising the money," Kate said as Ian drove them home.

"At least," he answered, "the elders didn't *veto* the whole idea of a school. From what Cyrus said, they could have. They just won't let it be part of the church budget. But a *stained glass window!* It's just a simple redbrick church, not exactly a cathedral! Don't they realize that a school is more important than colored glass?" He sounded more exasperated than annoyed.

"The elders did support the idea of a school," Kate said, trying to be fair. "And there's more to the stained glass window project than you know." She couldn't keep the sadness from her voice. "A church congregation is, well, kind of like a, how can I say it, an extended family, sort of. You look out for each other. There is a kind of…loyalty. And Amy and Theron Gilmartin have been there all their lives. They were married in that church and…"

"I gathered they were very VIP," Ian said, flipping on the turn signal for their corner.

"Not in the sense that you mean," Kate said. "They are very modest people. Theron works at the post office until he retires next year. Amy has always been a stay-at-home wife. She's the one who designs all the cuddle toys that the members of the Pastor's Aid Group make. Theron spends almost all day Saturday working at the church. He's the one who posts the hymn numbers on the boards. He does a lot of the scut work. He keeps the graffiti cleaned off the brick walls—not an easy job. They are VIPs only in their simple goodness, their faithfulness…and their strength."

She fell silent, remembering. No, the elders could not spare money from the church budget and still set aside the yearly amount for the stained glass window. The Gilmartins, two thin gray little people, were living for the day the rose window was installed.

The Gilmartins had not been blessed with a child until late. Amy was almost forty when Brenden was born, and if there was ever a perfect child, Brenden was. From some ancestral gene pool he had received corn-colored hair and clear blue eyes and a splendidly strong physique. And Brenden was a happy child, full of laughter. Seemingly touched by angels, Brenden combined being a straight-A student with a personality that made him class president from grade seven. He excelled in sports—tennis and swimming.

Nor did he peak in high school, for in his freshman year at university he began brilliantly. The Gilmartins sacrificed to give him the best they could afford. He was their idol.

Pledged to a leading fraternity, he was living his freshman year in the fraternity house, probably the most popular pledge the house had ever had.

The fraternity house, stately and old, just off campus,

had, flanking its wide doorway, two cement planters shaped like classic urns. Once they had held plantings. Now they held only old dirt and people walked back and forth between them, going in and out, never even looking at them anymore. The front balcony was just over the planters. And on a brilliant October afternoon an advertising blimp circled overhead, trailing behind it a long banner of glittering letters spelling out something. Somebody in the house—nobody now remembered who—noticed, and students began coming out onto the balcony. More students came out to see what it said. Nobody ever did make out the message as the blimp circled above. There was some pushing and shoving and jostling and—nobody could ever remember how—Brenden Gilmartin fell over the railing. It was just a short distance to fall, just the one story, but he landed with a crash on his back across one of the cement urns. He was arched over it, his head hanging down on one side, his spine shattered. He slid into a coma from which he never emerged. Such a useless, senseless death, and it devastated Amy and Theron Gilmartin.

Kate remembered the outpouring of love in the red-brick church for the Gilmartins. They aged overnight into being old, when they hadn't seemed old before. They walked through the days like wooden puppets, doing what was expected of them, going through the motions. The first spark of life seemed to return when someone among the elders suggested the Brenden Gilmartin memorial window. And now, after about five years, part of the annual church budget, part of the pastor's discretionary fund and the Easter Sunday offering were set aside for the memorial window. Soon the window would be a reality because Brenden Gilmartin had come among them, lived his brief brilliant life and gone.

No. They would have to raise the school money by other means. Kate tried to explain the situation to Ian and he agreed. They had driven into the garage and the automatic lights had gone off while she talked.

Ian reached down and turned the ignition key, which brought on the car's dash lights. "Your church means a lot to you, doesn't it?"

"Yes. I always come away stronger," Kate said, looking at the planes and hollows of his face in the dim glow. "Yes," she said again firmly. Some day she might need all the strength she could find.

Ian picked up the remote to switch on the garage lights again so they could go inside. "When I can get rid of all the travel I'll...I'll attend more regularly," he said, and Kate was pleased to hear this. Come November, if things went wrong at the custody hearing he might need extra strength, too.

Inside the kitchen they could hear the mutter of the TV in Raymond's room. Kate glanced at the wall clock. It was almost time for the kids' going-to-bed routine, but she had a few minutes left.

"Do you want a snack?" she asked, knowing he would. She, always watching her weight now that she had attained cute, never had snacks and tried not to miss them. Ian was worth the sacrifice.

"At least the elders went along with converting the old parsonage into the school building," she said, getting out the small flavored crackers he liked and slicing some cheese. His beverage of choice with this for some reason was cranberry juice. She put it all before him.

"Yeah, I guess they went as far as they could," he said, crunching into the cracker.

"And quite a lot of members do *want* the school. For their own children. That was encouraging. Pastor Ledbetter's going to pitch the whole idea Sunday in his sermon. If we could get everyone involved in it, you know, for fund-raisers—cake sales, car washes, all those money things. It's going to work, I'm sure.''

On Saturday afternoon Jill and Greg and their three children came over. Ostensibly, this was so Greg could lower the shelf on the service porch for Kate. Jill had volunteered his services. Greg was the family woodworker, and he enjoyed it. Once he had built a beautiful sailboat, the *Far Horizon*. But Kate, sensitive to family undercurrents, knew Jill had wanted to talk about something else, too.

"I'll help," Ian offered, "by staying out of your way. Since I'm the world's greatest dummy at fixing things, it's the kindest thing I can do."

Kate and Jill were both glad that the two men got along so well. Greg, efficient as always, had the shelf lowered in just a few minutes, and then to cover the place where it had been, he neatly glued on a strip of border print wallpaper Jill had found at the paint store.

"That looks lovely," Kate said. "It looks like a decorator job. Thank you so much. I'm sick of dragging the step stool out here whenever I want the detergent off the shelf."

When the children were out back playing and the two men were watching a football game on TV, Jill and Kate had time to talk.

Before Jill launched into what was on her mind, she mentioned the Thursday meeting. "What was all that about the stained glass window? Our little church just has that amber pebbled glass."

"I know," Kate said, and told her the story. "The window itself—I've seen a drawing of it. They put it in the newsletter so we'd all know. It's the classic rose window, round with the rose in the middle surrounded by some leaves. It will be set high, just under the peak in the roof over the pulpit. And luckily that end of the church is east, so the morning sun should come through. It will be lovely.''

"Yes, I guess it will, but…oh, well. I guess under the circumstances…'' She fell silent.

"Jill,'' Kate said. "I've waited a decent interval. What's on your mind? You've been jittery ever since you came in the door.''

"That obvious, huh?'' She pushed back her dark hair, so like Mom's, with a nervous gesture. "There's something you kind of need to know. And I hope you won't be…upset or anything.''

"Like what?''

"I think I'll just give it to you straight. Mom and Doug want to get married. But Mom's afraid you'll feel that…''

In the back of Kate's mind she had known this was coming, even accepted the idea, and she wasn't ready for this sense of rejection. *Not now! Not yet! It's too soon. Dad's only been gone a little over a year.*

"What's the hurry?'' she heard herself say sharply.

"Oh, Kate, I was afraid you'd feel that way. Please don't. Please think about it. I don't know how to say this, but…''

"I suppose this is the big love of Mom's life. Dad certainly wasn't,'' Kate said bitterly, and stopped at the shock on Jill's face.

"Kate, how did you…'' Jill's face colored. "Did Dad ever…? I mean, I know you and Dad were close, but he was *happy*.''

Kate got up from the kitchen table and went to the sink to look out the window. "He didn't have to say anything. I knew. I don't think Mom ever really loved Dad. I can't imagine why she ever married him in the first place." I shouldn't have said that, she thought.

"That's not true," Jill said steadily, but Kate could feel her sister's anxiety. "I saw him in the hospital…at the last. He said he'd had a wonderful life. He said he couldn't believe his luck in marrying Mom. He wouldn't have had it any other way. Dad was happy, Kate! Mom made him happy. Please believe that. And with Doug she…don't you like Doug?"

"Of course I like Doug," Kate said wearily. "I'm sorry I'm not…that I can't be enthusiastic about this. When I think how kind Dad was, how patient…" She stopped, fearful that she might cry. *Dad, I'm sorry. You and me, we never really make it, do we?*

Jill said gently, "Dad's at peace now. And…if he ever wanted anything in this world, it was to make Mom happy. You know that as well as I do."

"I know." Kate sighed, turning to look at her sister. "Is it definite? I mean, they've made up their minds?"

Jill nodded.

"Well, I guess that's that, then. What am I supposed to do besides act happy?"

"Just go along. Don't make Mom…feel bad about it. Can you do that?"

"Oh, sure. But just between you and me, just the two of us, I'm *not* happy about it. I knew it was coming, but—"

There was a roar from the TV in the living room as somebody scored something important. Both Ian and Greg shouted.

"Look, I'm sorry," Kate said. "Don't look so crushed. I'll go along. I won't spoil Mom's big day. When do they plan to take the step?"

"They're working on that now. They want it simple. I've gotten to know Doug better lately and he's really a nice man," Jill said, sounding hopeful.

"I know that. I'm not saying he isn't. It's just that Dad and I are such...*losers.*" She stopped herself, but too late. Jill was too sharp.

"What's that supposed to mean?" Jill half rose from her chair, looking at Kate intently. "Katie...isn't everything...all right?"

Kate went back and sat down at the table across from her sister. Both reached out at the same time and clasped hands. *Now what? What can I say?* She'd gone too far to backtrack, so she spoke carefully.

"A month before Ian asked me to marry him, he told his lawyer to file for dismissal of the custody suit because he would no longer be a single parent when the case came up. We needn't have bothered with the big make-over. He'd have married any old hag who was available." *I shouldn't have said that. I hurt my sister because she is protective of me. Forgive me, God.* She tightened her clasp of Jill's hands as Jill closed her eyes for a moment.

"Katie, what—are you going to do?" It was just a whisper.

"Hang on. The same way Dad did. We losers take what we can get. I love Ian and...he tries. I'll give him that. He says we're a good team. He pretends it's a good marriage. I think he wants to believe it. Anyhow...I've got a pretty good life. When I fall into a puddle of self-pity like this—and I apologize—I try remembering people who are a lot worse off. The Hyslops. The Gilmartins. Doug, too. Doug isn't happy, did you know that? Have you noticed that sometimes he's not really with us? He's a thousand miles away somewhere. Don't worry about me, Jill. I'm sorry I said anything at all." She made her voice brisk and matter-of-fact. "One thing I ask. Don't—repeat—don't tell Mom about this. No point in making her any less happy with life."

There was the sheen of tears in Jill's eyes. "I love you, Katie," she said simply. *Thank you, God, for Jill.*

Kate gave her hands another squeeze and got up. "Let's go into the other room and see the last of the game, whatever it is." She knew, without knowing exactly how she knew, that more than anything else Jill wanted to go into the other room and sit down close to Greg. *If only I could have that with Ian,* she thought. *That mutual devotion.*

Pastor Ledbetter's Sunday sermon was a blockbuster of persuasion. He was a good speaker, a very good preacher. He never hit his listeners over the head with the message. He got it across with a combination of kindliness and sheer reasonableness. And, as always, he had done his homework. He started out by telling them how many members of the congregation had children, and how many were in what grades. He spoke of their responsibility to "train up a child in the way it should go," and how difficult this was in an increasingly violent society.

Then he mentioned the big, nearly empty parsonage next door. He was good at dropping in small jokes, usually aimed at himself, which made them laugh and feel kindly and protective toward him. He told of school discussions he'd already had and of the pledges of help received. It was impressive. By the time he finished the congregation was convinced that a church school was not only overdue, but it was a project the whole congregation should be involved with. Preferably the day before yesterday.

During the coffee hour after the service people could talk of nothing else. Cyrus was surrounded by an ever-changing crowd of people, all wanting to help or offer suggestions. The coffee hour lasted almost an hour longer than usual and the ladies ran out of coffee and tea, and *all* the cookies were eaten, which had never happened before in the history of the parish.

"I think the school is a done deal," Ian said as he drove the family home.

"I do, too," Kate said with satisfaction. "All that's left for us to do now is the actual work of it."

"And as Cyrus pointed out, we only have three months to do it—June, July and August, since it has to open the Tuesday after Labor Day. So you're right, it'll take a lot of work. I wish I didn't have to leave—"

"Well, you can't help that," Kate said. "It's your job."

"I'll do what I can when I'm home," he promised. "I didn't get a chance to talk to Cyrus during that crush after the service, but I've decided what my contribution will be. I'll arrange to have the alarm system put in. There will be a lot of equipment in the building to be protected. And I can get the in-house TV monitors for the principal's office, so he or she can know by flipping a button what's going on anywhere on the premises. It's a rough world out there. They'll need all that stuff and I can get it at cost, or below if the model is to be discontinued." Kate was warmed by his enthusiasm.

In all the excitement at church Kate hadn't had a chance to speak to Beth, so she called her as soon as she could in the afternoon. She dreaded it and had put it off yesterday.

"Mom, Jill told me Saturday about you and Doug."

"Oh, did she?" Mom's voice was hesitant.

"I'm so happy for you both, and I want you to be happy, Mom. Please know that." She made her voice sound more enthusiastic than she felt. "When is the wedding to be?"

She heard Mom's sigh of relief before she launched into her plans. They thought they would marry just after Thanksgiving, as they wanted to take a short trip. Go skiing, perhaps. And she had reservations at her B and B through October. She wasn't taking reservations for November. Yes, they would keep the B and B. It gave her something to do—she loved the work. She rushed on, her happiness bubbling over. Kate let her talk, murmuring encouragement now and then, but eventually when they hung up, Kate stood alone in the hall, hunched over the phone, trying hard not to cry. *Life goes on, Dad.*

In the days that followed, Kate was grateful again and again as people came forward. Cyrus had asked her to coordinate the gifts and donations, which she was glad to do.

The church usually published the newsletter twice a month, but Bessie, the church secretary who wrote it, volunteered to make it a weekly during what she called "the big school push."

"Good PR," she said. "If everybody knows what other folks are doing, they'll do more."

She must have been right, because the day after the first weekly, Mark Bethune, a church member who was an architect, called Kate.

"You know, Mrs. McAllister, that parsonage isn't going to meet city codes for a school. Why don't I look into that?" Bethune would donate his time and expertise and up to a thousand dollars for actual work.

"Oh, yes," Kate said. Neither she nor Cyrus had thought of anything like city codes.

A fairly new church member, Sharon Ferguson, a widow, called Kate. "We've met a couple of times at coffee hour," she said. "I happen to be an attorney. No matter what you do, at some point you're going to need a lawyer. Let me know of any hassle that comes up. I'm available. I don't have any kids, but, well, just say, I'm a member of the team."

Old-time church member Duane Harvey, who owned a construction business, called. "You'll need some renovation in the parsonage. I mean more than baffles and room dividers. I took care of patching the roof a year ago—that'll last you a while yet. I can do any renovation needed, free of course, and I can get materials at cost."

And Jill called one morning when Kate was trying to get some housekeeping done.

"Pastor Ledbetter," she began, "said that since the parsonage had that nice big kitchen, he wanted to serve the students a wholesome lunch. He said kids' brains work better when they eat right. So guess what I've been doing."

"I can't imagine," Kate said, half knowing what it would be. Jill had been a successful restaurant owner and had been Mom's advisor on what to serve at the B and B.

"I've been sitting here for the last hour working out high nutrition and—get this—low cost…lunch menus. I've got six weeks of five-day menus. And it's food the kids will eat."

And on Tuesday afternoon Doug Colby stopped by, without Mom. It was almost five and she'd had a rather contentious meeting with the gardening service but had finally convinced them about the perennials, but she hadn't had time to change out of the pedal pushers and T-shirt she'd done her housework in. She had adopted

Jill's custom of changing clothes in the afternoon, putting on something attractive.

"Not only for Ian," Jill had advised. "For you, the self-respect thing. If you look good, you feel good." And as usual Jill had been right. Now here was Doug Colby on the doorstep, looking hesitant and uneasy.

She made her voice warm and cordial. "Come in. Mom didn't come with you?" She led the way into the living room. "Can I get you something? Coffee? A cold drink?"

"No. No thanks. I just stopped by to give you an update on my contribution to the school."

"How nice of you. How's it going?" She sat down on the couch so he would sit down. He had an old-world politeness and deference that was appealing.

"Well, your brother-in-law, Greg, came through. His art gallery client looked at my pictures and agreed to show them. He's booked me in for the whole month of July." Doug couldn't help but looked pleased.

"Wonderful! I'm so glad!"

"So that brings me to the real point of my call today. May I borrow back that one we gave you—not for sale, just to add to the show? It'll have a Sold sticker on it, so nobody will snap it up." He gave a self-deprecating grin.

"Of course you can borrow it. But do see that the Sold sticker is firmly stuck on. I love that picture." They laughed together and a little silence fell between them. Kate hurried to break it. "How many pictures will you be showing?"

"Probably about twenty by July. My guess is that on a couple of the canvases the paint will still be tacky. I was more than amazed at the prices the guy was talking about. But he said they peg the price high so they can come down if a prospect wants to dicker. This is all new to me. I never planned on actually *selling* any.''

Then both spoke at once and stopped, laughing.

''Sorry, go ahead,'' Kate said, half knowing what he wanted to say. If only he wouldn't. She braced herself, trying to think what a really nice person he was.

''I just want to…thank you. I understand you were very close to your father. He must have been a fine man. I've heard nothing but good of Ralph Bennett. And since…'' He paused, looking off into the distance and, seeming to forget what he had started to say, he added, ''He must have been a good father.''

''Yes, he was,'' Kate said steadily, willing herself not to cry. Grief hung on so long, and it had been only a little over a year. ''But if Mom, and you, of course, have a chance of happiness together I…knowing my Dad, he would be the last to question it. Do…do you have any children?''

''Yes. My wife died some years ago, but we had…have a daughter.''

''Where is she? She'll probably want to come to the wedding. Or have you already taken care of that?''

He looked uncomfortable. ''No. I think not. My daughter and I are…not close.'' He was silent for a moment and then went on, and Kate felt very sorry for him. He seemed—what? To be presenting his credentials? And apologetic about them? How deeply was he estranged from his daughter if he didn't expect her to come to his wedding? Before she could say anything he went on.

''I was away a lot. My work, early in my marriage, was as a lecturer in economics in our local college. I never made it to full professor—I was kind of a misfit in academia. But with that job I did stay at home, and it was a pretty good life. Then, since I couldn't really hack

it with the academics, I got a job as a book salesman."
He smiled slightly. "They didn't call us salesmen, of
course. We were agents. It was a textbook firm, and you
had to be a credentialed teacher in order to make the cut
for their sales staff. To sell instructional material to teachers and curriculum people you have to know what you're
talking about. I've volunteered my advice to Cyrus if he
needs me."

"Did you like that work?" Kate asked.

"Pretty well. But it kept me on the road most of the
time. I managed to get home...for my daughter's various
graduations as she went through school, but I missed
some birthdays. I...wasn't a very good father."

Ian travels and he's a good father, Kate thought. There
must have been something else. Poor man. He was regretting broken fences when it was too late to mend them.

"I feel...I should add one more thing." This was difficult for him, and Kate could feel it. "I wasn't a very
good husband, either. Being gone all the time didn't help
the marriage." He paused a moment. "But I will be a
good husband to Beth. I want you to know that." He
stopped, letting it rest there.

"Of course you will," Kate said, and the warmth in
her tone was genuine.

After she had seen him out she was just shutting the
front door when the phone rang. It was Ian. Her heart
rose as soon as she heard his voice.

"Kate, would it be inconvenient to have the Greers to
dinner tonight? Ray's grandparents are in town."

"No, of course not. But why? I thought they were in
Arizona."

"Not today." His voice was grim. "The colonel called

me this morning. I meant to call you earlier but a couple of hassles came up at the office. He thinks I should have let the Burgesses have Raymond for the summer. He wants to talk about it.''

Chapter Twelve

During dinner Kate had to admire Ian's composure. If he was worried he hid it well. Raymond had been pleased to see his grandparents again, she hoped not entirely because they always brought a present. This time it was a generous gift certificate from Seattle's leading toy store. They had picked it up after they arrived in town.

"I can't keep up with what growing boys want these days," Lydia Greer said in explanation. "So we thought he could just please himself." She had cleverly brought along a catalog from the store, which kept the children occupied after dinner.

Kate served them coffee in the living room. She liked both the Greers, although she didn't know them well. Marsha had inherited her beauty from her mother, who was still very attractive. The colonel was one of those lean strong men who age well. His hair was gray, but he moved with the ease of a much younger man.

"We might as well get to it, Ian," he said. "I think you made a bad mistake by not sending Ray to the Burgess farm this summer. It would have been an ideal chance for him to meet the Burgess family, and really get to know Chet.''

"We haven't ruled it out for some future summer," Ian said quietly. His manner was courteous, but Kate sensed his wariness.

Colonel Greer, who could never sit still for very long, got up and walked over to the mantel. He was standing at ease, with his hands behind his back. Even in civilian clothes it was a military stance.

"He can get to know them all some other summer," Ian added.

"Well, Ian, we've always been honest with each other, no mincing words," the colonel said. "I wish you would change your mind. There's still time."

"No." Even Kate was startled at the rock-hard quality of Ian's single word.

Lydia leaned forward in her chair. "Ian, dear, we know you were disappointed when—" she paused uncertainly "—when the marriage didn't work out." Then she stopped.

"Would you like more coffee?" Kate asked. *Remember me, Lydia? Ian's wife, Kate?*

"No. No, thank you, dear."

Colonel Greer spoke again. "Ian, we've been pretty good friends. Liddy and I were sorry when things didn't work out, and I think it's fair to admit that the blame lay with our daughter. Marsha just wasn't ready to settle down. She was not, let's face it, a good mother to Ray. In my judgment she is now. She's matured. She's grown up. She wants to meet her wifely and maternal obligations. I think, frankly, she should have that chance."

While he was talking Ian had stood up, too. He walked over to the front window and looked out for a moment at the front garden in the lessening daylight. "What are you suggesting, Justin? What kind of chance does this add up to? Keeping in mind that Marsha's and my custody arrangement for our son was dictated by Marsha herself. Keeping in mind that the Burgesses have now— ignoring this previous agreed-to arrangement—filed for full custody, where they appear to want to battle it out in court. Forgive me if I'm not too impressed with Marsha's sudden attack of mother love and need for her child. She was glad enough to leave him in my care until past his twelfth birthday. Do you have any explanation for that, sir?"

Ian, please. Don't lose your temper.

"Actually, I have," the colonel said evenly. "I thought we might discuss this in a civilized and sensible way. Try to put aside your resentment for the moment. Let's just look at facts."

"Fine. Give me a fact. I'm listening."

"We've already conceded that Marsha was, well, a late bloomer. She went through a lot of confusion. Some false starts. Now both Liddy and I are confident that she's found herself. And she and Chet have a good marriage. This is no criticism of you, Ian. You are a fine person. It was Marsha, she just wasn't ready for the responsibility. She is now. And we feel—we all feel—that Raymond's place is with her." He paused and added firmly, "Permanently."

Ian waited a moment to answer. Kate could feel his effort at control. "Permanently is not an option. That is *my* number-one fact. Do you have any further facts to present?"

Oh, Ian, don't be sarcastic.

Lydia spoke anxiously. "Ian, dear, please. We're talking about the *Burgess* family of Virginia. Don't you realize what a wonderful opportunity this is for Raymond?

And Chet is so generous. He's talked to Justin and me about it. He will adopt Raymond. Raymond will inherit equally with any children he and Marsha have together. Raymond will grow up with the very *best* people.'' She stopped uncertainly at the look on Ian's face.

''Raymond is already growing up with the very best people.'' Each word was a chip of ice. ''Now let's get down to the real fact. The *only* fact. The fact of the Burgess money. I never expected this of you, Justin.'' His tone was a lash of contempt.

''Ian!'' Kate said sharply, before he could continue. These were Raymond's grandparents and he mustn't alienate them completely. She had been so quiet that they turned to look at her as if they had all suddenly remembered she existed.

''Kate's right,'' Colonel Greer said quickly, his face pale with held-in anger. ''I'll forget you implied that the Burgess family fortune has anything to do with this. But I think we've reached a dead end here. It was useless to come. Come along, Liddy. Thank you for a lovely dinner, Kate.'' Then he turned to Ian. ''I'm sorry we can't get together on this, Ian. We've been good friends in the past. Lydia and I—and Marsha and Chet—only want what is best for Raymond. We'll just have to let the court settle it.'' He gave a stiff little bow toward Kate and, not knowing what else to do, Kate followed them to the door and saw them out. She watched them as they got into their rental car and drove off. When she went back into the living room Ian was sitting in a chair with his head in his hands.

''Ian?''

''I'm okay,'' he muttered, and she got the feeling he wanted to cry and was holding it back. Cry if you want to, she thought. You're entitled. There's no feeling of betrayal like knowing you've been let down by a friend, someone you trusted.

"I'm sorry," she said simply. What could she do? How could she help? She pulled over the ottoman and sat down in front of him.

He raised his head and looked at her. There were tears in his eyes. "Justin, of all people. I thought he was my friend. He always seemed…"

"But maybe they do think that Marsha is—"

"No way! They're both impressed out of their skulls by the Burgess family wealth and prominence. *Justin,* of all people, to suggest that I give Ray up permanently. Well, that's that, I guess. Cross him off my list." He sank back in the chair. "If things go our way in November," he said slowly, "and they could well *not* go our way, I'll still see that Ray gets to see his mother any time he wants to. You're right about that. I won't deny him. I would never use my child against his mother."

"You're a good father, Ian. Raymond—even with all the difficulties—is a lucky boy." Luckier than he had been, certainly. Perhaps Ian's own childhood, with its disorderly and impermanent relationships, had made him more aware of his son's needs. Remembering she hadn't cleared the table, she started to get up and Ian reached out to her.

"Don't leave yet, please. I'll help out later in the kitchen." He looked so beaten that it tore her heart, and they just sat quietly together holding hands. *Please God, let it be right for Ian in November.*

They had only a few minutes until they heard the children coming noisily down the stairs. Ian said, "Thank you, Kate," and released her hands.

"We finally decided," Raymond announced, coming into the room followed by Tommy and Joy. He looked around quickly. "Did they go already? So soon? I wanted to tell them what I'm gonna get."

"Yes. They had to leave," Kate said. "What did you decide on?"

Frowning slightly, Raymond extended the catalog. "We turned down the pages. It's like this. It's either two things, and I get thirty-four dollars in change. Or it's three things, but I have to con somebody into giving me seventeen more dollars. And both those totals include sales tax." He looked at his father speculatively. "What do you think, Dad?"

"If it's something you can share with Tommy and Joy, I think I'm probably good for the seventeen dollars."

"Share, yeah. More or less. But mainly with Tommy. But Joy could watch. Does that make it?" He paused, looking first at his father and then at Kate. "What's goin' on?"

Ian sighed. "For a twelve-year-old you're too sharp for comfort. Your granddad and I had a disagreement. I'm sorry."

"About me," Raymond said flatly. "You'd better level with me, okay?"

"All right. He thinks I should have let you go to the Burgess farm this summer." He stopped there, and Kate was relieved. She didn't want Raymond to know what else his grandfather had suggested. If it didn't happen, if the custody arrangement was confirmed in November, he need never know.

Talking about the toys was a good distraction until it was the children's bedtime. Joy's bedtime prayers were filled with requests right out of the toy catalog. Tommy almost fell asleep again during his prayers. When Tommy's day was over it was over. When she finally went into Raymond's room, he was sitting up in bed, holding his gift certificate in his hands and looking at it.

"I think I'm changing my mind," he said, climbing out of bed to kneel.

"About what? The gift?"

"Yeah. I had a better idea. I'll break the news to the other kids in the morning. I think I'll donate it to the new school. Everybody else is donating stuff. You're in charge of that, so here." He handed the gift certificate to her. "You take it."

Kate took it and sat down on the side of his bed. "That's a nice gesture, but what would a school need with toys?"

Raymond looked pained. "*Mom, sports* stuff! Bats! Baseballs! Soccer balls! Basketballs! The catalog's full of it. Top-grade stuff. If Pastor Ledbetter expects kids to beat their brains out in school all day, they need *something* in recess."

Kate took the gift certificate, but kept it a week in case Raymond changed his mind again. When satisfied that he wasn't going to, she put it away until they knew exactly what sports equipment might be needed.

When Kate conferred next with Pastor Ledbetter she was pleased to learn that Raymond's former teacher Mrs. Lundy had called at the church office, introduced herself and volunteered any help she could give.

"I'm so glad," Kate said. "She's really nice and she was so distressed about the deposition she gave the lawyers."

"She's also distressed about her job in the public schools," Cyrus said, his eyes twinkling. "Before we finished talking I began to think she might be interested in a private school job."

"You're kidding. This will be a church school. I don't

think she's even a churchgoer, is she?'' Kate said, laughing.

"Let's say she's not a churchgoer *now*," Cyrus said, grinning. "She may pick up the habit if she hangs out with churchgoers. It's been known to happen. And I must say she's well qualified to teach. I was thinking she'd make a terrific principal. She told me something I wanted to hear, since I'm an old teach-the-basics teacher myself. She doesn't worry too much about the child's self-image at first. She focuses on helping the child build the self through achievement, then the image comes in due course. What a concept. We've got to have a principal, as I can't do that and my other work, too. And since her first love is teaching English the way it should be taught, she could also take the English classes."

"Do you think she could do both?"

"Yes. At least while the school is still small. We'll have to double up. Later, as we grow, we'll add more staff." He was looking as pleased as the Cheshire cat. He had had to raise his voice because of the noise outside, the sound of pounding hammers and the agonized screech of ripping wood.

Then he got serious and fumbled in his desk drawer for a sheaf of papers. "Greg Rhys came over and we talked money," he said. "It's an enormous total just to get going, even with all the donations and free stuff we're getting, so it's going to be a little iffy."

"But we're going to do it," Kate said in alarm.

"Yes! That much is fact! But during the next three months we'll know exactly how big we can start."

"What do you mean?"

"We *will* start, but we may have to start small. What usually happens when a private school starts up is that they start with the primary grades and work up, as they can finance it. But I can't see the sense of that in our case. It's the middle school kids, grades six through eight, who need the help and guidance *now*. That's where the kids start getting into difficulty in our present culture. I'm thinking we should start there and, as finances permit, work up through high school. That's where the greatest need is.''

"Yes," Kate said. "That makes sense in these times." She was speaking loudly over the noise. Then, like a small epiphany, she identified the sounds. Hammers pounding. Wood tearing. And it was *next door*. The *parsonage.*

"They've started work! Haven't they!"

He grimaced. "Yes, in a sense. When the architect and the builder got together over there, the first thing they found was dry rot in the cellar. They're ripping that out now and putting in new support beams. No point in remodeling the top two floors and have it all fall into the basement. But Sunday I'll have the preliminary drawings of the school offices and classrooms posted all over the rec room walls. You haven't had a plumber sign on as a volunteer, have you?''

"No, we haven't. Is the plumbing over there bad?"

"Well, when that ten-room house was built they thought one bathroom was enough. About fifteen years later another was added off the downstairs service porch, but that's not going to do it for a school. We have to put in His and Hers rest rooms, which is going to cost the earth.''

"I'll ask Bessie to put a note in the newsletter about it," Kate agreed.

When Kate left the church office, she was elated. Never had the noise of pounding hammers and ripping wood sounded so good.

When Ian was home he spent a good deal of time with the architect, planning where the security equipment should go. Even at cost and below, he was spending a lot of money. Kate said nothing but paid the bills as they came in. Thank heaven the garden next door was thriving—it always cut down the food bills.

Ian had a haunted look about him these days and Kate knew he was regretting his lost friendship with Raymond's grandparents. Grief came in varying degrees. He didn't talk about it, but fleeting looks of sadness and defeat came in his eyes when he felt unobserved, and the set determination to get the school going revealed how he felt, and what he feared.

He sought her out one day after dinner, when she was in the garden next door, tying up snap beans, which seemed to have grown at least six inches overnight. It was a beautiful evening. The setting sun was down below the rim of mountains, but the sky still glowed pink for one of Seattle's long twilights.

"Congratulations," he said, smiling.

"Thanks. We're going to get a good crop this year," Kate said, brushing her hands together. Immediately after Jill's makeover she had tried wearing garden gloves, but had found them too clumsy and had discarded them. There was no substitute for plain fingers in working with plants. And now she had been so busy, she had forgotten to change into something pretty for the afternoon. *Sorry about that, Jill.* And she had needed a haircut for a week. *I'll find time, Jill. I promise. I won't regress to my rubber-band ponytail.*

"I wasn't referring to the snap beans," Ian said, sitting down on the wooden bench against the back fence. "I was referring to Raymond's sudden ability to actually save some of his money. How'd you manage that?"

"I had my own kids on the saving schedule when I lived next door. We just hadn't got started yet over here. He went right along," Kate said, sitting down next to him.

Ian laughed. "When I found out he was actually *saving* some of his money I almost passed out from shock. Ray's spending skills are fantastic."

"Well, I think my dad started it. When Jill's and my kids were born, Dad opened a college-fund account for each. He and Mom made as big a deposit as they could, living on a librarian's salary. It was up to us to keep it going after that. So as the kids get money of their own they have to chip in—one-third into the college fund, one-third into a spending fund for valentines, other kids' birthday gifts and so on, and one-third to blow on anything they want to. I think it's that one-third to blow on anything that keeps them hooked on the plan. We do make bank deposits of the college fund at frequent intervals just to be on the safe side."

"Thank you, Kate," he said softly. "You have no idea what you do for the McAllisters, father and son."

"I'm glad," she said simply. Right now, this minute, he didn't look haunted and sad. *Thank you, God.*

"Now let me ask you this, to change the subject. Are you working too hard? It's just for the summer, isn't it? After the school starts, it will level off, won't it?"

"I don't know. I don't think so. We're hoping for another infusion of cash from the fall bazaar, which doesn't happen until November. Don't worry about it. Work is good for the soul."

"Then your soul should be in pretty good shape," he said quietly.

You don't need to be grateful, Ian, she thought. I teach Raymond what he needs to know because I love him.

I'm his surrogate mother. But Kate felt a warmth at his compliment.

When they got back home there was a phone message to call Beth.

"Guess what," Mom said delightedly. "Serendipity has struck again. Ruth Threlkeld, your dad's old workmate, called. The city library is getting ready for another surplus book sale. She knows about our school project, and she's spotted a complete set of middle-school-level encyclopedias, only four years old, that the library is going to replace. We can get it for pennies on the dollar. Shall Doug and I go down and root around for other reference books, too?"

"Yes! Please!" Kate said. "Keep track of what you spend so I can reimburse you," she added, knowing they would spend as much of their own money as they could. Mom had always been interested in Dad's work, so had learned a great deal about librarianship.

Things were falling into place in a wonderfully happenstance way. Kate was cleaning out the attic for an extra rummage sale in midsummer when she found again Marsha's swirly peach-and-brown painting. On a hunch she asked Raymond about it.

"Do you think Marsha paid very much for this? Is it worth anything?"

"I would say yes, but I dunno how much."

"What makes you think that?"

Raymond grinned. "They haggled about it. Marsha wanted it, but she didn't think Dad could take the price, which I don't remember what it was. Anyhow, the decorator sort of spread it around among other stuff, so it didn't look so bad. I think—if you wanna know what I think—I think this is definitely *not* rummage sale, stupid as it looks. Why don't you call that guy at the art gallery, that Halloran?''

Kate called the Halloran Gallery and was stunned at the value of the painting. After checking with Ian to see if he wanted to donate the proceeds to the school, she put the painting in the car trunk and happily delivered it to the gallery. On the way home she detoured by Mom's house to give her some of last year's frozen peaches, as the new crop would be coming in.

"Oh, Kate, I'm so glad you stopped by. Yes, I can use the peaches, and I want to give my eyes a rest."

Beth had been seated at her large dining-room table, leafing through pages of the encyclopedia set. She was about halfway through the twenty volumes. The ones she had finished leafing through were in higgledy-piggledy stacks on two dining-room chairs. She had been making a list of missing pages. Kate had to laugh. It took her back, remembering Dad. How fortunate that publishers of encyclopedias and other reference books kept stocks of loose pages to sell to libraries for those reluctant scholars—skateboard at the ready—who *had* to write a report but didn't want to hang out too long at the library to do it. Missing pages, the librarian's everlasting burden. In a couple of weeks Mom would be sitting here at the same table tipping in the replacement pages. Kate felt a rush of love. Every body was working so hard.

Two days after that, and she told herself she would always remember the day, Mr. Kramer came. Stocky, sweating at the end of his work day, clad in dark jeans and sweat-stained dark-blue work shirt.

"I'm Joel Kramer," he said, suddenly remembering to take off his baseball cap. "I don't go to your church. Actually, I don't go to any, but my mother-in-law does. Go to your church, I mean. And don't start thinking of all the mother-in-law jokes," he added, grinning. "She's a neat lady. She's telling me about your school last night, and I'm very interested because I got kids. Mine are too little yet to go to school, but they're coming right along. Anyhow, she says you're the one to see about donations of time and work?" He ended on a questioning note.

"Yes. I am. Come in," Kate said, opening the door. "What were you thinking of volunteering for, Mr. Kramer?"

"Well, I can really offer only the one thing," he said modestly. "I'm a plumber."

In mid-July, in the middle of the showing of Doug's paintings at the Halloran Gallery, Seattle had one of its heat waves. This happened every few years, when Seattle's usually mild temperatures soared into the nineties, and wavered there for two or three days until the marine air moved in again. In Houston or Baltimore ninety and up could go without notice, but in Seattle, where almost nothing was air-conditioned, it became a city crisis. Even as Seattle-ites got hysterical over the occasional winter blizzard, they also got hysterical over the occasional summer heat wave. TV anchors ignored stories of national interest to talk about the temperature, and at least one tourist from Dallas was interviewed, having a good laugh at Seattle's expense. But even this paid off for the school.

"Is anybody coming to your showing?" Ian asked Doug one evening when Mom and Doug came over for a cold salad supper.

"Everybody," Doug said, almost smugly. "The gallery is air-conditioned—for the pictures, you know—so people come in to get cool. They've also been buying pictures. My snow scenes painted up in the Cascades went first."

But the good luck couldn't go on forever. Even with

the extra midsummer rummage sale, the cake sales, the car washes, the auction-for-services and the donated labor—Mrs. Lundy was going to work the first six months on credit, since her husband's salary could carry them—they were woefully short of start-up money.

"You see," Cyrus said at the early-August meeting of the school committee and the elders, "we have thirty-seven students for the first term, thirty-six paying full tuition and one on scholarship." He looked at them over his half glasses, which had slipped down over his nose. "We're taking one child who needs to come to this school, and before you say we can't afford it, I must tell you we can't afford not to take her. I'll pay for her books and school materials out of the pastor's discretionary fund. Taking this child into the school now will change her life, and her life needs changing." He waited for comment but none came, and he went on.

"Mrs. Lundy—" he nodded in her direction "—will function both as principal and English teacher. And a young man named Kirby Wallace, though he isn't here with us this evening, will sign on for math and science. He'll also act as coach and do playground duty. And I'm going to teach history and geography classes for the time being. Beth Bennett has volunteered to keep the library going and spend some time there. That's our beginning staff. We will start classes the Tuesday after Labor Day. On the Sunday before Labor Day we will hold open house at the school so all the congregation can see what we've accomplished."

After the wild burst of applause, he added, "And that's the good news. Now for the bad news. I'm sorry to tell you that a number of our members who have high-school-age kids are disappointed that we are starting with the middle school grades six through eight. There has been some…unpleasantness about the Rose Window Fund. This grieves me, as we have promised the Gilmartins this tribute to Brenden. I ask…indeed, I *urge* you to talk to any of your friends who feel this way. Remind them that we have a deep commitment here, and we must honor it. Cast your minds back. Remember when Brenden died we all wanted desperately to do something, anything, for the Gilmartins, and we did. Next month we'll have enough money to pay for the rose window and the installing of it. Don't worry about getting enough money for the school. We're doing fine and, with God's help, the money for the school will come."

"That's too bad about the Gilmartins," Ian said as he drove them home from the meeting.

"Yes," Kate said soberly. "I was at church last Thursday. It was our turn to pack up the bags for the food bank, and Amy Gilmartin wasn't there. She's never missed a day that I know of. I hope they're not being pressured. I'll ask Mom if she was at the Pastor's Aid Group Wednesday. That's really bad news."

Ian was silent a moment. She couldn't see much of his face from the dash light. "I had some other bad news today, if you haven't had enough already."

"What?" she asked anxiously.

"I got a letter today from Justin, addressed to me at the office. He's such a stickler for detail. He's notifying me that he and Lydia plan to offer testimony at the custody hearing in November. I suppose he thought it was only fair to warn me in advance."

Chapter Thirteen

Kate was disturbed when Beth told her that Amy Gilmartin hadn't shown up at the Wednesday meeting, either.

"Mom, we've got to do something. Are they being pressured about the rose window money?"

"Yes, I think so. I know Amy pretty well from all our Wednesdays together. I think I'll talk to her. If there's anything we don't need it's another church row that divides the congregation."

"I know," Kate said. "And there's already been some squabbling about what the school name will be. Let me know what you find out about the Gilmartins."

Then the whole thing was pushed out of her mind because Marsha called from Georgetown.

"Marsha, how nice to hear from you," Kate said politely. "If you want Ian, he's out of town until this weekend."

"No, it's better if I talk to you," Marsha said. Along with everything else, Marsha had a lovely voice. "What are we going to do about Raymond's birthday? It's August fifteenth, you know."

"Yes, I know." *I do keep track of the kids' birthdays, Marsha.*

"Have you made any plans?"

"Raymond's thinking about it. He hasn't decided yet what he wants in the way of celebration."

Marsha sounded diffident. "You know, as Ian reminded us last time, the original arrangement stands, at least until November. So I wondered if I...if maybe Chet and I could make another quick trip out there. Maybe we could give Raymond some sort of special day or something. I really..." She paused. "Kate, in the winter, in that snowstorm, it seemed I...he seemed to care about me. Then this last trip, I don't know. Children grow up so fast. They change or something. It seemed I didn't really know him anymore." Then she added, sounding desperate, "I can't let that happen. Please understand."

"Of course I understand," Kate said. Maybe Justin had been right. Maybe Marsha was growing up, or at least trying to. *Help me, God. What's the right thing to do here?* "Maybe we should ask Raymond what he wants. He's not here now, but I can have him call you this evening."

There was a little silence, then Marsha said in a small voice, "I'm not sure. Last time he seemed to be... pushing me away. I can't explain it."

"Would you like me to talk to him about it?"

"Yes, please. And...let me know? It wouldn't have to be exactly *on* his birthday, if you had other plans for that day. Maybe the day before, or the day after..." Her voice dwindled away.

After they had rung off, Kate stood with her hand on the phone for a long time. Chet's words came back to her. *Does he still love Marsha, or has she lost him?* Had Marsha lost Raymond because she had abandoned him for long intervals to his father? Maybe this was a last effort to get him back. Could she do that? Kate was remembering the Raymond she had first known, the lonely little kid next door, who had burrowed his way into her family by just hanging around. Was Marsha now thinking that she had lost her child? What must it feel like to have your child turn away from you? What had Raymond quoted? *"Home is where when you get there they have to take you in."* And Marsha hadn't been home.

Can I let this happen? What can I do to change it? She thought.

When Raymond came home she asked him about his birthday, only a week away. He was wearing his Seahawks T-shirt and his Mariners baseball cap, which was slightly too large. He sat at the kitchen table, twisting it around on his head, front to back, back to front, while he pondered his answer.

"It would be sort of like two birthdays," Kate said, rinsing some lettuce from the garden for dinner salad. "On your birthday, the fifteenth, you can have whatever kind of do you want here. And either before or after, you can spend with Marsha and Chet. What do you think?"

"Do you realize which birthday this is?" he asked, still twirling his cap. "My thirteenth. I'll be a teenager. Are you and Dad ready for that?"

Kate laughed. "I think we can handle it. But what about Marsha? They want to do something for you."

"Do you know that Chet has his own plane? It's a Learjet. Seats ten people. That's what they came out here in the last time. A pilot flew them, but he can fly it if he wants to. He knows how."

"No, I didn't know." She turned from the sink and

looked at him. He had put on some weight. He was look-ing better, healthier. And he seemed more confident these days, more sure of himself.

"Well, maybe if they *insist* celebrating my teenhood, I'll ask Chet to give me a ride in his plane. Would you and Dad do any nail biting over that?"

"We could probably handle that, too," Kate said, dry-ing her hands, then putting the bowl of lettuce in the refrigerator for dinner. She sat down opposite him.

"The last time we talked, you were thinking of just a family dinner. Is that still the idea?"

"A family dinner, with *presents,* yes. That's on the actual day." He widened his eyes dramatically. "The ac-tual *day* I become a teenager. Then if Marsha and Chet want to come another day, yeah, that'd be okay. Do you think Dad can survive that, things being as they are?"

"Why don't I talk to him about it? Or would you rather?"

"Uh…I think you'd better do it. That's adult stuff. And until the fifteenth, I'm just a little twelve-year-old kid." He gave her his most angelic smile, and she had to laugh.

That evening, after the children were in bed, Beth stopped by without Doug. Kate was glad to see her, as when Ian was gone there was a sense of emptiness in the house.

"Doug didn't come with you?" she asked, opening the door. More and more she was thinking of Doug as part of the family.

"No. We've got a full house. Two couples and that antique dealer from the Bay area. He comes up twice a year to buy collectibles. Doug's getting the breakfast stuff ready, setting the table and all. I wanted to talk to you about Amy."

"Come on in," Kate said. Mom looked younger, happier, and she had said "we've" got a full house. She missed the first part of what her mother said as they went into the living room.

"...really worried. There's apparently been a lot of pressure by two couples with high-school-age kids. The Gilmartins—you know what timid souls they are at best. Amy's dropping out of the Wednesday group. She says due to ill health. She seemed very upset and Kate, I have to tell you this, they seem to be blaming you."

"Blaming me for what?" Kate asked blankly.

"Well, you're heading the donations committee. Somehow they got the idea, or it was implied, that you think the Rose Window Fund should be diverted to the school."

"Nonsense! Of course I don't."

"I tried to explain that," Beth said, "but I don't think I convinced them. Can you talk to them? I'll come with you if we can do it in the afternoon. I've got my hands full until noon when I have guests."

"Yes, I'll see them," Kate said. "And you don't need to come with me, Mom." How odd. Somewhere during the past few months she must have picked up an extra allotment of courage. Maybe from all the committee work. Maybe Jill hadn't got all the in-charge genes, after all.

The next day, after Raymond had gone next door, where he was reading aloud a young-adult adventure novel to Mr. Hyslop, Kate took a couple of garden-fresh tomatoes, a cucumber and half a dozen tiny green onions—just enough for a salad for two—and drove over to the Gilmartins'. She had forgotten how drab their little house was. It needed painting, and there were old papers and circulars on the tiny front porch. The lawn was overgrown with patches of brown and tall, leggy dandelions. She rang the bell three times before she heard someone coming. There was the soft slip-slap of bedroom slippers and the door opened a crack.

"Who is it?" When had Amy's voice started sounding so old?

"It's me, Kate. Beth Bennett's daughter. She said you were feeling under the weather."

"Oh. Yes. Just a minute." The door shut and there was the sound of awkward fumbling with the chain. At last it opened. "Come in. I wasn't...really expecting anyone. Just... I'm not..." Amy Gilmartin stood before Kate in a rumpled cotton nightgown, covered with a much shorter terry robe that had seen too many wash days. "Please sit down," Amy said, as if suddenly remembering her manners.

"Maybe I should just put these into the fridge for you first," Kate said. "I brought you and Theron some salad makings from my garden. I'll be right back."

"How...kind," Amy said as Kate went into the kitchen. As she did, Brenden's beautiful face followed her, on the small table in the living room, on the mantel, on the dining-room sideboard. Brenden, laughing on skis in the snow. Brenden, about ten, poised at the edge of a lake. Brenden in his high school cap and gown. She had forgotten how *alive* Brenden had been.

The small kitchen was appalling. Kate stepped over the scatter of old newspapers and went to the refrigerator. I've got to clean up this kitchen for her, she thought. She went back into the living room. Amy was seated in a chair looking blankly at the wall. She was in the light from the front window, and she looked exhausted, her tired eyes puffy, as if she had cried for a very long time.

"Amy, what's the matter? Is it about the rose window?" Kate had difficulty keeping her voice steady.

"We have to give up the window," Amy said in a thin, shaky voice. "It's the right thing to do. Everybody says so. You're right, of course, we really must."

"No!" Kate said. "No, it's the wrong thing to do! We must not give up Brenden's window." And at the mention of Brenden's name, slow tears rolled down Amy's thin face. She wiped at them vaguely with her fragile hands.

"You see, if we had the window, people would know that...know that Brenden was *here*. Brenden was here..."

Kate took the sparrowlike form in her arms, hugging her, rocking back and forth, remembering when she and Jill had kept track of the condolence cards that came in honor of Dad. It had seemed so important that people *know* that Dad had been here, that he wasn't forgotten. And the rose window was a validation of Brenden's short, bright life. *The Gilmartins must have that.*

"Don't worry about the window. It's going in as scheduled," Kate said firmly, trying to convince the shattered little woman. When she thought she had, she helped her back to bed and tackled the sinkful of dirty dishes. She went through the small house like a whirlwind, cleaning up. When she noticed it was almost four, she realized she'd have to get back home. She looked into the bedroom, saw Amy in exhausted sleep and went back to the kitchen to write a reassuring note to Theron, then left it on the kitchen table.

She'd have to talk to Cyrus. They could set up some sort of celebration on the Sunday after the window was installed. Maybe Cyrus could speak more firmly to those who thought all monies had to go for the school. She drove her car into her own driveway and sat there a moment.

What about the school? Maybe she'd better talk to Greg tonight. He was the one keeping track of money, and how much more money did they actually need? But Cyrus had said they were starting on schedule, just starting small. How much more money would it take to, say, add the high school grades?

She saw Tommy walking across from next door. Mrs. Hyslop must be home, then, so it was well after four. *How much money?* In six months would Mrs. Lundy want her six-months salary in one lump sum, or would she want it prorated over the rest of the year?

"Why are you sitting in the car?" Tommy asked at the car window.

"I was just thinking a minute," Kate said. "Is Mr. Hyslop okay?"

"Yes, he's okay. I wonder how it feels to be…not with it," Tommy said soberly. "Do you think he knows?"

"What do you mean, dear?"

"Well, he likes to work the jigsaw puzzle, see. And we're sitting there doing it and all of a sudden, out of the blue, he says 'I have such a heavy schedule tomorrow, I must get downtown very early.'" Tommy shook his head, frowning. "Then he's right back and he says, 'I need a brown piece with a curved side.' I never let on, you know, that I notice when he goes out of sync like that."

"That's right," Kate said, opening the car door. "That's the best way." She looked at Tommy for a long moment. My son, Tom, she thought. He would probably go through life helping other people. Not a bad way to live a life. *"When you do it for the least of these, you do it for Me."*

Going toward the back door, Kate put her arm around Tommy's shoulders, loving him intensely. If only Marsha could know this, she reflected. If only she could have this sense of connectedness with her child, being part of the long flow of creation. She wondered if she could talk to Ian about it. He would be home Friday. Two more days. Her heart rose. But when Ian came home Friday his good news drove the idea out of her mind.

"Guess what?" he said, coming in from the service porch. She had heard the back door open and the thud of the two-suiter being dropped on the floor.

"What?" she asked, shutting the oven door and setting the timer.

"After January I part company with the two-suiter and catalog case. As of January first, no more travel! You're looking at the new sales manager, whose office is in Seattle!"

"Oh, Ian! Congratulations! How wonderful!" And she hugged him as he picked her up and held her close for a long moment. Then they sat together at the kitchen table, talking excitedly. He had worked hard for this; he deserved a moment of glory.

Later, when the children were down for the night, she brought him up-to-date on the home front news, the school progress, the Gilmartins. Then she told him about Marsha's call.

"Maybe she's trying to grow up," Kate said tentatively, noting his somber expression.

"That'll be the day."

"People can change, Ian. And if they go to the trouble of coming clear out here to Seattle again, just to give Raymond some sort of birthday celebration, I think…"

"What do you think?" He was looking at her intently.

"I was remembering during dinner something Chet

said when they were here the last time, when he was helping me try to find Mr. Hyslop. He said he'd rather settle things peacefully. So I thought...I wondered..." She took a deep breath. *What am I saying?* "I thought I'd like to talk to him. Just Chet and me. One on one. Would you have any objection to that?"

"I don't have any objection to anything you do," he said slowly. "Since we married...I've learned so much more about you. You are one of those strong, gentle women who...who go through life...quietly getting things done. With no fanfare. No asking for credit. Just doing...what needs to be done. And you're one of the kindest people it's ever been my privilege to know. Sure. If you think you can talk Chester Burgess out of something he wants to do, go ahead. With my blessing."

Kate was shaken by his words, so it was a moment before she found her voice. "I'm not sure it is what he wants," she said slowly. "I think it may have been Marsha, back in the beginning of their marriage, in February when she was rushing into a brand-new life, but...if Marsha is changing..." She let it rest there.

After the Sunday service, Kate managed to get a moment alone with Cyrus to tell him about her visit with Amy Gilmartin. His usually kind face set grimly.

"Theron did come to see me, offering the rose window money," he said. "I'm glad you told me this, because I was tempted. But now..." He paused. "Let me think a minute. The window's ready. I'll see if I can get it installed a week early—make a big production of it. Once it's a done deal..."

Kate was pleased and relieved to hear that the rose window would be installed as planned. Cyrus had been right weeks ago when he said the Lord would provide for the school. Now they need only keep that faith strong.

"How long do you think it will be before we can start phasing in the higher grades in the school?" she asked.

He sighed. "Well, Katie, if some philanthropist would drop about fifty thousand dollars on top of us we could probably phase in grades nine and ten next term."

"So much?"

"Kate, you ought to talk to Greg Rhys about money. You know, in all my planning, I never once remembered insurance. Schools have to have a ton of insurance, did you know that?"

"No. I didn't," Kate said ruefully. "Well, I'll start working getting the money for, say grade nine."

Raymond's birthday dinner was a smashing success. Kate had never seen him happier. And it wasn't only the pile of birthday gifts, although everyone had been generous. It was because of *family,* and they were all at the dining-room table, stretched to its full length, talking and laughing and together. Kate looked at him through a blur of tears. The lonely little kid from next door, hungry for family, had come a long way. Her eyes met Ian's across the table and she knew he was thinking the same thing. It was a good feeling.

The next morning early, Kate was surprised to see Ian packing up his two-suiter.

"I thought you weren't going out again until tomorrow," she said.

He grinned. "Put it this way. I think things will go better for Ray's second birthday bash if I'm in Albuquerque and they're in Seattle. So I'm going a day early. Besides, in Albuquerque, in the old section, you get the best Mexican food this side of the border."

"Maybe you'll miss traveling more than you know," Kate said, laughing.

"You could be right. I think I'll get a whole bunch of

different kinds of cookbooks for you this Christmas. You could experiment. In Nashville they serve hush puppies with almost every meal. Where in Seattle can you get hush puppies?''

With a feeling of contentment, she watched him drive off to the airport. A few months ago, if Marsha and Chet were to arrive within minutes, he would have been anything but happy.

Raymond had talked with both Marsha and Chet on the phone during the previous week, so for Big Day Number Two, the plans were made. Tommy had wanted to go with them. Joy hadn't. She was learning to tat from Mrs. Hyslop and was fascinated by it. So Chet had agreed to take the two boys up. When they got aloft Chet would take the controls, with both boys in the cockpit, and give them a sky view of Seattle as they circled above it. Marsha had elected not to go, as she didn't care for flying in the best of times. Kate was glad, as it would give her time to talk with Marsha.

When they were alone, Kate made the standard Seattle hospitality offer. ''I'll make a fresh pot of coffee.''

''Not for me,'' Marsha said, crossing her slim hands over her flat middle. ''I can't wait to tell you. I'm going to have a baby! And the weirdest thing is…I'm not scared anymore. I *want* to have it. Can you believe that!'' And suddenly her lovely eyes filled with tears. ''Can you believe that, Kate?''

Kate felt a wild rush of happiness. Some time, somehow, between February and August, Marsha had matured.

''How wonderful! I'm so happy for you! When did you change your mind?''

''I'm not sure,'' Marsha said as she and Kate sat down across from each other in the living room. ''I kept thinking about Chet, and I…I love him so much. I kept thinking—why not? I mean, even all the misery of it, all those long months, but I kept thinking for Chet I might be able to do it. And the more I thought about it the more I thought I *could* do it. And you know, the oddest thing, I'm six weeks into it now and I haven't been sick once. Not once. I can't believe it.''

They laughed together and fell to talking about it, comparing notes, asking and answering questions, the way women do who share in the act of creation. An hour flew by, and eventually they came to Raymond.

''I was talking to Chet about this...this custody thing,'' Marsha said at last. ''It's so odd, Kate. Ever since that snowfall this last winter I...can't help but think of you as a friend. That may be dumb, considering...everything. I need to...ask you something.''

''Ask.''

''I really do feel I have to set things right with Raymond. I—I wasn't... I was going to say I wasn't a very good mother. Actually, I wasn't *any* mother. And I have to...fix that. Only lately, since the last visit here, I'm not sure I can. I used to, you know, get him presents or something and things seemed all right, but—'' She stopped, her eyes troubled. ''Kate, tell me the truth, even if it seems unkind, or even rude, tell me the truth. Do you think I can get Raymond back?'' Marsha's hands reached out, and Kate clasped them.

Only the truth would serve here, and Kate spoke carefully. ''You have lost...his childhood, Marsha. And I don't think you can ever regain that. It's past. He's gone beyond that now, and it's over. But you haven't lost *him*. Raymond identifies as part of *this* family.'' Her hands tightened on Marsha's as Marsha closed her eyes. ''But you have the future, you and Raymond. He is feeling very secure here now. I think next summer, or the next, he could at least spend some time with you and Chet. Summer, or part of summer. Even if he doesn't identify as your child, your son, he might become the best friend you ever had. You and he can have a future, Marsha, because he *does* love you. And he's going to be a very fine person. I'm not saying this very well—''

''You're saying it very well,'' Marsha said softly. ''Oh, Kate, I've made such a mess of things.''

''You made mistakes. There isn't a living soul who doesn't. I've made my share.''

''What do you think I should do? I've made such a row about this custody thing.''

''I had planned to talk with Chet about this, but maybe I'd just better talk to you. I think you should drop it. If you won it would devastate Raymond. He's settled in here. This is his home. The last time you and Chet were here, Chet said he would rather do things peacefully, not have a big battle. I wish you would talk it over with him. You can't go back in time, Marsha. You can only go forward.''

''I'll talk to Chet,'' she said quietly. ''And thank you.''

When Chet came back with the two boys, they were both euphoric.

''I'm gonna be a pilot,'' Tommy declared. ''I decided!''

''I think I will, too,'' Raymond said, flinging himself into a chair. ''Chet knows everything in that cockpit, everything! He's had a pilot's license since he was twenty-two. How about that!''

And, as both boys were starving, they headed for the kitchen to make peanut butter and jelly sandwiches, to hold them until dinnertime.

''Thank you for taking Tommy along,'' Kate said to Chet.

"Tommy'd make a good pilot," Chet replied, sitting down by Marsha. "He's very deliberate—doesn't rush into things. He's steady, and that far above earth steady is what you want. Raymond was telling me all the progress you've been making with the new school."

"Yes. We're to open the Tuesday after Labor Day. So far it's only a middle school, but as we can we'll add the upper grades, nine through twelve."

"That's wonderful. Ray was talking about how everyone joined in, giving what they could in skills and money. I think it's a remarkable achievement. Any chance we could see it while we're here?"

"I—I guess so," Kate said in surprise. "I have a set of keys." She looked at her watch. "Why don't we go over after dinner? The workmen will be gone then. I'm assuming you will stay to dinner?"

"Yes. Thank you. We'd like to. Has Marsha told you our good news?"

"Yes. Congratulations, Chet. You must be thrilled," Kate said, fairly beaming. There was nothing like a baby to bring people together.

"I am," Chet admitted happily.

"Tell me about the school," he went on. "Where did you get the idea?"

"Actually, right after that dismissal of Ian's motion," Kate said frankly. "We didn't think the homeschooling thing would work. If nobody believed in it but Raymond and me. So we started talking private school and—it kind of grew from there."

"And it's all gone so smoothly," Chet said admiringly.

Kate laughed. "Not smoothly. Not at all. When you get a hundred or more people together you get—how can I say it—differences of opinion." And she found herself telling them about the rose window, and the angry parents of the high-school-age students.

"And the present battle is about uniforms. Pastor Ledbetter had his heart set on dark green pants for the boys and green-and-gray-plaid skirts for the girls, but I think navy blue is going to win. He's going to have to give in on that one. Then there's the business of the school name—that's just starting to cause a new bout of infighting."

When they stopped laughing, Marsha leaned forward. "Chet. Kate wants to talk about the custody case. I'm beginning to think...maybe..."

"I was recalling what you said when you were here last," Kate explained. "That you'd rather do things peacefully. And now that Raymond will be in a school—not my hometeaching—why can't we leave the custody arrangement as it is? There's no reason Raymond can't spend time with you and Marsha in the future—summers, perhaps?"

"McAllister agreed to that?" Chet's cool, clear gaze held hers.

"Yes. He's said Raymond *should* have time with Marsha. She's his mother. And I believe that, too. Will you think about it? Just consider it?"

Chet's glance flicked to Marsha, who was nodding. "I think it's best, Chet. I'll talk to Daddy."

"Well, it's always been up to you, Marsha. If this is what you want, then let's do it this way. For the record, Raymond and I got along quite well today. We had a good rapport. Maybe we could down here, too, in time." He really did have a nice smile, Kate thought.

After dinner Chet drove them over to the school. All three children wanted to come along, so it was a crowded ride. As they stopped at the front of the old parsonage, resplendent now with new gray paint, white window facings and a shiny black door, Kate began to have qualms. What kind of Ivy League prep school had Chet attended? Would this all seem too humble and makeshift for him? Well, it was too late now. She got out her keys.

"Be careful," she warned the children. "This is still a building site and there is stuff lying around. I don't want you falling over things."

Going up the front walk to the porch, she indicated the porch overhang. "That's where the sign is going to be. It will be a thick slab of cedar, I think. And it will have the school name on it, when we decide on the name, if ever."

They went up the steps and she unlocked the big front door.

Raymond spoke up. "We'll have the playing field in back. A baseball diamond. And in the church rec room, they're painting basketball lines on the floor, and they'll put in the hoops that they can take down when they want to."

"Very efficient use of space," Chet agreed.

"Now this, of course, is the entry hall," Kate said, turning on the lights. It looked quite good. Someone had swept out all the trash and leftover bits since she had last seen it. It looked like a school entry hall, with a longish table, some chairs, a rack of wooden slots for teachers' mail, a large corkboard for notices and a big round clock on the wall. She began to feel better.

"To the right is the principal's office." She opened the door. There was a roll of carpet to be laid and the refinished desk that Mrs. Lundy would use when she was being principal.

"Very nice," Marsha commented.

"And over here, to the left, is what used to be the

dining room. Fortunately, when this place was built they had big dining rooms. It's the study hall and library.'' She noticed that the only furnishing so far was a pencil sharpener that someone, probably Cyrus, had mounted on the wall by the window.

''And we'll be serving a wholesome lunch. Through here is the kitchen.''

She showed them the upstairs classrooms, glad to note that the refinished floors gleamed and some of the furniture was here.

''I guess they don't use chalkboards anymore,'' Chet said, looking at the newly installed white nonglare writing surface on the front wall of each classroom.

''No,'' Kate aid. ''They can write on these in color and they just wipe clean. We're using writing tables, too, instead of desks,'' she added, not mentioning that the tables had been cheaper and secondhand. They had been refinished by weekend work parties from the congregation.

''This is really nice,'' Marsha said, passing her hand over a gleaming surface. ''Much nicer than desks, or those silly old chairs with the big arm to write on.''

Kate felt a swelling of love and pride. So much work, so much planning, from so many people.

''This is really impressive,'' Chet said. ''All working together to create something of value out of nothing. It reminds one of the early settlers, getting together for a barn raising, things like that. If they needed something, and didn't have it, they got together and made it.''

''Chet's a history buff,'' Marsha said fondly.

They heard someone coming up the stairs, and Kate leaned over the banister to find Cyrus. ''Hi. It's me, Kate. I brought some friends over to see the school.''

''I thought it might be. I was working over in the

church and saw the light.'' He reached the top of the stairs slightly out of breath.

Kate introduced Chet and Marsha to Pastor Ledbetter, and they continued the tour, the men falling behind. Kate heard Chet say, ''My stepson told me you were still short of funding. Have you approached any of the foundations? They're always looking for worthwhile projects to help along, and what you've done here would certainly command respect.''

''No, I hadn't thought of that, but...''

After the tour Chet dropped Kate and the children at home and headed for the private airport. Kate was suddenly very tired. It had been a long day.

''Okay, kids, it's bedtime,'' she said, and the children, also tired, didn't quibble. I must call Ian, she was thinking with quiet exultation. It's over, all the worry and strain. She made herself listen patiently to the children's prayers after they had bathed. When she got to Raymond's room, he was sitting on the side of his bed, looking glumly at the floor.

''You know, you would think with all Chet's money that he just might have given a little donation.'' He stopped at Kate's cautionary raised hand. ''Wha-at?''

''Never mind a donation,'' she said. ''He and Marsha did something else much more important. They've dropped the custody suit.'' She waited a moment for this to register.

''You're kidding!'' He looked stunned.

''Nope. Marsha and I talked about it this afternoon and when Chet came home from the flight, he agreed. So you can just visit them from time to time—not this summer. But sometime.'' She wouldn't tell him about the baby. That was Marsha's privilege.

''Wow,'' he said softly. ''That's gonna take some get-

ting used to. It's been hangin' over our heads so long.''
He looked at her thoughtfully. ''You know, it could be
kind of fun. Chet's got two other planes at home. He's
got one of those choppers like a big bubble. I bet that'd
be something to go up in.''

''I think that sounds wonderful,'' she agreed softy,
pushing back his fair hair.

''I still think he could have come up with some
money.''

''Nonsense,'' she said briskly as he slid to his knees.

I think he will, probably from his own foundation, she
thought, but quietly, behind the scenes, so as not to em-
barrass Ian. But we'll just have to wait and see.

When Raymond was in bed with his book, Kate fairly
flew down the stairs to Ian's study, where his itinerary
lay on his desk, listing the phone number of that hotel in
Albuquerque. She could hardly wait to tell him the news.

Chapter Fourteen

The weather cooperated and the rose window was a blaze of beauty on the August Sunday morning it was first viewed by the congregation. Cyrus was at his best, pointing out how many *different* projects the congregation could carry to completion if they all pitched in and worked at it. It helped that he could also announce the prospect of a large grant coming from a philanthropical foundation in the east, which was devoted to education and other connected works.

"The idea came to me quite by accident," he explained. "But being a humble man who has lived a humble life, I had no idea how to get a grant from a foundation. Then I recalled all those little yellow cards everybody filled out when we started the school project, listing any skills they were willing to donate. And lo and behold, I came upon Emma Lockhart's card, listing grant-proposal-writing experience." There was a murmur of appreciative laughter from the congregation.

"Stand up a minute, Emma." There was a round of applause, and when it died down he continued.

"So Emma and I had a meeting and she put together a very impressive application for a grant, which we—now, get this—*faxed* to the foundation. Speed is everything these days. We've come a long way from the time when people gathered on the prairie to hack out big squares of mud to make a sod house for the new settler. But it's the same idea, people coming together for the benefit of someone else, to do good things for one another."

From where she was sitting in church, Kate could see Amy Gilmartin, her faded eyes fixed on Brenden's beautiful window. It didn't matter how many school supplies the money spent on the window could have bought. There must always be a place for a rose window, Kate thought. There was no knowing, in the years to come, how many people might glance up at it and gain pleasure or comfort or just find an excuse to pause in the daily rush.

After the service she turned to Ian, next to her. "I'm so happy we have the window," she said.

"I agree," he murmured. "And the day we can't find any time to just stand and stare, we're lost."

And on Rose Window Sunday the coffee hour was standing-room-only, with everybody excited, talking and laughing and walking all over the new lines painted on the floor for future basketball games. There wasn't a disquieting or critical word, because Cyrus had made it clear that the grant from the foundation insured the phasing-in of grades nine through twelve next term. And it was all free and clear, a gift that didn't need to be paid back.

Cyrus snatched a moment to speak to Kate as she and Ian and their brood were about to leave.

"Did you notice Mrs. Lundy in church today?" He was wearing his Cheshire cat grin.

"Didn't she come just because of the rose window?"

"She was here last Sunday, too," Cyrus said. "And the man sitting next to her today was Mr. Lundy. I told you, once she started she'd keep coming." Then he was swept away by a group of people who needed urgently to talk to him. It was always that way with Cyrus.

On the first day of September there was a heavy rainstorm, as if Seattle was saying in no uncertain terms that the short summer was over, and it was time to get down to the beautiful business of autumn. There was a nip in the morning air, and here and there a brown leaf—which surely hadn't been brown the day before—fluttered down from its trees.

Kate had shopped the whole previous week for school clothes and supplies. Raymond, of course, had his new navy blue pants, white shirts and navy sweater or blazer, depending on the occasion.

"You're sure I'm not supposed to wear a tie?" he asked. "We got the navy ties on the list." He was trying on his uniform for the third time.

"Ties on formal occasions, where a tie is appropriate," she read from the list of instructions. "You can wear the shirt open at the neck. I think they must mean when it's warm or something. We'll still have a few warm days left in September."

Joy and Tommy viewed Raymond's uniform with mixed reactions.

"I think wearing the same thing every day is dumb," was Joy's verdict.

"I dunno," Tommy said. "Pastor Ledbetter says it's a good thing to wear a uniform at school. Mom, why is it a good thing?"

Kate glanced down at the instruction sheet, which offered no help on the philosophy of school uniforms.

"Well, I think it has something to do with discipline or something. Get Pastor Ledbetter to explain it to you next Sunday."

And the school open house took place on the Sunday before Labor Day, the second of September. Mrs. Lundy and Cyrus had worked almost all day Saturday, setting the scene. It was a gray and overcast day, but the actual rain held off. And the thick wooden sign suspended from the porch overhang was shrouded in a cloth, hiding the new school name. After the service the congregation trooped over to what had been the old parsonage, passing under the draped sign, into the entry hall.

The long table in the entry hall held coffee urns, cold drinks, plastic cups and glasses, and plates of the usual Sunday cookies. The people were somewhat in awe of what they had accomplished in the three months past. They wandered around with their plastic cups of coffee or cold drink, munching cookies. And the new shelves in the library were quite well supplied with books, and the study tables were neatly arranged. On each board in each classroom was printed in big colored letters, Welcome! Here and there were open textbooks on desks, eighth-grade reading, sixth-grade math, seventh-grade history. And the whole place looked very satisfyingly like a *school*. When the open house was over—Cyrus figured about an hour would do it—they would all congregate out in front for the unveiling of the school name. Afterward Kate was sure that Cyrus had pulled some strings behind the scenes.

Gathered in front of the school, the congregation made quite a crowd, extending clear out past the sidewalk. Passing cars began slowing down to see what was happening.

"Now," Cyrus said. "Are we all here? Anybody else left inside?"

A few obliging people near the porch shouted into the front hallway, but got no answer, so it was time for the unveiling.

"I'm going to ask Theron Gilmartin to pull the cord," Cyrus said. "And when he does, that cloth is supposed to fall off neatly. We did it twice before to rehearse and it all went as planned. Where's Theron?"

Theron Gilmartin came from the back of the crowd, always willing to help whenever asked. He gave the cord indicated a firm pull, and the curtain fell away as the name of the new school was revealed in a sudden burst of good-hearted applause and a ragged cheer. As a way of making amends for unkindnesses past, it was the best they could do, and perhaps a lesson had been learned, for the sign read, The Brenden Gilmartin Academy.

Mrs. Lundy had proctored Raymond's entrance exams on one previous Saturday, in the half-furnished principal's office.

"I guess the homeschooling worked very well," Ian said, looking at the grades, which they received by mail a few days after the open house. Raymond had come through with flying colors, getting straight A's in everything but math, in which he did make a $B+$.

"Well, we managed to keep up," Kate said. "And let me give Raymond his share of credit. If he hadn't kept at the books as he did, it could have been a disaster."

Raymond looked self-satisfied to the point of smugness. He retrieved the report from his father to take it next door to show Mrs. Hyslop.

"Apparently his self-image is in pretty good condition," Kate said, laughing.

"His self-image is getting obnoxious," Ian agreed.

"But his personal world is so much better than it was, by a long shot, I guess I can put up with it."

When Ian left on his next trip, he started a countdown. "Four more trips," he said, "and that's it! I retire the two-suiter." He was more carefree and happy than she had ever seen him, and it was a good feeling.

The Brenden Gilmartin Academy had opened for the business of educating the young on schedule, the day after Labor Day, proving from day one to be a remarkably efficient operation.

"Could you believe it?" Cyrus asked Kate on Thursday when he stopped in at the rec room where they were working on packing up bags for the food bank. "There hasn't been a single crisis. I don't understand it. *Nothing* has gone wrong. Not one thing. I think we did it!"

"Maybe Mrs. Lundy is just the best principal in the world," Kate offered, reaching for a packet of macaroni.

"Or maybe our enrollment consists only of perfect, trouble-free children. Whatever. It's working. We have thousands of dollars of insurance and not one kid has fallen down stairs to break a neck. I don't understand it. Something should have gone wrong. Whatever happened to Murphy's Law?"

While Ian was away on his fourth-from-last trip, Kate had all her family over to a Sunday dinner. Mom and Doug. Jill and Greg and their brood. It was time to start thinking of the coming holiday season. Thanksgiving Day at Mom and Dad's had always been a big family get-together for the Bennetts. This year would be different again because Dad wasn't here, but Kate was getting used to the idea. Last year, after Dad's death, they had compromised and eaten Thanksgiving dinner at what had been Jill's restaurant. It had been a pretty good day. And now, in the way of families, there seemed to be an unspoken agreement that once again the big house on the hill that was now Mom's bed-and-breakfast would not be right for the family festival. It would be quite empty this year, of course, because Mom wasn't accepting any reservations for November.

Life goes on, Kate, she thought. And Doug Colby was a good man, and Mom seemed to care for him, and he certainly cared for Mom. *So, what's the problem, Kate?*

After Kate's excellent Sunday dinner, the adults were still at the table, drinking last cups of coffee, and there came a small lull in the conversation.

"Anybody going to talk about the holidays?" Jill asked. "And the leaves are turning red on our backyard maple tree is why I'm asking."

"Why don't we flip a coin?" Greg suggested.

"Well, my dears," Mom said. "Doug and I have decided to marry the Friday after Thanksgiving. It'll be a quiet ceremony, just family. I've talked it over with Cyrus. So we'll be taking off for the Cascades to ski for a few days. So from now until then, I'm going to be pretty busy getting ready, shopping, packing and so on. I'm hoping one of you two will volunteer—let me be a guest this year."

Unspoken among them was the knowledge that big family festival days in the big house were in the past. They had been so much Dad's days.

"What do you think, Jill?" Kate asked.

"Well, we had Christmas at my house last year. Why don't we switch it around? I'll do the Thanksgiving dinner and you can take care of the Christmas dinner. How does that sound?"

"That's fine. We'll do it that way," Kate agreed. So it was settled among them while Kate had a sudden intense longing to talk to her father, sitting beside him in the grape arbor, like old times. But the old times were gone. Hadn't she told Marsha not to try to salvage what was past, but to go forward?

Kate had a talk with Cyrus when she went to the church office to give him her records of school donations and other notes. It seemed such a long time ago that she and Ian had sat with him at his painted kitchen table to confer about the homeschooling.

As they went over the records and notes, Cyrus said, "I think I might use these to write a how-to book on starting a school. *How To Create a School with the Help of a Hundred Other People,* which I guess is kind of long for a title."

Kate laughed. "It would almost make a book, and there certainly are sad parts. I wish the Gilmartins hadn't been hurt by it."

"Yes," he said slowly, his face serious. "One wonders how God must feel sometimes, when his beloved go around hurting each other, causing each other pain and heartache.... The tears of God—it doesn't bear thinking about, does it?"

They were silent for a time. And the office was getting dim. It was a gray overcast day outside and he hadn't thought to turn on the lights. Then he said, "How's Kate doing?"

"Kate's doing very well," she said. "I've wanted to talk to you, but we've both been so busy with the school. But we're doing well. Ian's got a promotion at his company, and he doesn't have to travel anymore after January, so we're looking forward to that. Then the best thing is that Marsha and Chet have decided to drop the custody suit, so we're home free on that. They're satisfied with Raymond visiting from time to time. So things are all working out for us."

"I'm so glad. I can see the change in Raymond."

Kate smiled. "So can I."

"Blessed are the peacemakers, Kate, for they shall be called the children of God. I know it hasn't been easy for you, but, surely it's been worth it."

"Oh, yes, more than worth it," she said softly, and began pushing her papers and lists into the big envelope to leave with him. They both stood up.

At the office door he took her hand. "It's a privilege to know you, Katie. We're going into October now, and from here on till year's end, it's holidays and merrymaking—and I hope remembering to thank God now and then—but next year I hope we can find another impossible project to do. And *do* it."

"Oh, we shall. Never doubt it," Kate said, and they laughed together.

During the final days of September and early days of October, Kate was frantically busy harvesting the last of the vegetable and fruit crops. And the zucchini had grown with its usual abandon. She had far too much for family and neighbors. She hoped Seattle's street people who ate at The Millionaires' Club liked zucchini, because they were getting a lot of it this year.

Ian came home from his third-from last trip a day early, late at night. She was still working in the kitchen, in a convenient work outfit of shorts, T-shirt and thong sandals. *Sorry, Jill. All my pretty outfits are upstairs and too nice for cooking. I'll do better tomorrow.* She had heard the back door and the familiar thud of the two-suiter being dropped, and he came into the kitchen.

"Are you still working? It's almost eleven o'clock. Time to check out for the day, isn't it?" He was looking at her quizzically. His smile and Raymond's were identical.

"Well, things have to get done," she said, laughing. "And the apricot tree and everything else outdid themselves this year, and you have to do this stuff when it's ready. The yellow Delicious did great, too. I've put a bowl on the table there, if you're hungry. How did this trip go?"

He sat down at the kitchen table and took a bright yellow apple out of the bowl. "It went fine. Apples always smell so good and autumny. Only two more trips!"

Kate shut the freezer door for the last time, and sighed. It had been a long day, but Ian was home. *You have a very good life, Kate.*

She watched Ian, tall, lean, strong, get up from the table.

"I think I need crackers with this."

"In that cupboard." Kate pointed. "And there's some cheese and a bottle of cranberry juice in the fridge. I'm going to go take a quick shower."

When she finished she put on her gown and robe and, as Ian was still downstairs, she went down to join him. As she came into the kitchen he was putting his apple core into the disposal. There was a scatter of crumbs on the table and half a glass of red juice. They sat at the table while she began to bring him up-to-date about the home news.

"...so we all got together to plan the holidays. You know how it is with my family. We're going to have Thanksgiving dinner at Jill and Greg's. Then we'll have the big Christmas dinner here at our place...are you listening to me?"

"Yes," he said softly, pushing aside his glass and taking her capable hands into his, not seeming to notice that the manicure she had had last week for his benefit was history now, from the washing of all those apples and pears and the mountain of zucchini. "I always listen to you. It's one of the greatest pleasures of my life. I don't think you know that, do you?"

She didn't know what to say, but felt a tremor in his hands clasping hers across the table.

"I've been thinking about this for some time—in fact, I've done a lot of thinking…about us…about our marriage. You have to accept the fact that your husband is not a big brain. It takes a while sometimes for things to get through to me. Then suddenly I do finally get it."

"I don't understand."

"I'm not surprised. I'm not a very articulate guy. Coming back on the plane this time, I was thinking about how it was for us…in the beginning How I took advantage—"

"Ian, it doesn't matter now."

"It does matter, Kate. I…made use of you, tricked you into marrying me because of *my* need to hold on to my kid. It wasn't fair. Then I didn't even have the guts to lie about it. I had to clear my own conscience by telling you the truth, hurting you. I will never forget—*and I deserve not to*—when I came back from that first trip after our marriage. You were back here, working as usual, doing what had to be done. Do you remember what you said?"

She shook her head.

"You told me to leave the two-suiter on the service porch, as you had to unpack it and put things in the laundry. I felt like two cents. You were making the best of a bad situation. You were standing by your standards, when I hadn't. I wasn't worth it, but you would stand by me. Believe me, in that moment I learned firsthand what shame is. And I'm so sorry."

"Ian, it's all right, really...." She didn't want to hear this. She didn't want to remember those days.

"Do you remember what you asked me when we got back from our honeymoon? When you faced me down, demanding answers?"

She shook her head. "I was always sorry about that," she said, remembering that Raymond had been frightened by their argument.

"Kate, you needn't ever feel sorry about anything. You were entitled to demand answers. And I have a different answer now...if you want it?" He ended with a question in his voice.

"Answer to what? I've tried to forget about—"

"You asked me if you were the love of my life...and I couldn't or didn't give you the answer you wanted. I can now, if you want it."

"Ian, what are you saying?" she whispered. "My dear, you don't have to..."

"I don't have to, but I want to. I love you, Kate. I've been falling in love with you for months. I had the perfect wife, the perfect life, and I began to get the message. Kate, I hadn't had a lot of love in my life, so maybe I didn't recognize it when I met it. Real love. Generous love that doesn't ask a return. You loved Ray because he needed it. And you loved me, even if I didn't deserve it." His voice shook. "This is it for me. I just want you to know...that you *are* the love of my life, and it will never be any different. And, knowing you as I do now, I know it's not too late."

Her small strong hands gripped his. "Oh, no. It's never too late." She wanted to see him more clearly, but she was looking through a blur of tears. "It's never too late to love."

* * * * *

Dear Reader,

I hope you enjoyed reading Kate's story. In exploring Kate's character, I, as the writer, learned that Kate's strength lay in her ability to see her own obligations as hers alone. Ian, her beloved, could compromise his standards of integrity in arranging a marriage of convenience, but, despite her hurt, Kate did not see this as reason for her to lower her standards. Instead, she took to heart the words of her friend and mentor, Pastor Ledbetter, who said, "Look to Kate's vows."

So in concentrating on her own vows, her own duty to those she loved, Kate's confidence and strength increased, and the way opened for her to become what they all needed most—the peacemaker.

Somebody wise once said, "When God closes one door, He opens another." And when a door closed for Kate, she simply went on day by day, honoring her own personal contract with God, doing what she knew needed to be done, until she found her open door. It's something to think about.

May the peace of the Lord be always with you.

Blessings,

Virginia Myers